DESERT RAIN

JEAN HOLBROOK MATHEWS

DESERT RAIN

BONNEVILLE
BOOKS

An imprint of Cedar Fort, Inc.
Springville, Utah

This is a work of fiction. The characters, names, incidents, places, and dialogue are products of the author's imagination and are not to be construed as real. The opinions and views expressed herein belong solely to the author and do not necessarily represent the opinions or views of Cedar Fort, Inc. Permission for the use of sources, graphics, and photos is also solely the responsibility of the author.

ISBN 13: 978-1-4621-1826-7

Published by Bonneville Books, an imprint of Cedar Fort, Inc.
2373 W. 700 S., Springville, UT 84663
Distributed by Cedar Fort, Inc. www.cedarfort.com

LIBRARY OF CONGRESS CATALOGING-IN-PUBLICATION DATA

Names: Mathews, Jean Holbrook, author.
Title: Desert rain / Jean Holbrook Mathews.
Description: Springville, Utah : Bonneville Books, an imprint of Cedar Fort, Inc., [2016]
Identifiers: LCCN 2015045875 (print) | LCCN 2015049372 (ebook) | ISBN 9781462118267 (softcover : acid-free paper) | ISBN 9781462126286 ()
Subjects: LCSH: Murder--Investigation--Fiction. | GSAFD: Mystery fiction.
Classification: LCC PS3613.A84333 D47 2016 (print) | LCC PS3613.A84333 (ebook) | DDC 813/.6--dc23
LC record available at http://lccn.loc.gov/2015045875

Cover design by Rebecca J. Greenwood
Cover design © 2016 by Cedar Fort, Inc.
Edited and typeset by Justin Greer

Printed in the United States of America

10 9 8 7 6 5 4 3 2 1

Printed on acid-free paper

To Boyd and Margie Holbrook,
for friendship and occasional expertise
above and beyond the call of duty.

Other books by Jean Holbrook Mathews
The Light Above
Escape to Zion
The Assignment
Precious Cargo
Safe Haven
Run For Your Life

CHAPTER 1

His body was found on Wednesday in an arroyo near the city limits. I received a call at about four o'clock that afternoon from a Mesa homicide detective by the name of Steve Sutherland. He asked me if I'd come down to the county medical examiner's office and identify him.

"The wallet on the body says he's"—suppressed cough—"or *was* Lawrence Lattimer, and Lieutenant Glade Schmidt tells me he was CEO of LL Construction and that you worked for him. We haven't been able to contact his wife. The housekeeper answered the phone and said she was in Bermuda. Schmidt said he knows you well enough to believe that you could probably handle the ID even though it won't be easy."

My legs turned to rubber. I dropped into my desk chair like a bag of sand. I knew that something bad must have happened because here it was, Wednesday afternoon, and I hadn't heard word from him since Saturday. But this was the last thing I wanted to hear.

"How did he die?" My throat was suddenly so tight that it hurt to talk. My ears were humming and my head suddenly hurt.

"We don't know. A couple of thirteen-year-old kids were down in an arroyo taking potshots with a new .22 rifle one of them got for his birthday when they found him. The coyotes made the identification more difficult. We won't know much more than that until the County M.E. gets a chance to examine the body. I'm serving as lead investigator on the case. I'll be glad to come out to the office and pick you up so you can make the ID right away—if you're willing. It can be tough to drive after you've had to ID a body of someone you know."

I looked over at my office mate, Roger. My stomach was in one big knot. "It's the police. They found LL's body. They want me to identify him."

"LL's dead?" Roger was stunned. He looked at me with concern. "Lexi, I'll come with you if that will make it easier."

"Thanks, Roger," I returned to the phone call. "I'd appreciate a ride very much, Detective Sutherland." It still hurt to talk.

• • •

My name is Lexi Benson, and I'd been working as an executive assistant to Lawrence Lattimer, the founder and CEO of LL Construction, for the past three years. It was an unusual position for a 28-year-old woman but I'd gotten pretty good at it and learned to like it. LL did his best to make sure I was as comfortable as possible in the position. He never allowed any of the men to give me a hard time and he called any man down who gave a wolf whistle when we were inspecting a finished project. Of all the tasks I'd had to do since coming to work at LL Construction, this was going to be the most difficult.

Heavy, dark clouds had begun to gather by the time Sutherland entered the office at about a quarter to five. Though I'm seldom impressed with anyone's eyes, his were dark blue and seemed to be able to look straight into a person's conscience when he spoke to them. He held my gaze like a magnet, and I knew I'd remember those eyes long after he had forgotten my name.

I put his age at three or four years older than I was, somewhere in his early thirties. He was tall, well over six feet. He was good looking in a Richard Gere kind of way. He had even features with good cheekbones, a strong jaw, and a broad forehead, below a head of thick, dark hair. He wore a white dress shirt with a dark blue tie and a navy blue sport coat and looked more like a lawyer than a cop. When I shook hands with him, his was warm, dry, and strong.

He shook Roger's hand, and after we reached the dark green, unmarked sedan, Roger opened the rear door for me. As I slid in, I flashed a weak smile of thanks at Roger before he walked around to the other side and climbed in beside me.

The sky looked as if the entire metropolitan Phoenix area had been covered by a dark opaque dome that reflected the lights of the city back at us. I could feel the electricity in the air making the hairs on my arms stand up, even though no lightning was visible. I suspected that this was going to be one of those nights when the electrical surges in the air would turn on touch lamps in the middle of the night as a rumbling thunderstorm tried to intimidate humanity. November weather in the Arizona desert was usually marked by mild temperatures and sunny skies, but the last few days had been soaked by an unseasonable series of rainstorms.

As we pulled out of the parking lot, I took a deep breath and asked Sutherland, "Do you know any more about how he died?"

"The medical examiner says it looks like a shotgun blast, but the official cause won't be listed until the autopsy's done. That could be several days from now since the M.E. always has a backlog, but for the present, the investigation is moving forward based on the likelihood that it was murder."

"Oh" was all I could manage to say. Roger thoughtfully reached over and patted my hand. I appreciated his sympathy. At that moment, I needed it. He turned to look out of the window at the traffic. I studied him. He looked younger than his twenty-five years, tall and lanky, like a colt that hasn't put on much flesh. He had an enviable kind of energy that never seemed to lessen. He was a good-looking young man despite a few old burn scars, one on the left side of his face from his neck up to his hairline, and one along his left forearm. His dark brown hair had a big cowlick in the front, so it wouldn't lie down. It was a frustration to him but I thought it added a touch of perpetual innocence to his expression.

We rode in silence for about twenty-five minutes and I tried to close my mind to what I was about to see, but nature abhors a vacuum, so my thoughts began to fill with memories of the first time I met LL at a big Christmas dinner and dance at the downtown Marriott. The bank where I worked, and where LL had obtained his business loans, had been bought out by a mega bank from Los Angeles. The public reason for the big party had been to celebrate the formal changing of hands, but I and about half the crew were each being given two months severance pay and a lump of limestone with our name and years of service engraved on the smooth side. It would make a good paperweight.

While praise and tributes for the retiring officers of the recently purchased bank had continued to flow from individuals speaking at the podium, a chicken dinner was served.

Pete Uxbridge, the retiring manager of the main office where I worked, had waited until about half the crowd had left and the remaining folks appeared to be planning their exit before he took my elbow and pulled me over to LL. "Lattimer, this young lady has been the best office manager I or anyone else has ever had. I think I heard you say that you need a new executive assistant. If you need something done, she'll get it done. You won't do better than Lexi. And with her background, she'd be a quick study." Then he had simply walked off to bid his former staff members and friends good-bye.

I wasn't sure what to say. LL put out his hand and said, "How much do you know about construction?"

"A little—well, quite a lot. It runs in my family, kind of like brown eyes. My grandfather told me that it started with his grandfather when he came home from France after the First World War. He started building houses and his sons worked with him and eventually formed a company of their own."

LL had chuckled. "Where did all this happen?"

"In Northern Utah. My grandfather naturally became part of the company along with his two brothers and two cousins. They tell me it really boomed after the Second World War. Grandpa retired when I was twelve and, after my grandmother died, he came to live with us. My dad graduated as an electrical engineer from Texas A&M, and of course, he became part of the company. We talked construction around the dinner table the way some families talk politics or sports." He was watching me with a look that was half amusement and half approval.

I had paused, feeling that I was talking too much. "Does any of this count?"

He nodded. "It may count some—maybe a lot." He chuckled and looked thoughtful. "But maybe I'd be making a mistake, hiring someone whose sympathies could lay with a competitor." That amused look hadn't left his eyes.

"Not really. My dad and his brother sold their interest in the company a couple of years before my dad died. Shortly thereafter, it was gobbled up by a big outfit based in Southern California—hardly more than a little bite to an expanding, multi-state company. I have no loyalties there." I was feeling a little nervous. It was becoming important to me to earn this man's approval.

He smiled at me broadly, as if he'd made a decision. "I think your background means you've got the right talent somewhere in your genes. With a reference like Uxbridge just gave you and a family history like yours, you're hired—if you want the job."

As he had stood there grinning at me, I was reminded of a great golden bear. He was a stocky man of medium height, and the hair on the back of his hands was the same golden color as the thick hair on his head. His golden eyebrows were arched above eyes lined with golden eyelashes. Even the irises of his eyes were golden brown. I almost expected him to give me a great bear hug that would accidently break every bone in my body, but he just watched me with a grin until I figured out what to say.

I had nodded uncertainly and tried to return his grin. I said the only thing that came into my head. "Thanks. When do I report for work?"

A week later, as I traded my stiletto heels, expensive suits, and jewelry for jeans and casual shirts, I asked myself, *Lexi Benson, are you up for this? This job will be a challenge.* Then I remembered what LL had said, that maybe I had it in my genes.

It took me nearly a year of being LL's shadow to get a good grasp of his philosophy and the vocabulary, processes, and legal requirements of the industry, but he was a patient tutor.

In the three years I had worked for him, I found that he was a man with currents of energy that pulled him toward his goals. He was restless by nature, perpetually in motion. For me, every day was a learning experience.

I was pulled from my thoughts as Sutherland parked the car. He led us to an entrance with a set of double doors where he leaned on one, allowing us to enter ahead of him. The Maricopa County Medical Examiner's office building was a large, two-story, square pile of blocks, an architectural orphan, but the inside was clean and efficient. The air was permeated with the heavy smell of chemical disinfectants. Steel doors separated each department and fluorescent lighting glared off tile floors that were shiny enough to make me want my sunglasses. Staffers walked around quietly in crepe-soled shoes, as if they were afraid that making any noise would wake the folks in the refrigerated section.

An attendant in green scrubs led us to a room with a closed circuit television screen mounted in one wall. There were a few molded, plastic chairs within easy reach, but I was too ill at ease to sit. When the screen came on, I couldn't help but flinch. The picture showed the upper half of a body on a gurney covered with a green sheet. Roger put one arm around me to offer support.

Another attendant—this one with a shaved head and round, Harry Potter–like glasses—stepped into the room. "Are you ready?"

Detective Sutherland looked at me. I took a big breath and looked at Roger. He smiled and gave me a nod as if to tell me that I was up to it. I whispered, "Okay."

He pushed a button by the door. Two gloved hands on the screen pulled the sheet back and exposed the head, neck, and shoulders. The head was turned away from us nearly 180 degrees. Though he had been cleaned up, it was evident that the flesh on the far side of his face and one shoulder was torn and ragged, and out of consideration, his face had been turned away. His skin had taken on the gray-green pallor that marked the absence of the spirit and said that no one was home any longer. I had to find a chair quickly where I could sit with my hand over my mouth.

I knew it was LL. I didn't need to see his face straight on or even in profile to recognize his sandy hair and the port wine birth mark on the back of his neck that ran up into his hairline. Whenever he got a new haircut, I had teased him about his "stork bite." I had seen enough, but Roger seemed unsure. He motioned to have LL's head turned more toward us. The gloved hands did so. The more of the face that was exposed, the less likely anyone would be able to identify him. Roger quickly turned away.

I nodded and whispered, "Yes, that's LL."

I wasn't sure how I got back to the car. I vaguely remember holding onto Roger's arm. Sutherland apologized as he drove us back to the company office. "Did I mention to you that it looks like the coyotes had gotten to him? That kind of ID is never easy, so we appreciate your willingness to do it."

He pulled up in front of the company office at ten after six. The whole experience seemed to push me into another dimension. I felt light-headed as I opened the door to get out of the car.

"I was going to ask you some questions, but from the way the two of you look, I think I'd better come back in the morning. Do you have a business card with your phone numbers on it?" he asked of both of us.

I fumbled in my purse and handed him mine. Roger pulled his card case from his pants pocket and gave him one.

He continued, "Between now and tomorrow, I hope both of you will try to think of anything out of the ordinary that could give us a lead, or names of anyone who might have had a grudge against Lattimer." He handed each of us a business card with his phone number on it.

My mind disconnected from my body like a caboose separating from its engine as Roger and I walked toward the office. I mechanically pulled my keys out of my bag and ended up dropping them. Roger bent, picked them up, and opened the door. He was looking like he was recovering from the experience a little more quickly than I, but his normally ruddy complexion was still pale.

We sat in silence for a minute or two before I whispered, "I genuinely liked LL. He was easy to work for: organized, generous, not afraid to tackle any project. In some ways, I . . . I think he became a substitute for my father."

"Yeah, I know what you mean. He always treated me like a son." Roger's voice was quiet too.

I felt as if I had swallowed something with sharp corners. I hurt physically. Someone was guilty of wiping away the life of a good man. I gradually became angry, so angry that I'm sure my face grew red. I wanted to know who had killed him, and more importantly, I wanted to put my face in his—or hers—and demand to know why. I looked down at my hands. They were clenched into fists. I've always thought of myself as an open-minded, forgiving person, but I suddenly realized that where LL's death was concerned, I wasn't above carrying a very big grudge.

Roger was watching me. He cleared his throat and moved in his chair. "I'll drive you home, if you don't feel like driving."

"I appreciate the offer, but I'd have no way to get back to the office in the morning."

"That's no problem. I'll be glad to pick you up." He made an effort to brighten his voice. "I'd like to see where you live."

"That's really thoughtful of you, but I think I can manage. Thanks, though." I didn't feel like riding in his 1968 black Corvette with the 427 engine and the T-top. Somehow, riding in a car collector's dream seemed irrelevant right then—and almost irreverent.

"If you're sure you're okay. Look, if you need to talk, don't hesitate to call me—anytime."

I nodded, though I knew that the first person I would call in such a moment would be my sister, Percy.

He threw on his suede jacket and left, closing the door quietly as he did so.

I was glad to be alone. After another ten minutes of organizing my thoughts, I realized that I needed to let LL's wife, Tiffany, know what had happened. If the police reached her while she was in Bermuda without any warning, the news could be devastating. I called her cell number but she didn't answer.

I left a message. "Tiffany, this is Lexi in LL's office. It's really important that I talk to you right away. Please call me. It's urgent." I repeated my number twice to make sure she would get it.

I pulled out a lower drawer to prop my feet on and closed my eyes, concentrating on a slow head roll, trying to ease the tension in my neck and shoulders.

When that didn't seem to help, I left my chair and crossed the office to LL's desk, where I mechanically straightened it as if the physical task of ordering the clutter there would somehow help me arrange my thoughts and feelings. When I'm confused and I don't have answers, it sometimes helps me to organize the world around me. I put the pens and pencils back into the holder with the letter opener from the Rotary Club and picked up the clipboard with his notes from last week's on-site visits. After I scanned that, I put a bunch of loose yellow Post-it notes asking for phone calls to be returned under a medallion paperweight. I would have to get to those sometime when I didn't feel as if I'd been hit by a truck.

I arranged his awards, lining them up with the back edge of the desk a few inches from the computer screen. There were three from various Chambers of Commerce for his charitable gifts: a long-stay house for families of children who were having major surgery at a hospital in Las Vegas, a hospital wing in Tucson, and a new elementary school for handicapped children in Albuquerque, New Mexico. Each one was almost identical: a heavy orb of marble about three inches in diameter suspended on the shoulders of an Atlas-type figure. The base of each one was engraved the same: *To Lawrence Lattimer for his contributions as a community builder.* Under that was the name of the group presenting the award. The fourth one was a trophy he had received from his skeet shooting club a year earlier for taking first place in a shooting match. Skeet was the one distraction from work that he allowed himself. Even his golf games with clients were focused on projects.

He was so proud of that little trophy that just holding it in my hand brought a brief smile. After I had finished straightening his desk, I pulled out a tissue from my pocket and wiped the dust that had accumulated on his computer screen. Now the desk was ready for the man who would never sit at it again.

This office was his home base. It was just an insulated metal prefab building painted mesquite green attached to a much bigger prefab warehouse where the company's excess heavy equipment and bulky supplies were stored. It was much more utilitarian than attractive, a lot like LL. Roger and I each had a desk on the other side of the room.

Another nearly identical building sat about two hundred feet to the east of this one, but that building was the office used by the architects, engineers, accountants, company lawyer, and all the other folks filling jobs required by county, state, and federal government regulations. Both warehouses were so far to the east of the metro area that even though they were technically within Mesa City limits, little more than desert spread beyond them.

• • •

In a day when many company headquarters are housed in glass and chrome buildings in the high-rent districts of metropolitan areas, LL wasn't concerned with appearances. He could have had a magnificent office, but self-aggrandizement wasn't his style.

Roger still had a desk in the other office building, where he continued to work about half time as an accountant, the job for which he was originally hired. The balance of his time was spent in training as another assistant to LL. During that time, we had become friends. There had been a few times when I had the impression that he would like that relationship to progress to a more personal level, but I hadn't encouraged him. We really didn't have much in common other than our jobs and the loss of our parents. And frankly, I suspected that any romantic interest in his life would take second place to his Corvette.

My cell phone rang. I hurried back to my desk and searched my oversized purse, trying to get to it before it quit ringing. "Hello, this is Lexi."

"Lexi, it's Percy. Has something happened that I need to know about? I've had a dark feeling the last couple of hours, as if you were really upset or in trouble."

Percy was not quite two years older than I was and she and I had a sisterly closeness that some people described as beautiful. A few of our former school friends described it in less flattering terms, calling it eerie or even weird. We had experienced a kind of mental telepathy since the time we were kids, a kind of mood barometer, for lack of a better description. It didn't matter how many miles were between us, we could feel each other's emotional conditions, especially negative feelings.

My self-control crumbled. "Oh, Percy, LL's been murdered. I had to ID his body about an hour ago. I'm not sure . . ." I took a deep breath to stop my jaw from trembling and halt the tears that were threatening to overwhelm me.

She filled the gap. "I could tell something was terribly wrong. Are you at home?"

"No, I'm just getting ready to leave the office."

"I'll meet you at your place. Richard's here. He can watch the kids."

Before I could answer, she ended the call. I put the phone back into my bag and headed for the door where I flipped off the light switch. When I took hold of the knob, I paused and leaned my head against it. I couldn't stop the tears that ran down my face and dripped off my chin, "I'm sorry, LL. Somehow . . . somehow we'll find out who did this to you." I straightened up and opened the door slowly, realizing that my life was going to change, though I didn't yet know how much. "*Vaya con Dios,* my friend," I whispered.

CHAPTER 2

It was dark when I left the office. I wiped my tears with the back of my hand before I locked the door and crossed the graveled parking area to my car. After I climbed in, I put my arms on the steering wheel and leaned my head against them for a few minutes before I could start the engine and head for home.

The next thing I remembered was reaching out of my car window and punching in the security code at the wrought-iron gate at the Willow Glen condominium complex where I lived. My headlights cut the dark, making two bright tunnels as I drove past the row of wispy paloverde trees that lined the entrance drive. I parked under the long carport in my reserved slot.

There were no stars in the sky. The chill wind was a precursor to more unseasonable rain. As I sat there, I felt more than sad. I felt like an exhausted swimmer in a wide, cold lake.

Now that I was at my comfortable little condo, I expected to feel the normal sense of security that usually greeted my arrival home, but it was missing. As I started to get out of the car, Percy's minivan pulled into the parking slot next to mine. She knew the code to open the gate as well as I did. She climbed out and hurried to me. I couldn't say anything. We just gave each other a long embrace, despite her extended tummy. She was more than eight months pregnant. She didn't speak. We just moved up the sidewalk to my front door with our arms around each other's waists. I didn't even wave to my upstairs neighbor, Mrs. Bolton, when she peaked out of her draperies to see who was there, as was her usual custom. Percy waved for me.

When I managed to get the door unlocked, we stepped inside and turned on the lights. The tension inside me eased a little.

"Go sit on the couch." Percy's mother hen instincts had taken over. She had four little girls and another on the way and she knew how to mother someone with a "boo-boo," or in my case, a heartache. "Have you had any dinner?" I shook my head. "What can I fix for you? What sounds good?"

Nothing sounded good as far as I was concerned, so she settled on making me a cup of hot cocoa. "You're sure I can't fix you a sandwich or a cup of soup?" she asked as she handed it to me. I shook my head and patted the place next to me. She sat.

I was crying again, silent tears that I couldn't stop. "I didn't realize how much I would miss LL until now. His death has brought back the same pain I felt when we lost Dad and Mom—that overwhelming sense of loss."

Percy responded in a near whisper. "It's natural to feel a loss like this intensely. One loss brings other losses to mind. Even though we were adults, losing Mom and Dad was an awful experience. I guess it was a lot more painful for you than for me. At least I had a good husband and was looking forward to the birth of our baby."

My hand was shaking as I held the hot chocolate. I drank half the cup and handed it back to her so I wouldn't spill it.

"Lexi, is the light on your answering machine blinking? Do you want me to answer it?

"No, I can do it."

When I punched the numbers into the keypad, Sutherland's voice responded. "Miss Benson, I'll be at your office by eight in the morning and I'd appreciate it if you could be there to meet with me."

I moved across the great room and stepped out onto the covered patio. Percy followed me. We watched, or rather listened, to the sound of the rain falling in the darkness. The lightning was a series of jagged flashes in the southeast; the thunder sounded like movers were pushing a grand piano around in the unit above us. The world was as sad as I was about LL's death. Even the sky was weeping for him—and in a belated manner, for my parents.

We stood in silence as my thoughts ran like cats in the night, darting in and out of the light. After a few minutes the dampness penetrated our clothing, and we were chilled enough to return to the warmth of the condo. I closed and locked the sliding glass door.

"Percy, I appreciate your coming over more than you can imagine, but you need to be getting home to Richard and your girls. I'll be okay. Tell all of them that Aunt Lexi sends her love."

"Are you sure? I can stay longer if you need me."

I tried to make my voice sound firm and confident. "No, you go home. I'll be all right."

She gave me another embrace and told me to call if I needed her for anything. I moved into my bedroom wondering about the chances of getting any sleep if I went to bed.

I peeled off the jeans and sweatshirt I wore to the office and put on my fuzzy robe. I paused to look at myself in the dresser mirror. After I went to work for LL, a beautician friend cut my hair short in a minimal-care style and I discovered that I had a substantial amount of natural curl. But tonight my auburn curls were as limp as I felt. The dusting of freckles across my nose and cheeks stood out against my white face and I had dark circles under my brown eyes. I felt a hundred years old.

As I listened to the rumble of the thunder, I returned to the great room to stretch out in the recliner, and the memories of the last three years continued to wander in and out of my mind, uninvited. I couldn't have stopped them with the Great Wall of China.

LL had explained to me early in my apprenticeship that those of us in the main office didn't do any hands-on work. He had been forced to give up the physical side of the profession because of a back injury about ten years earlier, but it was his policy to visit all major projects and watch their progress closely. Our tasks focused on permit requirements, site selection, quality of work, construction schedules, and financial contracts.

LL flew his own plane, a Cherokee Six. He told me that in the early days of his marriage, Tiffany had accompanied him to job sites but had quickly grown bored. Since then, he had always taken his assistant with him. My first flight with him was to Albuquerque.

In addition to me, he often took the company's head accountant, attorney, chief architect, or any other staff member from the corporate office whose expertise might be needed for specific on-site problems. We could usually get to any of the building sites and back to Mesa in a long workday. He kept a rented space for the plane at Mesa Gateway Airport, which was about thirty minutes south of the corporate office.

The demands of the job were heavy, but I had grown to enjoy it. I owed LL so much and wanted to do a good job for him—but now I would never have the chance to repay him.

Roger came on about eighteen months after me, at first as one of the company accountants, later to learn the responsibilities of an administrative assistant. LL instructed him to interview some applicants and find a replacement accountant so he could move into the office to work full time with the two of us, but somehow he never found anyone who would be "just the right fit." He liked being involved in both places and it didn't seem to bother LL.

Trying to shut down my thoughts, I turned on the TV. I dozed a little while I tried to watch the national network talking heads as they reported on the natural disasters and wars in the Middle East that filled the news every day. I changed channels to the local affiliate for the ten o'clock news. The story of LL's death led the newscast. I sat up to watch it.

"The fifty-five year old CEO and founder of LL Construction, Lawrence Lattimer, was found dead early this afternoon. The Homicide Division of the Mesa Police Department is handling the investigation, causing speculation that the death was not from natural causes. At the time of his death, Lattimer had built his company into one of the most successful construction companies in the southwest. He was recognized as a leading civic figure and major financial supporter of many charitable groups."

At that point, the other talking head, an attractive woman wearing distracting gold hoop earrings that bobbed under her long, dark hair started the next local story. I hit the off button on the remote.

Hearing it summed up in that way—as though it were one of those impersonal reports on traffic conditions or an oncoming storm—made me want to cry all over again. If they had just known and worked with him, surely they would have given the story of his death more importance.

I leaned back in the recliner and must have drifted off to sleep. I was jolted awake by the flash of lighting that accompanied a clap of thunder that shook the sky. The touch lamp at my elbow flashed on. My heart suddenly seemed to double its rate. I took several deep breaths to slow it down to somewhere near normal while I noted the time. It was five after five.

Something in that news report from the evening before had stated that it would rain more today and the high would be no more than fifty. Though rain was welcomed by most everyone else, it intensified my grief.

I put on my sweats and my Nikes. When I'm frustrated, anxious, or in need of some intense thinking time, I walk—not just a light stroll, but a hard and fast walk. I've solved many of the world's problems between the distance of two and four miles. Personal problems sometimes take a few miles longer. Today was one of those days. I walked until six thirty. By the time I reached home, I was thoroughly soaked and chilled. I took a hot shower, used the hair dryer, and slipped on my blue sweatshirt, jeans, and a waterproof jacket. I grabbed a banana before I left the condo.

I arrived at the office at seven thirty. Somehow I expected that it would be different with LL gone, but it wasn't. I looked around the room at the three desks, each at a ninety-degree angle against the wall with a wooden, straight-backed chair sitting nearby for clients. The concrete floor was covered with dark green sisal carpet.

Along one wall were four file cabinets separated by a closet door and next to a big copy machine. Next to that, two long tables ran along the wall. They were used for spreading out the blueprints of active projects, which were usually rolled into tubes and stacked like paper kindling on top of the file cabinets. The pile rose nearly to the ceiling. There had never been any apparent system to them, but LL had always been able to put his hand on the right one whenever he needed it.

Under each of the tables were wide, specially built, shallow drawers for blueprints and plans that needed to be stored flat. Long fluorescent ceiling fixtures cast a bright, clear light throughout the large room, where metal shelving that looked as if it had been made from an industrial strength Erector set covered the other two walls. The shelves were crammed with binders, technical manuals, project reports, specs, and plans of completed projects.

It was not a glamorous environment, but after I had been hired, I had added a few softening touches to my workspace. When I brought a small arrangement of artificial flowers for the top of the two-drawer file cabinet next to my desk, LL had tried to hide his smile. With his permission, I hung a landscape my father had painted a few years before his death above my desk and I placed a framed photo of my parents next to my computer screen to remind me who I was. Despite the general masculinity of the office, I had a little space of femininity and had come to feel at home here.

On the wall behind LL's desk was a gallery of framed and autographed photos, including photos with three present or former governors and two US senators. Most of them had been on a first name basis with LL. Below them, he had hung a dozen photos in plain frames arranged in two rows with him in his white dress shirt and dark tie, tan slacks, and hard hat, standing in lines of differing businessmen, each one in a hard hat with one foot on a shovel.

I picked up the frame he kept on his desk. It was a smaller photo of him and Tiffany that must have been taken on their honeymoon. It was about five years old. They were smiling at each other, the age difference making it look like a photo of a father and daughter.

I put it back on his desk and moved over to mine. I decided to try to get some telephone calls made before Sutherland arrived.

I was immediately distracted by the sound of Roger's car. As he entered the office, he pulled off his European driving gloves and stuffed them in the pocket of his jacket. He looked at me. "How're you doing this morning?"

"I'm doing better. I think I've got my act together." I tried to confirm my words with a smile. "Thanks for asking."

He seemed to be in silent agreement with me that whether or not we ever found out how or why LL had died, there were several major building projects that needed to be completed. Dozens of jobs depended on them, not to mention the final payments that wouldn't be forthcoming if they remained unfinished. It was what LL would have wanted.

The telephone rang. It was the company's head accountant, Ted Jorgenson. He was so loud that I almost had to hold the receiver away from my ear. "Lexi, what happened to LL? What should we do? Everyone over here is looking for an explanation as to why they had to hear about LL's death on the news."

"I'm sorry, Ted. Please tell everyone over there that when we heard about it we were just too stunned to even think about spreading the word. I offer my wholehearted apologies. Will you contact each of the satellite office managers and let them know about it? Just . . . just tell everyone to continue as if LL were still here. The present building projects need to be completed. No one's job is in jeopardy." *At least, not that I know of,* I told myself.

"The news broadcasts are saying that he might have been murdered. Is that right?" His voice was only slightly calmer.

"It . . . probably," I said lamely. "You can expect the police to come around asking questions. Give them all the cooperation you can."

I hung up and the phone rang again. It was Tiffany. This was the call I was really dreading. She had finally listened to her messages. Her voice was shrill. "What's happened, Lexi? Has something happened to Lawrence? I had a message from a police detective right after yours. I was afraid to call him. I'm sure it is bad news, so I wanted to call you first. What's going on?"

"Tiffany, I'm not sure how to break this to you, but that detective was calling to tell you that—that LL is dead." The silence on her end of the conversation was total. "Are you still there?"

"Yes, I'm here. How did he die—a car accident? Did he drop over from a heart attack—a stroke?" The shrill quality had begun to modulate, but her voice was only slightly easier to listen to.

"The police are investigating, but they don't know very much yet. They won't know until the autopsy is done. His body was found in the arroyo that runs along the west side of the golf course that's part of the Sunnyville project. They think he'd been dead for about three days. The homicide division is investigating."

"Homicide! I'll be on the first plane out of here. I'll call you when I get home."

"Do you want someone to pick you up at the airport?"

"No, I'll grab a cab. Make yourselves available when I get there. I'll want some answers." She ended the call abruptly.

It was clear Roger realized who was on the other end of the line, and he sat quietly and watched me. When it was over, I looked at him and shrugged. "I hope we have some answers by the time she gets back."

CHAPTER 3

As I hung up, I heard the crunch of car wheels on the gravel parking area. Detective Sutherland entered a few moments later, nodded at both of us, and looked around. He noted the nameplate on LL's desk and motioned for each of us to pull up a chair near the front of it. As he sat behind the desk, he started to go through everything on top of the desk.

When he pulled out the first drawer, he looked at me. "Do I have your permission?" he asked perfunctorily.

"Of course, anything that might help."

He continued working through every drawer until he seemed satisfied that there was nothing to grab his attention.

"I'm sorry for your loss, but I hope you're both feeling up to answering some questions." He began with personal questions, asking for our full names and home addresses, and then asked how long we had worked for LL.

I responded first. "My full legal name is Alexis Aurelia Benson, but I would appreciate being called Lexi. Only my mother used my full name." I added my address and told him I'd worked for LL for three years.

When Roger gave him his address in the historic Evergreen section of town, Sutherland asked, "Is that Corvette outside yours?"

Roger's face turned bright pink. "Yeah, she's my pride and joy."

"Was Lattimer a tough man to work for?" We both insisted that there couldn't be a better boss than LL. "Did he have any enemies that you know about, any clients that were unhappy with the projects his company built?"

We looked at each other, and I responded. "I guess anyone who heads a company like this one might have some unhappy clients, and there are a few that owe money. Most are claiming that the downturn in the real estate market is making it tough to pay what they owe." When his face lit up like a dog that had spotted a bone, I tried to let him down easy. "LL wasn't pressing them beyond their ability to pay. He had worked out payment plans with those that were really hurting."

"I need a list of any companies or individuals that haven't paid what they owe, or have fallen behind on the provisions of their contracts by tomorrow noon. Can you get it by then?" He was looking at me as he spoke.

I nodded. "I'll get it done by then."

"When was the last time you saw Lattimer?" Again, he directed the question at me.

"Saturday morning. We had a contract signing here at the office at about eight." I responded.

"Who was here for it?"

I thought about it for a second or two. "LL, Stan Bergman, who directs the Phoenix satellite office; Roger and I; a writer and a photographer from the local newspaper; and a representative of the sports equipment company that's expanding into the area with one of its big box stores, a man named Jack Maulding. He's the regional manager for the company." I looked at Roger. "I didn't miss anyone, did I?"

He shook his head. "No, you mentioned everybody."

"Anything special about the event?"

Both Roger and I shook our heads. "The article about the contract ran in the Sunday edition, the same day you said he was killed," I added. The irony was not lost on any of us.

"How were his relations with the trade unions? Some of them can play hardball. Did Lattimer ever have to deal with strikes or other intimidation tactics?"

I shook my head. "Not while I've been here. LL paid union scale and it was his rule to treat his employees fairly so they would never need a union to lean on. Maybe that wasn't always so with some of his subcontractors, but LL had earned a remarkable personal loyalty among the men who worked on company projects."

"Have there been any unusual incidents lately that might have affected Mr. Lattimer?"

I was ready to shake my head when I remembered the auto accident. "About two weeks ago, LL totaled his SUV. It was only a year old, and he had kept it in good condition, but the investigating officer said that he must have lost control coming down the cul-de-sac from his home. He hit two cars parked at the bottom of the hill and took a hard hit on the head. The next day, he came into work with a bandage on his forehead and said that he really didn't remember much about the incident. He laughed it off as no big deal."

He looked at me closely, as if this matter might have some importance. "What did they do with the wreckage?"

"I suppose it was towed, probably by the company the city uses, since he had been taken to the hospital."

He made another note. "What kind of a relationship did he have with his wife? Did they fight? Is she a big spender?"

"She's a spender, but that wouldn't be a chafing point with LL. As long as it kept her happy, it was fine with him."

"Do you think she married him for his money?"

"I wouldn't go so far as to say that. I think she really loves . . . loved him. She's just the kind of person that enjoys the luxuries money can buy. By the way, she called a little while ago. She's catching the next flight back from Bermuda. Did she return your call? She told me you'd left a message."

"No, she hasn't returned my call. I'll need to talk to her as soon as she gets here."

He turned to Roger, who said, "I'll give it some thought, and let

22

you know if I come up with any ideas, but it's like Lexi said: LL was a great guy."

Sutherland turned back to me. "Just get me that list of clients who aren't paid up—by tomorrow." Sutherland stood and headed for the door.

As he put his hand on the knob, I asked a bit timidly, "Would you show me—ah, us, if Roger's interested—where his body was found?"

"Right now? Sure. Why?" I crossed the room and he held the door for me.

Before I stepped through the doorway, I looked at Roger. "Do you want to come?"

"No, it's not necessary." He moved to his own desk. Evidently his experience at the medical examiner's office was more than enough for him.

"I'm not really sure why I feel like I need to see it." I walked with him to the car. "I guess I'm hoping that it'll help me accept the situation a little more readily. I just can't get my mind around the idea that he's dead."

"Climb in." He opened the passenger side door of the front seat.

He drove through the gate where the property of LL Construction meets East Adobe Road and eventually made his way onto Highway 202, which looped around to the south to where he could exit onto Highway 60.

"How quickly the world has changed." I mused out loud. "He was here Saturday and—oh, I've got to contact Roseanna and let her know." The thought hit me like a slap. "She needs to be told. I should have thought of her sooner. By now, she may have caught a news broadcast, but I should've been the one to break it to her."

"Who?"

"Roseanna Gardner. She does the cleaning of both offices. LL has always been good to her. She's usually in about five o'clock every Saturday morning and gone by the time any of us get there, though I did get a chance to talk to her for a few minutes last Saturday, before the contract signing. When Roger and I got there about seven thirty, she and LL had their heads together in serious conversation. They broke off when we came in."

"I'll need her address and phone number. I may need to talk to her."

"Sure. I'll get it to you when I can look it up."

We rode east until we reached an undeveloped area, almost out of Mesa City limits. There, he took the exit onto McCurdy Road and turned right. The black top continued for about two miles past several neglected houses and then petered out. The dirt portion of the road continued, winding in an unplanned fashion through a few rolling sand hills that were dotted with saguaro cacti and mesquite. The tires made a hollow thump-thump as we crossed a wooden bridge over the dry arroyo.

I broke the silence. "When Sunnyville Estates was in the planning stage, LL and I drove out here to examine the area. I had been with the company about a year."

"What brought you out here?"

"LL said that 'Fast Eddie'—er, I mean, Ed Gomes—had gotten a clean bill of health for the project from a geologist who filed the required report with the county planning commission. It said that the runoff from the golf course was expected to be minimal and wouldn't worsen the erosion in the arroyo. The report concluded that it would have little impact on the topography of the immediate area.

"LL doubted that report. As we stood looking over the area, he said it looked like a pretty fragile ecosystem to him, and he couldn't see how the runoff from the golf course couldn't help but erode the immediate area."

Sutherland's department car bumped over some of the rocks that poked up through the hard soil, and he braked at a spot where yellow crime scene tape was stretched from a saguaro cactus to a leaning fence post and from there to a mesquite bush, where it fluttered in the wind.

After we climbed out of the car, we stood looking at the area. To the north, we could see where the arroyo began, about two hundred and fifty feet from where we stood. It deepened rapidly to about twenty feet. At its widest point, it was well over sixty feet wide, filled with tumbleweeds, mesquite, cacti, lizards, and other things that crawled or slithered. In my mind, I could visualize the effects of a heavy storm, how the rivulets of rainwater would roll down the sandy hills and meet in a turgid, churning stream at the base of the gorge, wearing away the fragile sandy slopes.

"I took some earth science courses while I was at ASU about eight years ago, thinking I would become a high school science teacher, so I enjoyed having him ask my opinion on the matter. Even though I wasn't a real expert, I told him that even I could see that an increase in runoff from the golf course would do tremendous damage to the area. In a couple of years, we'd be able to sell tickets to our own Grand Canyon. That set up the first real confrontation between LL and 'Fast Eddie'—I mean, Mr. Gomes."

Sutherland looked at me, and just said, "And?"

"I've only seen LL really angry on two occasions in the three years I worked for him and that was one of them. When he got Ed on the phone, he told him that the project wouldn't go forward unless a reputable geologic firm was brought in to re-evaluate the impact on the ecology of the site. After a lot of yelling at LL on the phone that I could hear on the other side of the room, Ed finally agreed. The second evaluation was a real blow to the project. That geologist said that it was imperative that a large catch basin be built to store the runoff from the golf course, and the potential overflow had to be piped from it into the Salt River canal, about four miles away. It would increase the cost of the project by more than a million dollars. LL told Ed that he would have to come up with the extra money or LL Construction was halting the project."

"Why didn't Gomes just change contractors and ignore Lattimer?"

"LL is . . . was a man of conscience. He made it clear that if Ed tried that, the second geologist's report would make its way to the county planning and zoning commission and the City of Mesa, as well as to the biggest newspaper in the metro area. That really tied Ed's hands. It had been a complex process just getting all the necessary permits, because the new homes and a portion of the golf course are in the county, but the rest of the golf course and the arroyo are in the city limits of Mesa, so he had to please both government entities."

"So Gomes was able to get the financial backing to put in the catch basin and pipe the water into the canal?"

"Yes, he put the arm on some buddies who had invested in the project to come up with the additional funds."

Sutherland said nothing. While he was thinking, he studied the slope that dropped down to the bottom of the arroyo. Apparently, the storm had been light in this area as we could see footprints and other marks left by the CSI team in the sand and among the rocks and brush.

I interrupted his thinking. "Can I go down there?

"What for?"

"I don't know. I just need to."

He took off his suit coat and laid it in the back seat of the car. He started down the slope, offering his hand to me to steady my steps as I moved over the rough places. It was a short, rough hike. When we got to the bottom, I could see the broken mesquite and dark streaks that might have been dried blood on some of the rocks. I was repelled but surprised there wasn't more.

I stood very still and looked around at the scene that might have been the last thing LL ever saw. I felt as subdued as if I were standing in a cemetery. After a minute, I asked, "Can I look around?"

"Sure, if you want to. It looks like the CSI team is finished." He added, "But be careful of things that sting or bite."

I walked farther into the gorge, moving in a southerly direction, trying to avoid clumps of prickly pear cactus with leaves the size of ping-pong paddles. It deepened a little as I stumbled over one rock and climbed over another. I don't know if I expected to find anything, but I let my eyes run over the rocks and mesquite. I halted when I saw a rattler sunning itself on a flat rock about six feet in front of me at eye level. As I stepped backward to put more distance between it and me, I bumped into Sutherland. Without turning to look at him, I said, "Sorry. Didn't know you were there."

"You think I'm going to let you wander around a crime scene without keeping an eye on you?"

"No, I guess not." As I turned to move away from the rattler, the sun glinted off something about a yard to the left of the snake. I picked up a long stick, long enough to keep the snake at bay, if it got unnecessarily friendly.

"Hey, what're you doing?"

"There's something on that slope to the left of that rattler. Maybe it's just a piece of a broken beer bottle, but I want to see what it is. Do you mind driving that snake away while I get it?" I offered the stick to him.

The snake opened its eyes with those narrow slits for pupils and gave me the look a predator gives to a potential snack.

He shook his head like a frustrated parent. "Miss Benson, I think you're . . . Never mind, just give me the stick." He grinned at me as I handed it to him. He stepped closer to the rock, where he could reach the snake with one end.

The long reptile, decorated with interlocking diamonds its full length, looked irritated and raised its head with a hiss. He poked it, and the rattles made that sound that can cool anyone's blood in a fraction of a second. The creature was not about to give up its place willingly on that warm, flat rock. It required several more pokes with the stick before it unwound and, with sinuous S-curves, slid into the underbrush.

I made my way carefully over to the spot where I was sure I had seen the shiny object. I visually searched the area carefully, noting that whatever it was, it wasn't shining any longer. I ran my fingers over the coarse sand and gravel and found something. It was a brass button.

When I turned, Sutherland was holding out his hand. I looked the button over thoroughly, noting that the thread would have been put through the dual holes in the back, which were hidden behind the sculpted front. It was emblazoned with the graceful form of a leaping deer and looked like the button from a blazer or a sport coat. I regretfully dropped it into his outstretched hand. He examined it carefully before he pulled a small plastic bag out of the front pocket of his slacks and dropped the button into it. He sealed the little bag before it went back into the same pocket.

"Do I have your permission to look around a bit more before we leave?" He could probably tell that I was a little miffed to have to give up the button so quickly.

He shrugged. "Sure, why not?" He handed me the stick. "Just don't step on any snakes."

That cooled my enthusiasm, but I did look around a bit longer, not expecting to find anything more. After all, the CSI team had probably covered the ground more thoroughly than I could. I probably found the button because the sun was at the right angle at the time.

He helped me climb back up the steep slope of the arroyo. When we reached his car, he pulled the bag with the button out of his pocket and briefly studied it again.

I offered a little apology. "I didn't think about fingerprints when I picked it up. I'm sorry."

As he tucked it back into his pocket, all he said was "Interesting. Couldn't have been here long or its finish would have been weathered, and don't worry about fingerprints. On television, the CSI types can raise fingerprints from thin air, but in the real world, it isn't that easy. It's highly unlikely that there were any usable prints on it."

We were both quiet while he drove me back to the office. As I climbed out of his car, he said, "When LL's wife gets into town, let me know right away just in case she doesn't. I have some questions for her."

As he started to drive away, a thought came to me. I waved him down and ran a few yards to catch up with the car. He rolled down the driver's side window. I bent so I could look at him more directly while I asked, "Where's LL's SUV, the one he bought after his accident? Has it been found?"

"What make and color was it?"

"A new Lincoln Navigator. It was midnight blue."

He pulled out a little notebook he kept in his shirt pocket and made a note to that effect. "Do you know the plate number, off hand?"

"It's a vanity plate—LLCON." He added that note.

"If we find it, we'll let you know." Then he was gone, a little dust cloud following him. He had forgotten to get Roseanna's contact information, but I was tired and decided that I could give it to him the next time we talked.

I returned to my desk and sat down to rub my temples in an attempt to ease a lingering headache. Detective Sutherland could have told me he was too busy to show me where LL's body was discovered, but he had taken the time to drive me out there, even though he apparently didn't understand my need to see the place. Was he interested in helping me obtain some closure . . . or was he interested in watching my reactions? Was I possibly a suspect? That thought made me pause for a moment as a cold chill ran up my spine.

CHAPTER 4

After Sutherland left, I copied down Roseanna's home number and address and was putting it in my purse when it occurred to me to check LL's calendar. There were two appointments listed for today. The first one was at eleven with Bud Hebestreet, the owner of the warehouse project that was technically finished according to the contract specifications. There were dollar signs after his name as a cue that the meeting would be about the cost of the add-ons he had recently requested.

The local Phoenix office under the direction of Stan Bergman had turned an old, cavernous building into sixteen large lofts of more than two thousand square feet each. They were designed to sell to folks who wanted to live near the state university, or the "bistro" section of the metro area where they could party at night in some of the glitzier clubs, or attend the symphony or opera if classes or clubbing weren't their style. The light rail would soon be extended to within a block of the building. It looked like it was going to be a potentially profitable project for him.

A week earlier, Bergman had called LL, who had put the call on the speakerphone so Roger and I could hear both sides of it, though he hardly needed to. We probably could have heard Stan without it.

"LL, I just can't put up with Hebestreet any longer. He's as hard

to please as a fussy old woman. In fact, he *is* a fussy old woman."
Stan's voice was edgy and stressed. "He's demanding suspended
ceilings in the lofts to hide the vents and ductwork after I've gone to
the trouble and expense of having all of it spray-painted black as per
the original agreement. The entire proposal is an expensive add-on to
the project and he wants us to eat the cost."

LL had soothed Bergman and then spent an hour on the phone
with Hebestreet. When he hung up, he grinned. "If the guy wants
suspended ceilings, then we'll give him suspended ceilings, but they
won't be free." Then he shook his head in mild frustration.

Bud arrived at five minutes after eleven. He was a short man and
couldn't have weighed more than a hundred and twenty pounds. He
wore glasses with thick lenses that gave the impression of vulnerability.
The thought crossed my mind that there must have been occasions
when business associates had attempted to take advantage of him
because of that impression.

I offered him the chair next to my desk and smiled at him to help
him relax as he sat down. Within an hour, he and I had come to an
agreement as to the added cost of the suspended ceilings. As he rose
to leave, he gave me a sympathetic look. "I'm really sorry about LL's
death, Lexi. He was a great guy."

I nodded. "Thanks, Bud," was all I managed to say around the
lump in my throat. I couldn't figure out why Bergman had been so
mad at Bud. He was reasonable with me.

The other entry in LL's appointment book was set for one-thirty
and was likely to prove more challenging. We were supposed to
meet with Ed Gomes to set up a schedule for him to cover a missed
payment, as well as the one due last Friday.

After Hebestreet left, Roger got a phone call from Ed, who
begged off the appointment that day. He wanted to meet for lunch
the following Wednesday.

"Okay, okay." Roger's voice sounded resigned. "Let's make
it at noon on Wednesday." He hung up and turned to me. "He
insists that he's got an appointment with the loan officer at his bank
tomorrow and if we give him a few more days, he's sure he can pay

the back amount owed plus a healthy installment on what was due last Friday. When we meet, I'll pin him down to specific dates and amounts."

I had always harbored some doubts about having Roger handle such a big account, but LL had faith in him. "Okay, but don't let him pull the wool over your eyes."

About one, he stretched and yawned. "Lexi, do you think you and I can hold it together?"

"You mean the company?"

"Yeah, it's a lot of responsibility without LL."

"Maybe it won't be up to us. LL probably had a will specifying what's to happen if something happened to him."

"You think so?" He was leaning with his elbow on the desk top, rubbing his forehead. "I'm going to head over to the other office and put in some time if you don't need me here. Will you be okay here alone?"

"Sure, I'll be fine."

Frankly, I was wondering if he intended to spend much time in the other office or was planning to head out early. Roger was a steady worker, but every day for the past couple of months regardless of which office he was working in at the time, he took long lunches and stopped what he was doing at four o'clock. We were both on salary—good salary—and when LL had something important that required my attention, I didn't hesitate to put in whatever time was required, but Roger obviously had other interests in his life. I was just a little bit envious.

On a few occasions, LL had taken Roger with him to shoot skeet or play golf with clients. They were both a five handicap in golf— good players. I wondered if Roger was using his free time to perfect his golf game. Sharing an interest in golf had given him time with LL that I didn't have, as my handicap had to be about fifty.

I was opening a small carton of yogurt for lunch and reassessing the paperwork on my desk when the phone rang. I jumped and grabbed it as if another ring would bite me. "LL Construction," I answered in a tight voice.

"Hey, it's just me again." It was Sutherland's baritone voice. "I just read the medical examiner's initial report and thought you might find it of interest."

I nervously cleared my throat. "Yes, of course. What does it say?"

"It verified that he was killed by a shotgun blast. The pattern of the blast suggested that the shooter was standing no more than three or four feet from him. That's why the side of his face was such a mess. The coyotes didn't help, but it was largely the damage inflicted by the double-ought pellets."

I let the air slowly out of my lungs. "So your suspicions were right."

"No doubt about it. The body was dumped in the arroyo. The CSI guys are sure of that because of the lividity and the fact that there was so little blood at the site."

"Do they know anything else?"

"Not yet. Do you have that list of clients who are behind in their payments yet?"

"Not yet. I'll have it by tomorrow, before lunch."

"Call me when you've got it."

"I put Roseanna's name and address on it, too, along with the other names."

"Roseanna?"

He had apparently forgotten about asking me for the information on her. "Roseanna Gardner, the woman who cleans our offices. You had asked for it."

"Frankly, I had forgotten. Thanks for remembering."

After he hung up, I plunged into some more paperwork, and when my back began to complain, I checked my watch. It was after four and I didn't feel that I could accomplish much more if I stayed any longer. I was emotionally exhausted, so I locked the office. As I walked to my car, I noted that Roger's Corvette was gone.

The wind was stirring, filling the air with dust as fine as mist. The clouds were gathering again. Lately, it was common for the rain to clear in the morning, allowing the sun to shine from an azure sky for a few hours, but by four in the afternoon, the sky was the color of pewter, bringing on an early twilight. Right now, the darkness felt smothering and the smell of the coming rain filled the air. The southwest might not get much rain, but when it does, it can come by the barrelful, often creating flash floods and turning streets into rivers and retention basins into small lakes.

In the heavy traffic, it would take me nearly thirty minutes to get home, so I decided to get a move on. At the halfway point in my drive, the rain was a staccato rattle that sounded like someone was throwing intermittent handfuls of shingle nails at the roof of my car, but it eased by the time I pulled into the driveway, slowing to a light drizzle that made the surface of the pavement glisten with reflections of light.

I was hanging my jacket in the coat closet when Tiffany called. She had chartered a small private jet to bring her home. I should have known that she wouldn't wait for a seat on a commercial flight.

"Lexi, I'm home now, and there was another message on the phone from that same homicide detective that left the message when I was in Bermuda. He was insistent that he needed to talk to me. His name was Sunderland, or Sutherland—Steve Sutherland, I think. What do you know about him?"

"He's leading the investigation into LL's death, and he asked me to let him know when you got back to town. I'm sure he'll want to talk to you right away."

"Will you try to put him off until tomorrow? It was a long flight and I'm just beat."

I thought it was odd that she didn't have a bunch of questions for him that she wanted answered immediately, as that was what she had seemed to want when she called from the island, but since she apparently expected me to be her go-between, I responded, "I'll call and ask him if that's possible, but he may insist on seeing you tonight. If that is the case, will you see him?"

After a long exhale of resignation, she said in clipped tones, "If he insists, make it about eight thirty here at the house. That will give me time to shower and grab a few minutes to lie down." She hung up without waiting for my response.

I dug around in my handbag and located his business card with his phone numbers. He answered simply, "Sutherland."

"Detective Sutherland, this is Lexi Benson."

He broke in. "Just call me Steve. It's a lot easier."

"Okay, Steve. You wanted to know when LL's wife, Tiffany, got back in town, in case she didn't call you. She just called to let me know she's here. Can you wait to talk to her tomorrow or do you need to see her this evening?"

"I'd appreciate it if I could see her tonight. What time?"

"She suggested eight thirty at her home, if you couldn't wait until tomorrow."

"Will you be there?"

"You want me there?" That was a surprise.

"I think having you there might make her a bit more comfortable. After all, she knows you, but she's never met me."

"Okay. I'll meet you there. By the way, the code for the entry gate to the house is 9911."

"I'll wait for you at the gate and let you open it. That way, the lawyers won't have any questions about the circumstances of my entering."

I called and told Tiffany to expect us at eight thirty as she had requested. Her voice had just a shade of resentment in it, but she agreed.

I fixed myself a peanut butter and honey sandwich, my comfort food from childhood. It was what I turned to in times of stress. I downed it with a tall glass of cold milk. It always reminded me of my school days when I would drop my books on the kitchen table and fix myself a sandwich like that to soothe the tensions that came with the social interactions required to survive public school. I had been a good student, but I never had any real idea how to make friends. It was Percy that made friends easily.

I rinsed the sticky honey off my fingers and then showered and put on my best electric blue pantsuit with the embroidered collar. With a white turtleneck under the jacket, I felt ready to meet anyone up to and including the governor. I ran a brush through my short curls and touched up my lipstick. I was still looking pale, about like I felt, but I picked up an umbrella and made my way out to my car.

On the way to Paradise Valley, I wondered if Steve had told me the whole reason he wanted me present when he questioned Tiffany. *Is Tiffany a prime suspect? Maybe he thinks we're in this together.* That was an unpleasant thought, but my mind continued down that same road. *She would have a bunch of lawyers at her beck and call—but she'd been out of town at the time of the murder.* I didn't like thinking that he was looking at either of us with suspicion.

Without stars or a moon, it was the kind of dark that you can feel on your face. I made my way through the streets with care since most of the cities that made up the metro Phoenix area have enacted ordinances prohibiting what they consider light pollution, but I wondered if the issue didn't have more to do with size of the payments to the local electric utility company than any kind of ecological reason.

I moved northward onto Highway 202 and made the interchange onto the 101, eventually reaching Indian Bend Road. In the lighter traffic, I made it to Paradise Valley in twenty-five minutes. It was an incorporated community tucked between Phoenix and Scottsdale where homes started at about two million and went up from there. Frankly, calling it a community was doing it a disservice. It was more like a small, very rich country. I turned on to a feeder road that, after a few minutes of twists and turns, led me into a cluster of homes that backed onto Camelback Mountain. Most folks would covet any one of these homes—at least until they received the annual tax bill.

This was another suburban community with ordinances to prevent light pollution, which the residents combated through the installation of at least one stylized lamppost in the front yard of their all-electric homes.

I wound my way through the narrow streets designed to discourage anyone who didn't live there until I located it, a rambling structure on a large lot nestled against the hillside, designed for Tiffany by a Frank Lloyd Wright wannabe. It was meant to be a copy of Wright's

Scottsdale home "Taliesin West." The architect had tried to imitate the long, low lines and uplifting planes of the original, even using desert rock for the walls. Like most copies, it fell somewhat short of the grace and beauty of the original.

A three-tiered fountain fed by a circulating pump sat in the middle of the sweeping lawn. There was a lot of lawn. The vast majority of homes in the suburban portions of the metro area had been built after 1960 and had been designed with "desert landscape," which meant a yard of gravel and a few succulents, exotic cacti, and palms. In an area where water is the most valuable resource, only the rich—or foolish—bothered with lawns to water.

When I arrived at the gate, Sutherland was sitting in his car, waiting for me while he studied a map. I pulled up to the post where the security camera and the keypad were located. I punched in the code and waited as the gate rolled open. With Sutherland's unmarked car almost literally on my rear bumper, we entered in tandem, driving two hundred feet up the long driveway to the half circle that ran under the spacious portico where we parked.

I had only been in LL and Tiffany's home on one previous occasion, to deliver a contract. At that time, I had expected my visit to be brief, but LL had wanted to show me the whole place.

We met at the front door and I rang the bell. While we waited, I could hear the dry palm fronds of the three trees in the front yard as they snapped and thudded in the wind.

He chuckled. "Without the GPS in the car, I'd never have located this place."

The housekeeper, whose name was Emma, if memory served me, opened the door and led us across the large foyer tiled in white marble. She motioned for us to enter the sunken living room on the right.

"Mrs. Lattimer said to put you in the living room." At that, she left us.

I felt a little bit like a potted plant, being "put" in the living room. I couldn't help but notice again the whiteness of it all: white marble tile on the floor with just a whisper of beige swirled in it.

The white area rugs that made islands of the two furniture groupings looked more like patches of deep snow than carpets. The twelve-foot ceiling was bordered with a wide, carved crown molding above walls papered in the palest of beige silk fabric. All of the wood furnishings looked like they came from a very expensive furniture store where the price tags made a person squint and wonder if too many zeros had been added by mistake. Three white leather couches formed a U in front of a fireplace, which burned brightly.

We stood while we waited for Tiffany. When she entered, she made a striking appearance. She had on a pair of white silk lounging pajamas that flattered her slender limbs. She was a remarkably beautiful woman. Her perfectly arched eyebrows gave her gray eyes a slightly astonished look. Her hair was ash blonde and cut in a sculpted fashion so no matter how she tossed her head, it slid back into place against her jaw line.

I had gotten to know the wives of many wealthy businessmen who were clients of the bank while I worked there, and had learned to recognize a well-done nose job. It suddenly hit me like a stab of electricity that she probably "went to Bermuda" to spend more time with plastic surgeons than with her friends. Why hadn't I seen it before? She had a finely shaped jaw, apparently the work of a master surgeon. There was just the faintest purpling under her eyes, suggesting that she may have had them done on this trip—or to be fair, perhaps it was from grief and stress.

She was hardly more than thirty. I wondered why a woman that young would feel the need to redo what nature had so generously given her. Was it boredom—or perhaps, an attempt to induce her overly busy husband to give her more attention?

I admired Detective Sutherland for his ability not to look overwhelmed by the display of wealth. His eyes swiftly took in her and the room. She led us to the couches in front of the fireplace, where the detective and I sat on opposite ends of one and Tiffany sat across from us on another couch that almost swallowed her small form as she pulled her legs up and folded them on the cushion next to her.

"Well, Detective Sutherland, what can you tell me about my husband's death?"

The question sounded more abrupt than she probably meant. She softened it by adding, "I don't mean to be a poor hostess. Can I have Emma get you something hot to drink? After all, it's wet outside."

I shook my head. He waved her offer away and answered her in a direct manner. His expression was alert, neutral, watchful. "Mrs. Lattimer, there's really no way to make this kind of news less painful. Your husband's body was found yesterday in an arroyo that runs parallel to the new golf course his company is building at Sunnyville Estates. Are you familiar with that area?"

"No, I know nothing about that project."

She shook her head again. It was apparent that she was not interested in unnecessary details, so he verbally painted the situation with broad brushstrokes. "He was killed by a shotgun blast, probably sometime Saturday evening or Sunday. His body was dumped in the arroyo, where it was found by a couple of kids who had cut school yesterday morning. We were unable to reach you, so we requested that Miss Benson do the necessary identification so the investigation could move forward. I'm directing the investigation, and I have the full resources of the Mesa Homicide Department at my disposal."

"Do you have any idea, any clue as to who would do such a thing?" Her right hand played with a tissue she had pulled from the breast pocket of the silk pajamas. It was the only sign of emotional tension.

"No, the investigation is in its earliest stages. Can you give me any insight into his life? Do you know of any enemies he had?"

"Everyone liked Lawrence. I really mean that. He had no enemies—at least, none that I know of."

Sutherland cleared his throat. "This may seem intrusive, but I need to know if you are his primary heir."

"I . . . I suppose I am. I insisted on signing a prenuptial agreement before we were married, so no one could say I married him for his money. If we divorced, I would receive nothing, but it made no reference to what would happen if he died. I suppose I'll inherit his estate."

"Is there a will?"

"Frankly, I don't know. I've always hesitated to show any interest in my husband's legal or financial matters, for fear it would be interpreted as . . ." she searched for a graceful way to put it but finally seemed to reach for the only words that came to mind, "self serving—or greedy. I figured that I would just have to trust that he had made all the necessary provisions for my future if he died."

"If he died intestate . . ."

"Intestate?" She paused and delicately dabbed at her eyes. "What does that mean?"

"That he died without a will. If that's the case, the estate is likely to be divided in equal portions among his immediate family members. Who would that include, other than yourself?"

"There isn't anyone else, except his older sister, who is in a facility for . . . for those who can't live independently any longer. She's suffering from dementia. She's been well provided for."

He was quiet for a moment before saying the obvious. "Then there isn't anyone else you can see who would benefit by his death?"

She blanched almost as white as the furnishings in the room. "Does that mean I'm a suspect?"

He softened his tone. "We have to consider all the options, Mrs. Lattimer, no offense intended." He pulled the small notebook from his shirt pocket. "Would you be able to furnish me with the name and phone number of your husband's lawyer?"

She nodded, unfolded her legs, and rose from where she sat. "I'll get it for you." She pulled an address book from the middle drawer of a dainty desk with legs like swans' necks. "Here it is. Corstelli and Associates." She read the office and cell numbers and the office address. "Brandon has handled all of my husband's personal and business matters since Lawrence and I married."

He wrote down the information before asking, "Have there been any unusual incidents recently that stand out in your mind?"

"I don't understand what you mean."

"Any kind of incident that Mr. Lattimer might have mentioned as unusual or odd, the kind of thing that he might have wondered about?"

She returned to the couch and sat again. "No, not really. He wrecked his car a couple weeks ago, but that can happen to anyone."

He closed his notebook. "If you remember anything that might be of use in this investigation, please call me." He offered her his business card as he looked at me. "Has anything occurred to you, Miss Benson, that you might want to ask about?" Startled, I shook my head.

She took the card as the three of us stood. She led us through the foyer to the front door. By the time she put her hand on the knob, she was dabbing at her eyes again.

I impulsively put my arms around her. "I'm so sorry, Tiffany. We all loved him, but you face the greatest loss. Is there anything I can do?" I knew it was a timeworn question meant to offer some comfort, but what else do you say to someone in those circumstances?

She put her head on my shoulder and quietly sobbed for about a minute. When she pulled away, she whispered with a stiff little smile, "Just keep the company going, Lexi. That's what Lawrence would want."

Several questions pushed their way into my head. *Did she have the legal authority to extend that assignment to me? Would I need some kind of written authorization to back up any actions I took? Would LL's lawyer support her request? Was I even ready for such a big assignment?*

Steve watched the two of us with an objectivity that told me things were going on behind his composed features.

I took a deep breath. "Are you sure that's what you want, Tiffany?"

"Lawrence put his trust in your judgment, Lexi. I think it's what he would want." She looked reproachfully at me, as if she thought I didn't want the job. Actually, I didn't. It scared me, but I tried to soothe her feelings.

"Tiffany, if this is what you really want—and what you think

LL would have wanted, I'll do it, but I think LL's lawyer will need to draft something to legalize the situation. I need a foot to stand on if someone challenges any decisions I make."

"Of course, of course," she murmured. "I'll call Brandon in the morning and tell him to do whatever is necessary."

"Tiffany, he'll want to know if this situation is going to be temporary—perhaps you'll want to sell the company at some future date—or if you want it to be more permanent." The enormity of her request was just beginning to sink in and I suddenly felt that I would be several inches shorter by the time I reached my car due to the sheer weight of it.

She thought about it briefly. "Let's just leave it open-ended for the time being, something revocable, until the estate is settled. Then some more permanent decisions can be made."

As she opened the front door for us, Steve thanked her for her time and offered the usual comment under such circumstances. "I'm sorry for your loss."

"I'll have Brandon—Mr. Corstelli—call you," she said to me as she watched us step out onto the wide porch.

"I'll expect to hear from him." I didn't know what else to say.

As she started to close the door, she paused. "Lexi, who's going to write his obituary? I don't know how to do anything like that."

I turned back to her. "I've written a few." *What I really meant was that I had written the obituaries for both of my parents.* "Why don't you write up everything you want the public to know about him, and email it to me at the office? I'll format it and add anything about the company that I think should be included."

Her face relaxed a little. "Yes, yes, I'll do that in the morning. Thanks for your help. I'm sure you won't let me down."

After she closed the door, Steve followed me to my car and opened the driver's side door. He had something on his mind. I could tell by his slightly narrowed eyes. After I slid in behind the steering wheel, he stood holding the door, looking off in the dark. "Didn't she say that she had never asked about LL's will or other legal matters?" he asked. I nodded. He continued, "That's what I thought. Seems a little funny that she knows the lawyer well enough to call him by his first name."

"They probably move in the same social circles," I said with a shrug. He didn't look entirely satisfied with my response when he closed my car door.

Traffic was almost nonexistent as I drove home in the continuing gusts of wind and rain. In the darkness, my headlights made a path of light that I rushed into. I was exhausted. When I stretched out on the couch to watch the last part of the ten o'clock evening news, I listened to the anchorman speculate about LL's death until I made myself get up and go to bed.

I couldn't sleep. I felt as if my brain was being churned by a herd of wild horses all trying to gallop in different directions. In a futile attempt to calm myself enough to rest, I adjusted the blankets and changed position repeatedly. I felt hot and fevered one moment and threw off the blankets, but then I quickly became chilled. I pulled up the blankets beneath my chin, but soon grew hot again. I turned on my side with my knees drawn up, but when I finally drifted off to sleep, the sight of LL's crumpled body in the arroyo forced its way into my dreams. Tears began to sting my eyes. I got up and spent the rest of the night in the recliner with the word "Why" repeating in my head.

CHAPTER 5

The sky was heavily overcast Friday morning, a brooding gray, roiling in the southeast, where the thick mass was threatening another hard rain. The whole scene had the somber look of an under-exposed old black-and-white photograph. The cloud cover made it feel more like evening than morning, spreading a gloom across the expanse of desert to the east and south that matched my feelings.

I pulled on my sweats and decided I needed to walk again. I walked hard and fast for an hour. I believe sweat is better than depression, any day. But the sweat I produced in the cold was minimal. Back at home, I took a shower, dressed, and headed for the office.

My car had been dirtied by the dust carried by the early morning wind. As I backed out of my parking place, a pigeon passed judgment on my windshield, so on the way to work, I put my car through the car wash to get rid of the smeared half moons the wipers made.

I took a special pride in my car, a white 2010 Chrysler Sebring coupe with a retractable hard top. I hated the water spots that trapped the dust that came with the rain. I had it washed often enough that I knew the guys at the car wash by name. In good weather, I could press the button that folded the top into the trunk and the wind would play with my short auburn curls while I drove.

As I parked in front of the office, I wasn't surprised to see Roger's Corvette shiny and clean in the parking lot. When I entered, he was going through one of the project files in the drawer marked In Progress.

I stopped in the doorway. "Good morning, Roger."

He straightened up and rolled his shoulders as if they were stiff. "Hi, there. I'm looking for the Sunnyville Estates file to make sure we have a complete record of all of Ed Gomes payments. Do you know where it is? The last time I talked with him, he insisted that except for the payment due this week, he'd made all but one of the payments the contract required. I'm just trying to verify that. I think he's missed two. He doesn't have any documentation to prove his claims so I'm trying to get it all straightened out so I can pin him down when we have lunch next week."

"Well, if he's been making his payments by EFT, then the bank will have a record. Don't let him mess with your thinking. I'm sure that he missed one payment back in March and then there's the one due last Friday. At two million each, that's a substantial amount of money."

"Yeah, don't I know it. I'll check the records in the other office. The file on his project is probably more complete over there. Don't worry about it. I'll get it figured out before the meeting with him. If necessary, I'll call the bank so I can document everything." The phone rang, and when I sat down to answer it, he headed to the other building.

I spent the rest of the morning answering or returning calls from alarmed project managers who had heard about LL's death from Ted Jorgenson. Their questions and my answers were nearly identical, no matter who was on the other end of the line. "Yes, it's a terrible thing. Yes, the police have called it a homicide. No, the police don't have any idea who did it. No, nothing will change on your project. Keep it moving toward completion. LL's widow wants the company to continue to function as it always has. No, I don't know when the services for him will be scheduled. Yes, we'll keep you in the loop so you can be there."

The one variation in those conversations was with Stan Bergman. He asked, "Who's in charge now that LL's dead?"

"For the time being, Tiffany has asked me to keep the company running and make sure that the projects in process aren't halted or hindered in any way."

"*You're* in charge?" His response was skeptical.

"Yes, until further notice. Tiffany wants things to continue as if LL were still alive."

He exploded a burst of air. "Huh, what a laugh," he muttered.

"Stan, I know I don't have the years in the construction business that you have, but this is a policy-making position. I can analyze economic trends, growth projections, and potential future property values in the same way LL would."

I hadn't pacified him. He hung up without saying any more. I had always suspected that Stan only tolerated me when I had accompanied LL to the various project sites he supervised, and now his tone of voice on the phone made it abundantly clear that he held no warm or fuzzy feelings toward me.

I returned to working on the computer, bringing up the records of all the finished or nearly finished projects, looking at the payment records, when the phone on my desk rang again. I began to wonder if I was going to get my task done before lunch as I had promised.

"Ms. Benson, this is Brandon Corstelli, LL's attorney. I just spoke with Mrs. Lattimer and she requested that I complete the necessary paperwork to give you legal authority to act in LL's stead to keep the company functioning while the estate is probated. Because he died intestate, I'll be forced to file the matter before the probate court and wait for a decision, a process that may take some weeks. In the meantime, I'll write up something that will pass muster if anyone challenges your right to make decisions in LL's stead."

"What's the probate court likely to decide?"

"In these situations, the court usually rules that the estate is to be divided equally between any first degree relatives—that's usually the wife and children." His voice reflected a slightly condescending quality, as if he were explaining things to someone not likely to grasp them. "Sometimes, there's a challenge from a sibling of the deceased, but with LL's sister declared *non compos mentis* and previously provided for, that isn't going to happen. Since it appears that Tiffany is the only relative in line to inherit, we will approach the matter as though it's a foregone conclusion. I heard LL refer once in our early association to a marriage that was dissolved a long time ago, but I did a records check on the first wife and she died several years ago, so that's a non-issue. Do you have any other questions I can address?"

I asked the obvious. "Were there any children by that marriage?"

"No, LL said there weren't."

"How soon do you think you can complete the paperwork authorizing me to act in his stead?"

"Knowing how long legal matters can sometimes take, I think that's excellent, Mr. Corstelli. Thanks for your help."

"Glad to be of assistance." Though he had been a bit condescending up to that point, he sounded sincere in his last statement.

After the call ended, I sat with my elbow on the desk and my head in my left hand, feeling my pulse pound steadily in my temple. I listened to the *click, click, click* of the second hand of the big clock on the wall above me as it unendingly measured the circumference of the clock face, and reminded me of the fleeting nature of the present. There's nothing like listening to a clock while you deal with death. I couldn't help but note that each click I heard was only briefly part of the present moment. It immediately slid into the past, and the next click briefly became the present then joined its brother in the past.

I heard my cell ring from inside my bag. It gave me a start. I scrambled to get to it. "Hello, this is Lexi."

"Lexi, this is Uncle Bob." He didn't have to tell me who it was. I could tell immediately by the faint, residual Texas drawl. "Betty and I just got back in town and heard about LL's death. We're just appalled at the news. He was such a nice guy. Is it true that he was murdered?"

"Yes. I'm here at the office trying to keep things going. I don't understand why anyone would kill him. His wife wants me to continue to run things as if he were here. Frankly, it's almost overwhelming."

"I'm sure it is. Is there anyone you can turn to if you get in a tough spot?"

"Yes, any of the satellite office managers are experts. I won't hesitate to ask their help or advice, if I need it."

I could hear Aunt Betty's voice in the background. "Hold on, Lexi," Uncle Bob said, "your aunt wants to talk to you."

I could hear a few muffled words before she asked, "Lexi, sweetie, how are you holding up? We're just heartsick to hear about Mr. Lattimer's death. I'm so sorry. Is there anything we can do? I know you thought a lot of him."

"Thanks for your concern, but I'll be okay." I tried to sound firm. All I needed was to have Aunt Betty fussing around me. She was a dear, but when she took it into her head to mother someone, they'd need a tank of oxygen to survive her smothering ministrations. "The police are investigating the case and I'm sure they'll find out who's behind it fairly soon. Please don't worry about me," I emphasized.

"Take care of yourself—eat properly, get your rest. I'm sorry if I sound like I'm nagging, but we do worry about you."

When I ended the call, I returned to the computer search of the construction projects that Steve had requested. I found several that were not paid up. The first was the loft project owned by Bud Hebestreet. I remembered that Bud had really riled LL when he came into the office about six weeks ago to solicit a big political contribution for a congressional candidate that LL didn't like. That had been another one of the few times I had seen LL really angry. When Hebestreet pressed the matter, LL had said with a stone face, "When you're paid in full on the loft project, I might consider a contribution to one of the candidates you're supporting, but even then, it will have to be a candidate I respect. If you press me again, I'll tell the newspapers what I've heard about that guy."

I started the list with his name, even though I couldn't imagine him as a threat to anyone. He was just a small man who wanted, more than anything, to be a big wheel in political and social circles. He was manipulative at times but basically harmless.

Payment for a highway project for the state in the Four Corners area was still outstanding, but that wasn't a surprise. The state was often late on contractual agreements. Unlike the feds, the state constitution prohibited the spending of money that was not in the tax coffers. Nothing there of interest.

I continued looking over the accounts for another hour before I reached the Sunnyville Estates Project. When I changed screens to the accounts receivable page, it wasn't what I had expected. The payment entries hadn't been kept up to date. Here it was, November, but the last entry was in early July. Surely Roger was aware of that—or had he delegated the task to one of the other accountants? It looked like he really dropped the ball on this account. I made a mental note to have a long talk with him about it.

I searched the rest of the projects, and then I had an "aha" moment. I came across the payment record of Chet Huddleston, the former owner of Hud's New and Used Autos. He had contracted with LL to build a home for his third wife. LL had said that Chet often told him "not to spare the horses, as nothin' was too good for his little woman."

Just seeing his name brought a picture of him to mind. He was a man in his late forties with receding brown hair and a waistline that had pushed him into suits with 56-inch waists. After having enjoyed the life of a prosperous—if not entirely honest—car salesman, prison was probably proving hard on him.

I also remembered his wife. She colored her hair brick red and stood at least half a head taller than him. She was dressed "to the nines." Maybe the way she dressed was part of Chet's financial problems.

Two years earlier, he had talked LL into building that large house. After it was finished, Chet never made any further payments after the initial one. Every time he was approached, he insisted that the payments would have to wait a few more weeks, when the economy was sure to improve and he expected that car sales would increase. LL had been on the verge of taking him to court when he was arrested for embezzlement and fraud by state authorities. He had been selling new models to folks who were still up to their ears in the loan payments on their present vehicles. I remember seeing his TV ads where he had cheerfully looked into the camera and promised that anyone could buy a new car from him, regardless of the amount still owed on a present loan. But he had overlooked a little thing called paying off the previous loans. He'd also aggravated the folks at the state tax commission when he hadn't forwarded the sales tax on the sale of the new cars.

If you murdered your neighbor, maybe your lawyer could keep you out of jail for months or even years with delaying tactics, but not if you withhold state sales tax. You'd get shut down and sent away with a speed that will make the pace car in the Indianapolis 500 look sluggish.

LL had been subpoenaed to testify at Chet's trial for fraud. The prosecution had asked that LL tell the jury about Chet's refusal to pay for the house, so there were undoubtedly some hard feelings on Chet's part.

I didn't know LL at the time, but coincidently, I was also subpoenaed to testify against him. The vehicle I purchased from him had long since gone to its grave, but it was my complaint about not getting the title to the car when I had paid it off that triggered the state's investigation. Not long after my complaint, others began to trickle in, effectively setting the state revenue dogs on him. He went on the list, even though he was sitting in the state pen.

There were three other projects around the metro area where the owners had fallen behind on the contractual payment schedule, plus one in Tucson and another in the Flagstaff area. Nothing really big, but I added them to the list. I sat back for a minute and then, on an impulse, I added Ed Gomes's name. Maybe there was nothing to be concerned about, but it wouldn't hurt for him to answer a few of Sutherland's questions.

At that point, I picked up the phone and called Steve. "I have that list you wanted. Can I fax or email it to you?"

"Fax it. Here's the office number."

After I had sent the list marked to his attention, I decided to close up the office, go home, and fix another peanut butter and honey sandwich on wheat bread for a late lunch. I was really feeling the stress of the past few days. On the drive home I realized Tiffany hadn't sent me any information for the obituary.

•   •   •

After licking the honey off my fingers, I called Tiffany and left a message with Emma that I needed the information for the obituary right away. Then I spent much of the afternoon preparing a Sunday school lesson for a class of fourteen- and fifteen-year-olds. I wanted to hang in as their teacher for another year, and I really liked every one of them individually, but at the end of nearly an hour of dealing with them as a group, I was always heavily perspiring and deeply relieved that I had not chosen a career as a junior high school teacher.

CHAPTER 6

On Sunday morning, standing at my front window I could see a storm front rolling in from the southeast, dividing the sky into layers that varied from smoke to sunlit, pearly gray. Soon the rain would be pounding, leaving full gutters and flooded streets rushing to the grassy depressed catch basins that served as city parks, and as I drove, I knew the water in the streets would blast the undercarriage of my car.

After church, I returned home and took a well-earned nap while lying on the couch. About three that afternoon, the ringing of my cell phone woke me.

"Miss Benson, this is Steve Sutherland. I tried to locate Roger today. Do you know where he is? He isn't answering his phone, and when I went by his place, his neighbor said he hadn't seen him for a couple of days."

"No, I don't. He doesn't share much about his private life."

"If you see him or hear from him, have him give me a call."

• • •

I spent Sunday night getting my exercise tossing and turning, so on Monday morning I decided to get up at five thirty and go to work early. When I reached the office, I was surprised to see Roger in so early.

He greeted me. "You're looking better. You must have gotten some rest over the weekend."

I laughed. "Yes, I needed it."

As I sat, he appeared to take a minute to gather his thoughts. "I came in early so I could look for any kind of document or . . . or directive from LL that would give us some guidance in a situation like this." He ran his hand through his dark hair. "I've looked through the files but found nothing. How does he expect us to keep the company running without some direction?"

"Tiffany has asked LL's attorney to draft the legal document that will give me the authority to keep the company running while the estate is probated. It's expected to be ready on Wednesday. Until then, we won't make any major decisions."

He looked a little surprised. "So Tiffany has asked you to run the company?"

"At the present it's an open-ended commitment until the court makes the disposition of the estate final. After that, she may want to sell it."

"Yeah, I can see why she might want to do something like that," he responded. He looked around and then added lamely, "Then I guess that I won't need to come back into the office until Wednesday when your decisions will be official." As an after thought, he asked, "Is that okay with you?"

"Sure. We won't be making any important decisions before then."

At that, he picked up his jacket from the back of his chair and headed for the door.

I suddenly remembered that I needed to pass on a message. "Hey, Detective Sutherland wants to talk to you. You need to give him a call—and we need to talk about the Sunnyville Estates account . . ."

He raised his hand in admission that he'd heard me but made no verbal response. The door closed behind him and I heard the gravel spray toward the office as he drove away.

The phone on my desk rang. "Lexi, I need some help planning the memorial for Lawrence. I've worried about it ever since I got home from Bermuda. What should I do?"

I was taken off guard. Tiffany had never previously asked my advice on anything—except the obituary. In fact, she and I had hardly had any more than a shallow, nodding acquaintance. Here she was asking my advice about his memorial service. Well, I was willing to do what I could.

"What kind of service do you want? A religious service held in a church, or maybe something a little less formal?"

"I just don't know. What do you think? I'm having him cremated because of the condition of the body. The funeral director recommended that it be handled that way."

"I didn't realize his body had been released to a funeral home yet. Detective Sutherland seemed to think that it might take sometime before the medical examiner would be finished with it."

"Since LL was on a first name basis with the governor, I made a phone call and got someone in his office to encourage the medical examiner to release it right away. I just can't stand the stress." Her last sentence was nearly a wail. She calmed down before she continued; "They allowed the funeral home to pick him up this morning. I've decided to have a wake here at the house for his closest friends and associates immediately following the services. I think that's the right thing to do, don't you? Do you think Veterans' Hall would be appropriate for the memorial service? Do you think it will be big enough—without being too big?"

I thought about it for a moment. "Yes, it ought to work. Because of the publicity and the way he died, I think you might want to keep the service private—by invitation only, with no public announcement of when and where. You might want to limit the program to a few tributes by people who knew him. I think you could invite the governor to speak, and if he can't make it, Congressman Jeff Skidmore might be available. They were good friends, and the congressman is known as a man of faith. You might want to invite County Commissioner Don Harvey to speak. I remember his eulogy at the services for state Senator Cowan. It was outstanding, and he knew LL well." I added as an afterthought, "Maybe you ought to consider inviting the head of the Metro Interfaith Council. I'm not sure who that is right now, since that position rotates among the different local denominations, but LL was always generous to them. He'd want them included."

She exhaled as if she were very weary. "Let's schedule it for Thursday, at one. I know that may not give some people time to arrange their schedules to be present, but I need to get this all behind me. Right now, I can't even think straight. I just want to get this over with."

I circled the date on my desk calendar. "I'll contact the company office managers and let them know. By the way, do you have your thoughts down on paper for the obituary yet? I'll need to get it to the paper in time for tomorrow's edition."

"Thanks for the reminder. There's just too much on my mind right now. I'll get it to you right away."

When I hung it up, the phone immediately rang again. It was Sutherland. "I just heard that the county medical examiner's office has released LL's body to Tiffany. It takes clout to get the autopsy done and the body released that quickly."

"She got someone in the governor's office to hurry the process."

"Why doesn't that surprise me?" he muttered. "I've looked over the list of deadbeats that you faxed over to the office."

"Now wait a minute." I jumped to their defense. "Some of those are just guys who have fallen on hard times. The term 'deadbeat' probably only applies to Chet Huddleston and maybe Ed Gomes."

He chuckled. "Okay, I'll be a bit more discreet in the use of that term. The thought occurred to me that I ought to interview anyone who might have felt that they were in line to step into LL's shoes. Can you make me a list of them?"

"That's easy enough. Got a pencil? There are really only three of them. I'll read you their names and addresses." I lifted a roster of the satellite office managers from the right-hand drawer of my desk.

"There are five satellite office managers, but only three that might have believed that they could move into LL's shoes if something happened to him. Stan Bergman runs the Phoenix office, and Rocky Steelman runs the Tucson/Casa Grande operation." I gave him their addresses and phone numbers and a brief background on each. "Jed Ralston, who runs the Vegas office, is a capable man as well. I think he or Rocky would probably be willing to relocate for that kind of a promotion."

"You said there were five satellite offices. What about the other two?"

"Frank Conley oversees the Northern Arizona projects out of the Flagstaff office but he and Bill Wilson, who runs the Albuquerque office, are just holding on until retirement."

"I need to get a fix on each of them without drawing attention to any of them. Can you bring them into your office for some reason—maybe to explain to them how the company will be run until the estate is settled and Tiffany can decide what she wants to do with it?"

"Tiffany set the memorial service for LL for Thursday. I'll email each of them and urge them to get here for the services and the wake that'll follow. Then I'll schedule a meeting for them with Corstelli, Tiffany, and me to follow the wake. I think that'll be okay with her. Then you can get a feel for each of them and take them aside if you want to. Will that be soon enough?"

"That should work."

After I hung up, I called Uncle Bob and Aunt Betty to let them know about the services. Aunt Betty answered. "Lexi, sweetie, you know we'll be there. We know LL meant a lot to you. Do you want us to pick you up?"

"No, I'll be coming from work. That's too far out of your way. I'll look for you there."

I checked my email and found some notes from Tiffany for the obituary. In response, I tried to call her, but had to leave a message. "I'm working on the obituary and I'll get it emailed to the newspaper so it'll be in tomorrow morning and run through Friday, if that is all right with you. I'll get the word out about the services to the satellite office managers. Let me know if there is anything else I can do."

• • •

I was not going to be "official" until Wednesday, but I decided to call "Fast Eddie." I really needed to stop calling him that, I scolded

56

myself. I called Ed Gomes. "Ed, I'm going to join you and Roger for lunch on Wednesday. That way the three of us can talk about the payments you've missed and come to an agreement as to a repayment schedule."

His response was what I had expected. "Lexi, you know I'm good for it."

No, I don't, and what does he mean by "good for it?" Does he mean the entire amount or just the last payment?

Ed had earned the label of "Fast Eddie" by developing a reputation for being slow to pay on his contracts. He continued in a wheedling tone, "You know as well as I do that this down economy has slowed home sales. I'm sure that if I can have a few more weeks, things will pick up. By spring, I'll have the geological problems on the back nine of the golf course fixed, and the clubhouse completed. Sales will pick up and I'm sure that most of the homes will be sold by then. I'll be able to pick up that missed payment as well as the one due this week."

"I hope you're right, Ed, but I still want the three of us to meet on Wednesday afternoon to work out the details."

He hung up so abruptly that I sat and stared at the telephone receiver. Something he said bothered me; it felt like a cobweb brushing my face—but I couldn't quite put my hand on it. Then it hit me—he had said "that missed payment and the one due this week." According to Roger, as of this week there were technically three missed payments. A difference of two million was not to be overlooked. Come Wednesday, "Fast Eddie" had some questions to answer.

I called Roger to tell him that I was joining his lunch with Ed on Wednesday. There was no answer, so I left a message.

I turned to my computer screen and took an hour to complete the obituary, scan in LL's photo, and send it off to the paper. Then I wrote the five satellite office managers giving them the details of the services and the wake for LL as well as the meeting to follow. I reread it and hit send.

Then I turned my attention to an environmental impact report on the Albuquerque high school project. I had to spend nearly three hours rewriting it before it was suitable to be sent in to the EPA, as required. That took the balance of the afternoon.

• • •

On Tuesday morning, I arrived at 7:30 and spent the morning returning the phone calls that had been on the Post-it notes on LL's desk. The conversations were lengthy, since the callers had heard of his death and wanted my assurance that the company projects would continue.

I lunched on a small container of Greek yogurt, but that didn't pick up my energy level. I pushed myself to contend with the pile of paperwork that had accumulated on my desk. By three, I was tired, so I folded my arms on the top of my desk and laid my head down on them. I was well into fragmented dreams when the phone at my elbow rang. I came to consciousness like a diver decompressing too fast after a deep dive. I yawned as I picked up the receiver.

"Miss Benson . . ." It was Sutherland.

I interrupted him. "Please call me Lexi. That would feel much more natural."

"Lexi, we found LL's SUV. It's just a burned-out wreck in the mountains north of Cave Creek. Someone drove it out there and torched it. Some hikers came across it and called it in to the county cops." Steve's voice was hard.

"You're sure it's his?"

"The VIN and the license plate were still readable. We're sure."

"Is anyone speculating as to why someone set it on fire?"

"Probably to hide fingerprints or blood spatters. The crime lab will see if they can find anything, but with all the recent rain, I don't think they'll find much. By the way, I assigned a man to locate the vehicle Lattimer wrecked two weeks before he was killed. He found it at a salvage yard. We had it hauled in and the crime lab guys are going over it too."

Was he expecting to find evidence of tampering? I wondered.

He continued, "I sent a team out to the state pen yesterday to interview Chet Huddleston's cellmate. He's due to be paroled in about six weeks. They called in and gave me their report. Apparently, Chet has been trying to find someone with contacts on the outside who would take a contract out on LL on a promise of future payment. What money his lawyer didn't get after the trial, his wife got in the divorce, so up to now, he hasn't had any takers. His cellmate says that no one showed any interest. In the meantime, I'll keep my eye on Mr. Huddleston through his cellmate."

"You think this cellmate was being totally honest? Perhaps someone took the contract and Chet wants to direct suspicion elsewhere now that LL is dead."

"I suppose that's possible, but for the present, we'll continue to look other places for more leads. "Anything new on your end?"

I listed the events that came to mind. "I've set up a meeting with Ed Gomes for Wednesday to see if Roger and I can make some arrangements for him to get caught up on his missed payments— and to come to an agreement on just what the total of those missed payments is. LL's services will be on Thursday afternoon at one in Veteran's Hall by invitation. The obituary was in this morning's paper and it will run through Friday morning. That's everything in a nutshell."

"Keep me posted. I'll need to be at the services. Thanks."

Why would he want to be at the services? I wondered.

I got up and went to the restroom to splash some cold water on my face. I noticed that Roseanna hadn't emptied the wastepaper basket. In fact, there were other signs that she hadn't cleaned recently.

That reminded me that I needed to call her. I hurried to the phone, but after a dozen rings, no one answered. I was not invited to leave a message. I decided to try again from home that evening.

CHAPTER 7

I pushed papers around on my desk for a few more minutes, trying to get something accomplished, but my concentration wouldn't stay focused. The thought occurred to me that it might be useful to drive out to the Sunnyville Estates and Golf Resort to take a look at the geological problem on the back nine that Ed Gomes had mentioned. Maybe he was just pulling my leg about it, looking for a reason to procrastinate payment. I put on my jacket and turned out the lights.

As I stepped outside, I was startled by the lateness of the hour. The day had gotten away from me. The twilight was sneaking up on the area and I'd soon need to use my headlights. I hurried my car along Adobe and eventually reached Highway 202, where I was soon moving south watching the rush hour necklace of headlights traveling northbound.

As I drove, my mind involuntarily called up the history of LL's involvement with Gomes. There was something that didn't sit right with me whenever we met with him. Maybe it was the way his eyes didn't meet mine, or the way he pumped my hand too long and too hard. He even slapped Roger on the back, as if he were his godfather or uncle.

I couldn't put my finger on what bothered me about him, but it was like that grit you run across in an otherwise good bowl of clam chowder, so I had given in to my protective instincts in an attempt to divert LL from what I had felt could be a bad contract. I had resorted to calling Glade Schmidt, a twenty-year veteran detective with the Mesa Police Department. Four years earlier, two nut cases had tried to rob the Mercantile Security Bank where I was the loan office manager and I had gotten to know Schmidt before the FBI took over the case.

I had called him, intending to ask him to do a background check on Ed. I took the time to ask about his wife, kids, and the two new grandchildren before I eased into my need for information on Ed Gomes. Schmidt had said succinctly, "Tell LL to stay away from him. He's as crooked as a dog's hind leg. Word is that he's recently been the defendant in a couple of big lawsuits. In both of them, he settled out of court and his lawyer got the records sealed. We're sure he's guilty of fraud and misrepresentation, maybe even embezzlement, but with the court documents sealed, it's tough to prove, and his victims aren't inclined to come forward and press charges because no one wants to look like an idiot in the press."

Why had I cared one way or the other about one contract, considering that my boss was worth nearly as much as King Midas? I had cared because he had worked to build a company that had become one of the most respected and profitable construction companies between Albuquerque and Vegas and a reputation as a solid, honest businessman. I didn't want him walking out on a limb to take on a contract with anyone known as "Fast Eddie."

After my conversation with Lieutenant Schmidt, I had rushed to work to tell LL to reject the contract, but he had said a bit sadly, "I can't, Lexi. This guy is married to Tiffany's sister's best friend. I've got to work with him to keep peace in the family."

My thoughts returned to the present as I took the long curving exit off 202, entering Highway 60 in the eastbound lane. After about six miles, I exited onto Gilby Road and followed it to the graveled strip which Ed Gomes called Sunnyville Estates Drive.

Where it separated from Gilby, he had placed a large billboard advertising the luxury homes at Sunnyville Estates. It was the dominant item on the rolling desert landscape.

At some future date, the road would be paved and dedicated to the county when the properties were all sold. In the waning light, I could see the changes that had occurred since the last time I was there. The road curved up the rolling hills about a mile and continued between two massive stone pillars connected by a wrought-iron arch where the words *Sunnyville Estates* were spelled out in curlicue iron letters. Inside the project, the road had been lined with at least thirty eight-foot palm trees transplanted from some local nursery.

A forty-foot mobile home converted to a project office sat parallel to Sunnyville Estates Drive about fifty feet inside the main entrance. It was apparent that the project had been planned so the streets followed the terrain and were shaped by the gently rolling hills like streamlets flowing from the higher elevation to the main drive. I could see clusters of finished or partially finished houses on lots adjacent to the streets that branched off the main drive. They were short streets, varying from five hundred feet to about eight hundred feet in length, and each ended in a cul-de-sac. As I drove past them on the gravel that had been spread to minimize the mud, I noted that they were named Sunnyvalley, Sunnyway, Sunnyhill, or some other sunny something. There appeared to be eight to twelve lots on each of them.

In the intensifying dusk I could just barely make out the two streets farthest from the entrance but closest to the golf course, where heavy equipment was sitting, waiting for the go-ahead to dig additional foundations when the remaining lots sold.

At the far end of the main road, three quarters of a mile from the stone pillars that marked the entrance, was another matching set of pillars. In my headlights, the arched iron sign connecting the two of them read *Sunnyville Golf Resort* in more curlicue wrought-iron letters. A billboard about eight feet long and six feet high stood next to the east pillar. It was a cartoon-style diagram showing the finished golf course with an Elmer Fudd–type character pointing to the drawing of the finished clubhouse with a nine iron.

From what I could see in my headlights as I approached, the first nine holes looked nearly complete, just waiting for the sod to be laid. Beyond the expanse of what would be the fairways, I could see the depressions that would be the sand traps. About two hundred feet from that point, my headlights revealed the recently poured slab for the clubhouse.

The darkness smothered the light, so I was forced to click on my high beams. It occurred to me that I should have taken a look at the place much earlier in the day, but now I was here I might as well see what I could see.

I noted a path the width of some of the heavy equipment that ran past the clubhouse foundation and over a low hill. The back nine would be over that hill, where more heavy equipment was probably being used to shape the fairways and greens and to scoop out the additional sand traps. I drove carefully down the rutted path, avoiding some of the larger depressions where water from the recent rains was still puddled. When I crested the hill, my headlights picked out the shapes of a yellow bulldozer and a smaller backhoe sitting like crouching animals in the darkness. I figured that they were probably parked near Ed's "geological problem."

I drove carefully around the bulldozer to where the ground opened up in some kind of a deep excavation about a hundred feet beyond the 'dozer. The hole looked at least twenty feet deep and it must have been at least twice that wide. I could see a large pile of earth on the far side. I killed the engine but kept my headlights pointed at the site.

I pulled a four-battery flashlight from beneath my seat and climbed out of the car. I made my way to the edge of the excavation and pointed the beam into the gaping hole. There, I could make out the reflection of the beam in the pool of water in the bottom. As I swept the beam around the excavation, I could see a steady seep of water oozing from three different spots.

A natural spring must be the geological problem Ed was referring to.

This isn't a geological problem; it's a gift! All he has to do is line the hole with clay and it becomes a natural water feature. Admittedly, it would add to the cost of the project, but it could be a great asset.

My thoughts were taken up with this new development as I carefully made my way around it. When I returned to the car, I put the flashlight on the passenger seat before I turned the key in the ignition and began a careful turnabout in the rutted ground. As my headlights picked up the foundation of the clubhouse, I turned on the radio, which was always set to KBAQ, the university classical music station. It was my bad luck that Tchaikovsky's 1812 Overture was playing. Though not my favorite, I did enjoy it, so I turned up the volume.

As the musical instruments drove the composition toward the climax, I had the strange sensation that the percussion section was different than any other recording of it I'd ever heard. The thundering timpani and the cannon explosions were underwritten by a low rumbling that was not normally part of the score.

Suddenly, two great headlights flashed on the passenger side of my car, nearly blinding me. They were about four feet off the ground. I realized they had to be attached to the bulldozer I had passed. Almost immediately, I felt an impact that made my Sebring heave and shudder. My head whipped back and forth. The steering wheel jerked out of my hands as my left front tire hit a deep rut. Fear came at me like a tidal wave.

The 'dozer was angled around to my right and was pushing my car toward the big hole, regardless of how I turned the steering wheel. A terrifying thought flashed into my mind. *The driver of that 'dozer means to push me into that hole. He could easily bury me, and my car. In the morning, there would be no sign of what had happened. I have to get out of this car.*

Just thinking about all that dirt being pushed in on me made it hard for me to breathe. Claustrophobia was the last thing I needed to interfere with my thinking. My car was bouncing and sliding sideways. I opened the driver's side door, but realized that if I tried to jump out, the car and the 'dozer would flatten me.

A voice in my head shouted, *Run, Lexi! Run or you'll die!*

I punched the button that retracted the roof. It began to lift and separate in slow motion. I grabbed my bag, stuck the heavy flashlight in it, and pulled the strap over my right shoulder. As the music ended, the bulldozer halted.

But the gears ground and the front blade that had been pushing my car started to lift. Past the glare of the headlights, I could just barely make out a figure in the cab.

The car had stopped moving, but the big blade was lowering onto the rising hardtop. As I heard the crunching and snapping of the disarticulated pieces of the roof, I rolled out of the car and onto my knees. I reached for the flashlight where it had fallen out of my bag.

As I stood, I screamed at the driver. "Who are you? What do you want?"

By now, I was shaking as much with anger as with fear. In a surge of adrenaline, I ran toward the bulldozer, swinging at one of the headlights. The sound of breaking glass and the loss of the beam of light was heartening. *I have to blind him.* I swung wildly at the other, but it was a long reach. While I tried to stay away from the blade, I managed to knock the other headlight out of alignment. Now it pointed to the right at a ninety-degree angle.

I heard the gears grind. *Is he going to swing the 'dozer around to try to run me down?* It seemed to be remarkably agile for a machine weighing twenty tons. I started a stumbling run through muddy ruts in what I hoped was the direction of the clubhouse foundation. I turned the flashlight off so he couldn't use its light to follow me, and made my way by the indirect, unsteady light of his one remaining headlight. On that rough and muddy rising ground, I couldn't outrun him for very long. The five miles an hour that 'dozer was moving wasn't very fast, but it kept a steady and relentless pace and was closing the distance.

My shoes were caked with mud and I felt as though each foot weighed fifty pounds. I stumbled into a deep rut and fell hard on my knees. Pain like fire shot through my right knee, but I was too frantic to let it stop me. As I labored to stand, I realized that I was at the crest of the hill and could make out the lighter stone of the pillars beyond the clubhouse foundation. If I could just make it that far, I might be able to hide from him long enough to catch my breath.

I was gasping for air and my lungs felt like they were on fire when I slid behind one of the pillars to the left. I was soaked with the perspiration of exertion and fear, and adrenaline was surging into my brain, driving out rational thought. I began to shiver uncontrollably, whether from the chill wind or nerves—or both—I wasn't sure. I pulled my cell phone from my bag and hit 911. The screen glowed and politely stated *No Service*. I felt an impulse to scream in frustration, but didn't have the strength.

The bulldozer continued its growling, lumbering way toward my hiding place. I leaned out from behind the far side of that rock pillar and saw it coming straight toward me with the blade lowered. It was going to demolish the pillar and me in one hard push.

I took two deep breaths, trying to still the pounding in my chest and ears. When the scoop was within a yard of the pillar, I bolted out from behind it and took a hard whack at the remaining headlight. My flashlight hit it so hard that it not only went out, it was left dangling by a couple of electrical wires when the scoop hit the pillar. I made a rolling dive into the mud, and then took off running down the gravel road in the near total darkness.

I ran until my adrenaline glands had no more to give. I couldn't tell if I had run a quarter of a mile or ten miles by the time I realized that I couldn't hear the sound of the bulldozer any longer. The driver must have killed the engine and climbed out to try to find me on foot. I slowed and stopped to breathe deeply before I started to walk as quietly as I could, minimizing the sound of the crunching gravel underfoot, looking for a place where I could rest for a few minutes and get my thinking straight. Panic was jamming the gears in my brain.

Looking behind me, I could see three lighter lines where the gravel of the roughed-out streets contrasted with the surrounding landscape. In front of me was a turn into a Sunnysomething cul-de-sac, actually the second from the entry gate. I remembered that those homes were nearly finished. I turned to the left, and as the ground rose, I could see darker shapes against the night sky. I made a stumbling approach toward the second house. It was an invitation to the homeless to seek shelter there and right now, I felt that I qualified. It had no garage door and no doorknob on the door into the kitchen.

As I put my hand on the door, I realized that if I could find the house that easily, so could the driver of the bulldozer. I went out the back doorway of the garage into a yard piled with lumber and sheetrock debris. In the dark, I discovered a pile of concrete left from the pouring of the foundation by stumbling into and over it, hitting my elbow and banging my forehead. I held my breath as my elbow sang with pain. I'm sure I whimpered. I put my hand up to my forehead and felt the sticky warmth of blood. After a search of my pockets, I found an old tissue, which was quickly soaked as I dabbed at the cut. I could feel the bump swelling.

I located a spot behind one of the larger piles of lumber scraps in the yard where I could either see him coming if he was using a flashlight, or hear his feet on the gravel. I pulled a piece of sheetrock from a pile of debris that had been protected from the rain and sat on it, pulling my knees up to my chest. My neck hurt and my head was pounding. I wrapped my jacket around me as best I could and tried to keep my teeth from chattering. They were trying to make so much noise that I wouldn't be able to hear him coming.

Between the cold and my exhaustion, I must have briefly drifted off to sleep. I woke as the clouds separated, and the weak starlight turned the world into black shapes surrounded by varying shades of dark gray. I was so cold and stiff my joints ached. For a minute, I thought about trying to make my way out of the subdivision and onto the road that would take me back toward town, but I realized I would be fair game if he were waiting for me somewhere along the way in a gully or behind the stone pillars at the front of the subdivision. I decided to stay put and wait until I had a better idea where he was.

As I sat there, I adjusted my position to see if my legs would move. As I muffled a groan, I heard something. I froze and listened intensely. It came again—a soft crunching sound. I couldn't suppress an all over body shudder. I struggled into a hunched position and made my way to the rear exterior corner of the garage where I could see the main road. The dark figure of a man in a jacket and cap was moving toward the main entrance. I stooped into a squat and watched him. Had he been looking for me this whole time?

He walked briskly, without showing much concern about being seen. The dark clothing hid his body type. I couldn't tell who it was.

When he disappeared over the next rise, which separated the first cul-de-sac from the one where I was hiding, I crept out. Trying to stay off the gravel, I stooped and limped up the gentle rise, trying to minimize the weight on my hurting knee, until I could see over it. He continued to walk away from me, passing the temporary office, moving through the entrance of the subdivision.

I ducked down in case he looked back over his shoulder. After a few minutes, I heard the sound of a car engine. I peaked over the crest of the hill again and saw headlights blink on. In the darkness, the vehicle was a nondescript dark lump parked on the far side of the road that connected Sunnyville Estates to Gilby. The driver made a U-turn and sped away, leaving a trail of dust lingering in the air.

Now what am I going to do—hurt and without a car?

CHAPTER 8

I limped my way toward the entrance pillars as fast as I could, which wasn't very fast. In the weak moonlight, I could still see the cloud of dust thrown up by the car. I figured he must have reached Highway 60 by the time I passed between the entry pillars and started down the road.

I spent the next forty minutes limping toward Gilby Road. When I reached it, I tried my cell again. Still no service. Another slow and painful half mile finally brought me to a spot where my cell found a signal. I pressed 911. At that point, I was condemning myself for not programming Steve Sutherland's number into my phone. I shook my head at my own lack of foresight, but how was I supposed to know someone was going to try to kill me?

When the emergency operator responded, I explained my situation, my name and location, and the attempt on my life. Then I requested that she notify Detective Sutherland of the Mesa PD as my situation might be related to a murder case he was investigating. She promised she would pass the message on to the Mesa PD.

My relief was nearly overwhelming when, twenty minutes later, I could see a county police car coming toward me with lights and siren going full blast. The car slid in the gravel when the officer braked. He sprang out and asked abruptly, "You made the 911 call?"

I nodded. That made my head hurt. How I wanted to make some flippant remark to show that despite my appearance, I was still in control, but my normal independence had been reduced to humility.

He looked me over in the beam from his headlights. "You look like you need an ambulance." I looked at my jeans where the knees were torn out. They were caked with mud and spotted with blood. The palms of my hands were bloody as was one elbow, but I had forgotten that I had blood smeared on my face from the cut on my forehead. I probably looked a lot worse that I was.

"No, I think it's all superficial."

"You're sure?" He sounded dubious.

"I'm sure. Can I sit in your car? I'm so cold."

"Of course." He took my uninjured elbow, and led me to the passenger side door, which he opened. "Slide in here. I'll put the heater on high." He talked into the radio clipped to the shoulder of his uniform jacket as he crossed around to the driver's side door and slid in. I caught the words "refused an ambulance, but I'm taking her to a hospital."

As the siren went on again, I laid my head against the headrest and closed my eyes. "I'm taking you to Banner Baywood." He didn't ask, he just told me. "You need to have a doctor look at you."

"Okay." I began to shake. I knew it was just a nervous reaction, but I think it really scared him. He was young—no more than twenty-three, and maybe I was the first bloody mess walking along the side of the road in the dark that he had picked up since putting on the uniform. He hit the gas pedal.

I was weary, cold, and hurting everywhere, but I was still conscious enough of my surroundings to be grateful that traffic was very light. When I briefly opened my eyes, I watched his speedometer slip past ninety when he reached the 202. I closed my eyes again. A thought crept into my mind. *It must have been Ed Gomes. After all, it was a bulldozer on his project . . .*

As he slowed down and made his way through the traffic on Power Road, I asked without opening my eyes, "Can you get a message to Detective Steve Sutherland of the Mesa PD Homicide

Department? I asked the dispatcher but I don't know if the message will get to him. Tell him that Lexi Benson is at the hospital and I need to talk to him."

"What's this about?"

"I think I know who tried to kill me tonight. It might be related to a murder case he's investigating."

"I'll contact him. When he gets to the hospital, maybe you can talk to both of us at the same time. I'll need information for my report."

"Thanks," I whispered.

We pulled up under the emergency entrance portico in about twenty minutes, covering a distance that usually took thirty-five. As I was helped out of the car, I gratefully accepted a wheelchair.

• • •

The cut on my forehead was stitched, and my hands, knees, and right elbow were disinfected and bandaged. While all this was being done, I was asked about my health history, including inoculations. My antenna should have gone up, especially at that question about my last tetanus shot. While I was watching the doctor wrap my injured knee, a nurse entered the curtained cubicle and slipped me a shot in my arm with a needle that felt ten inches long.

"What was that for?" I asked as if I had been punished for something I didn't do.

"That was a tetanus booster," she said with a smile. "It won't be much more than a mosquito bite by tomorrow."

After the doctor had completed his ministrations, he told me that he wanted to keep me overnight because of the bump on my head. Did anyone else see the irony in that? It was near midnight. There wasn't much night left. I doubted that I could count on a discount.

But I nodded, grateful that aside from bruises and aches that would follow me for days, I was in pretty good shape—especially since I might have been dead and buried. I was put into one of those backless, shapeless gowns, the ugliest robe on the planet, and told to sit in a wheelchair. When the nurse who gave me that tetanus shot pushed me out of the exam room, I was relieved to see Steve a short distance down the hallway, standing next to the county officer, where they were talking with one another and undoubtedly waiting to talk to me. I raised my hand and said to the nurse, "Wait up. I need to talk to these guys."

"The doctor told me to see that you were put to bed right away. After you're in your room, if they don't make a lot of noise, they can talk to you for a few minutes, but only a few minutes. The doctor doesn't want them to tire you out." Now there was another little irony. Hadn't anyone noticed my exhaustion?

They followed us to my room and after I was helped into bed, she stepped to the door and waved them in. They each pulled up a chair and Steve opened the interrogation, scowling as he looked me over. "Lexi, what on earth did you get yourself into?"

Was I hearing a slight tone of genuine concern in his voice? I hoped so. I was feeling in need of some genuine sympathy.

"I went out to the Sunnyville project to see what Ed Gomes was referring to when he mentioned a geological problem that was holding up the completion of the golf course." As I described the way the bulldozer came at me and tried to push me and my car into that big hole, I began to shake again. Even my teeth began to chatter as if I were freezing. I was thoroughly embarrassed. "It's . . . it's all over now. I don't know why I . . . I'm shaking like this."

Steve stood and lifted the blanket from the foot of the bed. He draped it over my shoulders. "Don't worry about it. I've seen cops with twenty years behind them react similarly. This is just part of the unwinding process." He patted my shoulder in a paternal manner. "You told Officer Bowles here that you wanted to talk to me because you thought there was a connection between Lattimer's death and this attempt on your life. Is that right?" He sat back down.

I was having second thoughts. "Maybe I'm all wrong. Maybe I just interrupted someone trying to vandalize the property. Gomes should have fenced it off but he didn't want the additional expense. Maybe someone was just trying to scare me."

"But that isn't what you were thinking when you had the County P.D. contact me. What were you thinking then?"

"I was wondering if Ed Gomes waited for me after I closed up the office, and then followed me out to the site. While I was out there walking around, he could have hiked onto the property. He would probably know how to operate heavy equipment. If he had buried me and my car in the big hole on the back nine, there would have been no trace of what happened to me in the morning, and Ed would have been free to do a snow job on Roger. If I weren't around, Ed could pull the wool over his eyes and get the back payments forgiven—or at the least, get an extension on what he owes—but now I just don't know . . ."

"So you didn't see the driver well enough to make a positive ID?"

I shook my head. "It was too dark, but who else could it have been? Who else would benefit by my disappearance? Gomes knows that if the company takes him to court—which is likely to happen, to force him to make the back payments he owes—it could leave him in a bad way financially. If I disappeared, maybe he could get more time."

"How much money does he owe?"

"Including the payment due this week, it looks like three payments of two million each."

The two men looked at each other and each nodded slightly. "A few million dollars is a pretty good reason for murder." Steve sounded positively pleased to have such a lovely motive presented to him.

The nurse stuck her head in the door and motioned over her shoulder with her thumb. "Out, gentlemen. It's time we let her rest." I wholeheartedly agreed.

Steve paused in the doorway and turned. "Give me a call when they're ready to let you out of here. I'll take you home—unless there's someone else you'd rather call." He added quietly, for my ears only, "I'm really glad that you weren't hurt more seriously."

There was no one else I'd rather call. I didn't want to panic any family members, and I would feel safer with him. I nodded.

After the nurse closed the door, my mind drifted. I was awakened by someone trying to take my blood pressure and temperature. The residual pain from my injuries and strained muscles increased as I grew more aware of my surroundings.

I drifted off to sleep again and was reawakened for breakfast, and despite my weariness and the fact that it was hospital food, it tasted good. I was starved. I went back to sleep again, until eleven when they woke me up and told me that I was being released.

I struggled out of bed and brushed my teeth as best I could with the brush included in the little packet of items given to every patient coming in through the emergency ward. I was hindered greatly by the knot on my right arm where I had received that tetanus shot. It hurt as much as anything else on my battered body. Mentally I added another item to my "Do Not Ever Do Again" list, which up to then had included getting another root canal and using a bedpan. Now getting another tetanus shot was number one on my most dreaded hit parade.

My cell phone rang. I could hardly hear it since my bag had been stuffed in the top shelf of the narrow wooden cabinet near the sink.

I hobbled over and pulled it out. Even before I saw the caller ID, I knew it was Percy. There was that unexplainable emotional tether again.

Now, speaking of Percy, don't presume that there are two people like me in this world. First of all, her real name is Persephone, but woe unto anyone who calls her that. We're like night and day, as different as two sides of a coin. She's entirely emotionally based. She cries when she hears sentimental songs or watches movies with tender moments. I'm more the type who analyzes the reason the director or the singer was able to get such a response.

Where I'm moderately tall at five eight and I have brown eyes. Percy is 5'5" and has worn her dark blonde hair in a ponytail since she was six. She's the picture of my mom with the same blue eyes. After four babies in the last nine years, she carries a bit of weight. In fact, I've heard her described as "buxom." To add to the differences, she is also 36 weeks pregnant.

"Lexi, where are you?" I was right. It was her. "Something

has been keeping me awake all night, telling me that you were in trouble."

"Well, you can take a nap now. I'm not in trouble." *At least not anymore.*

"From the sound of your voice, I can tell that something happened. What was it and where are you?" The last question was a demand. She could probably hear the hospital PA system paging a code blue in the intensive care ward.

I took a big breath and decided to fess up. "I'm in Banner Baywood Hospital, but"—I tried to calm her fears—"but I'm okay, I really am. I had a little accident last night, but I'm being released right away. Just a few cuts and scratches. I promise to tell you all about it when we have a few minutes. Please don't say a word about this to Aunt Betty or Uncle Bob—at least not until I can talk to them first."

"I'm coming right over this minute."

"No, no, Percy. I'm checking out right now. It'll take you too long to get a sitter and I'll be home in a little while. If you need to see that I'm okay with your own eyes, you can come over this afternoon."

"But who will pick you up and take you home?" she demanded.

"I have instructions to call Detective Sutherland and he'll drive me home."

She reluctantly agreed before I hung up. I called Steve and he said he'd be there to pick me up within a half hour. It was nice to use his first name.

I slowly and painfully dressed myself. When I was finished, I looked worse than a homeless person who had been mugged. Everything was torn, muddy, and smeared with blood. After I completed the necessary paperwork, an orderly pushed me to the front door, where Steve was waiting to assist me into the car.

As Steve pulled out onto Power Road, he looked over at me. "How are you feeling?"

"Like someone tried to kill me last night."

"But we can both be glad that he didn't." His voice became more businesslike. "By the way, one of the crime lab boys is a good mechanic and he found something interesting when they went over LL's SUV, the one he totaled. He found tie rods—" He looked at me directly for a fraction of a second. "How much do you know about cars?"

"A fair amount. I dated a mechanic for a couple of years and that was all he could talk about—and my uncle likes to talk auto mechanics when he's restoring one of his muscle cars."

"Then you may know that the tie rod on each front wheel is held on by a nut. The nuts are held in place by a cotter pin."

I nodded, having seen a couple of cotter pins in Uncle Bob's garage.

"If the pin is removed and the nut loosened—or gradually vibrates itself loose, it can gradually work its way off. If one came off at any speed, it could cause the vehicle to roll or veer unexpectedly."

"Is that what happened to LL's SUV?"

"Both cotter pins were missing. The mechanic that checked out the wreck thought it was probably deliberate. He thought that maybe, just maybe, one cotter pin could be missing through the carelessness of a mechanic, but not both, and one of the nuts was missing. The other nut had nearly worked itself off. If he had been driving at high speed on the highway instead of in his cul-de-sac, he might have taken out another vehicle and the results could have been . . . well, you can imagine."

"So someone tried to kill him a couple of weeks ago." The question of *why* made its regular route through my mind again.

He rubbed his chin for a moment. "Do you have any place you can go until we get this problem solved?"

"You mean leave my condo?"

"Yes. If that incident with the bulldozer wasn't a case of vandalism or mistaken identity, then someone wants to harm you." He seemed to be choosing his words carefully—as if he didn't want to scare me. "Whoever it is may know where you live or could find out easily enough. I'd like to see you move in with family or a friend for your own safety. Do you have family close?"

"I have a sister but I can't involve her. She has a husband who is out of town a lot with his job and four little girls. My folks are both dead. I guess I could go to stay with my aunt and uncle, but I feel the same about not endangering them. Frankly, I feel safer in my condo, which is in a gated community and where I have a watchdog for a neighbor."

He still looked concerned. To pacify him, I added, "Would it help if I promise to get a security system put in right away?"

He exhaled. "Well, that would give you some protection."

He said no more at the time, but I felt sure that the subject would come up again.

CHAPTER 9

When Steve pulled up to the gate, he punched in the security code I gave him. As the gate rolled open, I guided him around to the parking stalls for my building. I pointed him to my slot under the long carport.

My condo was one of the units in a flat-roofed complex of three two-story, Southwestern-style buildings that LL's company had built long before I knew him. They were all painted a sand color with chocolate brown doors and brown trim around the windows. The three buildings made up a big U and each held eight units, four up and four down. The area between the buildings did have some grass about the size of a giant's handkerchief with three orange trees in the center, a remnant of the citrus grove that had once occupied that land.

"Nice place," Steve commented as he took my elbow and gently helped me get my hurting body out of the car. "Been here long?"

"I bought the place four years ago."

I located my keys and handed them to him, pointing to my door, which was about twenty-five feet away. I noticed my upstairs neighbor watching from her front room window. I was hurting almost too much to wave at her, but I made the effort.

"Who's that?"

"Mrs. Bolton. She's the watchdog neighbor I mentioned. She keeps an eye on the condo complex. She's our no-cost security system. If I didn't wave to her to let her know that everything was okay, she would call me or be down to my place in just about one minute to check on me."

"A neighbor like that can be a blessing." After he unlocked the door, I slowly limped my way inside. "Can you make it by yourself?" *There's that concern in his voice again. I like that.*

I grinned weakly and nodded. "I think so. Thanks for giving me the lift home. By the way, where's my car?"

"It was taken to the county impound lot. It's totaled. The frame is bent and the retractable hard top is beyond repair." I know the look on my face gave away my feelings. "I'm sorry. It looked like it was a nice car."

"You've seen it?"

"Yes, I was out at the project site before dawn this morning to watch the county crime scene guys at work and I stopped by the impound lot to have a look at it."

"I just made the last payment on it about four months ago." I felt as if I had lost a good friend.

"Get some rest. If anything new develops that might throw some light on the situation, I'll let you know."

I closed the door. He immediately knocked on it. When I opened it, he ordered, "Lock your door. Put on the chain. Take precautions."

I nodded dutifully. "Will do."

He turned and started for his car. I did as he had ordered. As I dropped my battered purse on the table by the door, my cell phone rang.

"Ms. Benson, this is Brandon Corstelli. Mrs. Lattimer has signed the paperwork she asked me to draft. I think you can consider yourself endowed with legitimate power to act in LL's stead now. We will revisit the matter when the estate is probated. I'll put a copy for you in the mail to the company office. Will that be acceptable?"

"That will be fine, Mr. Corstelli—and please call me Lexi. Thanks again for your help."

I ended the call and hobbled my way into the bathroom, where I turned the water into the tub and poured half a canister of Epsom salts into it. While the tub filled, I examined my battered face in the mirror on the medicine cabinet. The bump on my head was purple and still swelling. It felt nearly as big as half an Easter egg.

Someone began to pound on my front door. I turned off the water in the tub and limped to the front room. When I looked through the plantation shutters on my front window, I recognized Mrs. Bolton. When I opened the door, she looked at me as if I had been up to no good.

"Lexi, why didn't you answer your phone?"

"I'm sorry, I didn't hear it. I was in the bathroom with the water running in the tub."

She was standing there with her arms folded across her ample bosom like a school teacher, which she had been at one time, giving me what must have been her "You've been a bad girl" look.

"Please, come in and sit down."

"You look like a train wreck." She scolded. "What happened? I saw you come home a little while ago with that man. Who is he?"

"He's a policeman, Mrs. Bolton, a detective." She stepped inside so I could close the front door.

"Are you going to tell me what happened? I noticed that you didn't come home at all last night."

"Please, sit down. I spent last night in the hospital."

She sat, clearly determined to hear the whole story. But before I could continue, she demanded, "Tell me the rest of it."

I had a teacher in the third grade who could make me feel just like Mrs. Bolton did, so I decided to tell her the whole story. I was sure she wouldn't leave until I did.

"Last night someone almost killed me."

She kept her arms folded as I talked, but her expression changed from one of an interrogator to an appalled and sympathetic friend.

When I finished, she labored to stand and put her arms around me. "You poor thing. I'm just an eighty-year-old woman, but I'm not helpless. I'm sure there's something I can do." She turned away from me and began to pace, albeit slowly, and I could see that she was thinking out loud. "I'm going to insist that the condo board hire a night watchman. If each one of the 24 unit owners paid an additional $40 a month, we could hire one. And until they do, I'm going to hire my granddaughter's husband and pay him out of my own pocket."

"Good grief, Mrs. Bolton. Can you afford that?"

"He's out of work and I'm practically supporting them right now, anyway. At least this way, he'll be working. He was a security guard for a big company out in Glendale until they moved their operations to China. He's got his own uniform and gun, and knows how to use it. I don't know about you, but I'll sleep much better knowing that there's someone here at night."

I made her stop her pacing and turn to face me. I put my arms around her and quoted Steve. "A neighbor like you can be a real blessing."

"I'll call Tommy and have him here tonight." She brushed my arms away as if she had work to do and had to get right to it. "When he gets here, I'm going to take him around to meet everyone who's at home."

She bustled out of my front room, and I closed and locked the door behind her. I returned to my bath where I added a generous stream of bubble bath to the pouring water, soaked a washcloth in cold water for my forehead, and then peeled off my jeans and sweatshirt. I dropped them into the trash basket I kept under the sink. When the water was near the overflow and the bubbles were ten inches deep, I sank into the hot water. I didn't care if the bandages got wet. I'd replace them later. I put the cold, wet cloth on my forehead, rolled up a towel to use as a makeshift pillow, and put it behind my head. I decided that I might never get out of that tub again.

When I awoke, the water had cooled. I struggled into a sitting position and turned the hot water on again. After another fifteen minutes, I had to face the fact that it was time to drag my weary body out of the tub. My fingers were all pruny.

After I re-bandaged my knee and elbow, I dressed in a pair of warm sweatpants and pulled on a turtleneck sweater. I gathered the down comforter from my bed and limped into the living room, where I turned on the TV, wrapped myself up in the comforter, and sat on the couch.

Someone pounded on my door and called my name. I recognized Percy's voice. I hobbled to the door calling, "I'm coming, I'm coming."

As soon as I opened the door, she flew at me with more speed than I thought a woman so pregnant could manage, almost knocking me over. She hugged me so hard it hurt. Then she stepped back and stood there with her fists on her hips, looking for all the world like a very large teapot. "Lexi, you look terrible. Tell me what happened right this minute!"

"Come in and sit down—and calm down. If you get too excited, I might have to deliver the baby right here."

She pushed her way past me and plopped down on the couch with her mouth set in a tight, narrow line that told me she meant business.

I told her about the events of the night before in a streamlined fashion, minimizing the details and when I finished, I added, "Now you can see that I'm okay and not mortally wounded."

"Someone really tried to kill you?" Her eyes were big and her face had grown pale.

"I don't know. It seemed that way at the time. The police are investigating and they'll find out, I'm sure. Now tell me how you're feeling."

She was not to be distracted so easily. She started to cry. "Oh, Lexi, I know I've said it before, but why don't you just find a nice guy and settle down and have babies like me? Then you wouldn't get in such terrible trouble. You worry me. I don't know what I would do without you." Her last statement was a plea.

"Percy, you know that if I ever find Mr. Right, that's just what I hope to do. I'll have a whole bunch of babies and catch up with you." I sat on the arm of the couch and patted her on the back. "Now wipe your eyes, and quit crying. You'll upset the baby."

"I want you to come and stay with us. You'll be safer if you're hidden away."

"Steve . . . er, Detective Sutherland said the same thing, but I won't put you and your little girls in danger—and I'm not going to go into hiding and put my life on hold because of last night. At least for the present, I've got to keep the company running. There are a lot of jobs on the line. I already promised I'd get a security system put in right away, and Mrs. Bolton is going to hire her granddaughter's husband to serve as a night watchman for the time being. That should put your mind at rest."

"But Lexi, can't Detective Sutherland put you in a safe house or something?"

"You watch too much TV, Percy. With Mrs. Bolton's granddaughter's husband on duty at night and a security system, I'll be as safe here as anywhere." She grew a little calmer. "Now go home and tell those little girls that Aunt Lexi is just fine and not to worry . . . please." We gave each other a big hug, and I could feel the baby kick. "Now promise me you won't worry."

She sniffed and gave me a half-hearted smile. "I'll try not to, now that I've seen you. But until the police catch whoever did that last night, I'm not going to be able to sleep a wink. Maybe you should stay with Aunt Betty and Uncle Bob."

I shook my head. "I'm not going to get anyone else involved in this mess, especially not you or them. That reminds me; please don't talk to them until I can, so they don't worry unnecessarily."

She nodded. "That's what you always say." Her voice sounded resigned to whatever I was going to put her through.

"I'll call them later tonight, after I've had some rest."

After she left, I wrapped up in my comforter again and drifted off to sleep on the couch. For the first hour, my sleep was dark and deep, but the realization that someone might want me dead started to magnify every noise, make each change in temperature noticeable. Shifting shadows on the interior louvered shutters made me start.

I roused at about five with something tickling the back of my mind. It was Wednesday—wasn't it? Something about Wednesday . . . I suddenly remembered the appointment Roger and I had set up with Ed Gomes for lunch. *If he really tried to kill me, I doubt that he even showed up, but if he did, then Roger could have handled it. I hope he didn't agree to anything that was going to cost the company big money.*

I lay back down, but realizing that I had put off the inevitable long enough, I picked up the phone and called my aunt and uncle. After I had reassured both of them repeatedly that I had suffered no permanent damage except the loss of my car, Uncle Bob made me an offer I couldn't refuse. He had four rebuilt old muscle cars sitting in his oversized garage.

"Well, Lexi, you're gonna need another vehicle. I'll let you borrow one of mine. Which one would you like to use—now I want you to know that this is only until you can get your insurance company to cough up a check for your Sebring."

"Uncle Bob, you're a dear. I know exactly which car I want to use, the 1966 Pontiac GTO." It was fire engine red and could do zero to sixty in less than ten seconds, at least that was what Uncle Bob had said more than once.

"Sure, honey. You just take good care of it."

We agreed that he would drive it over to my place in the morning. Then I called my insurance agent. When I explained why I was calling and how my car had been damaged, he let out a whistle. "Are you really all right?"

"I'm bruised and sore, and my knee will take a while to heal, but I'm basically okay. There will be some hospital bills as well as the loss of the car to deal with."

"We'll find out where it was towed so I can take a look at it. I'll get back to you, but it sounds like it isn't repairable. In the meantime, you'll need a rental."

"Don't worry about it. My uncle is going to give me a loaner for the present. Will my insurance policy cover it until I get another car?"

"Yeah, I'll take care of it." He got the required information from me to put the policy in place before he urged me to take care of myself.

After he hung up, I lay back down to watch the rest of the newscast with my comforter pulled up to my chin. The ringing of my cell phone disturbed me.

It was Roger's voice. "Hey, Lexi, where are you? I've been worried. You didn't come into the office and you didn't call. What's up? Didn't the lawyer get the legal papers drawn up?"

"He did, but I wrecked my car last night and I'm sitting at home in a great blue funk of self pity. I'll see you tomorrow. By the way, I'll need a report on your lunch with Ed Gomes."

"What lunch with Ed Gomes? He never showed up."

"Could you give his office a call and find out why—and set up another meeting with him for Friday when I can be there?"

"Okay. Look, do you want me to pick you up in the morning? It wouldn't be any trouble."

"No, but thanks for offering. I'll have another car by then."

I put down the phone and pulled the comforter around my shoulders only to have it ring again. It was Stan Bergman, and he was a very unhappy man.

"Lexi, there was some vandalism on the Sunnyville site last night. When I called the office, Roger told me to call you. The bulldozer was driven around and the headlights were broken and some other damage was done. Will the damage be covered by insurance?"

"Not if it's under five thousand dollars."

"That's what I figured. What's really odd is that there was even some crime scene tape out there when I got to the site this morning at 7:30."

"Ah . . . yes. The police were called and they've already investigated. Stan, I know you won't like this, but you may have to lay off the men working on that site for a week or two until Roger and I can work out something with Ed Gomes. He's getting behind on his payments and we're getting worried." *Not to mention the fact that I suspect that he might have tried to kill me*, I thought.

Stan let loose with a string of words I didn't want to listen to, so I ended the call.

As I've mentioned before, when I'm looking for answers, I often clean and straighten; anything to give external order to mental disorder. As sore as I was, I got up and with cautious movements at first, my stiffness gradually lessened. I gave the bathroom my full attention. Scrubbing the tub and toilet bowl is a wonderful way to seek solitude when I want to think. I did some soul searching, asking myself if I had jumped to a conclusion about Ed Gomes. *Who wanted me dead? Who would benefit? What made me think it was Ed behind the wheel of that bulldozer? I never really saw him. Was I doing him an injustice?*

As I watched the water swirl in circles around the tub drain, I wondered how Steve would ever get all the pieces put together. I had a clean bathroom but I didn't have any answers.

When I'm at home, I'm usually suffused in a bubble of security, as if all must be right with the world if all is right within my four walls. But I still couldn't capture that feeling, so I wrapped up in my comforter again and watched an old movie, falling asleep after midnight.

• • •

In the morning I still hurt, but I decided to make myself get back into my usual routine. I could get in a half day of work before the funeral services for LL.

I dressed my bruised and achy self in a navy blue dress suitable for a funeral. It covered my damaged elbows and came below my scraped knees. That hid much of the damage. My big problem was the bruise on my forehead, which was draining into my right eye socket, making it swell and darken. I looked like someone had hit me in the head and then in the eye.

Before Uncle Bob arrived with the car, I worked for a half hour with a good base makeup and cover stick that camouflaged ninety-five percent of the rainbow on my face. I grabbed my curling iron and strongly encouraged two curls to cover the stitches in my forehead. By the time he had arrived, I felt almost presentable.

When I opened my front door, Uncle Bob insisted on giving me a big hug. It was a painful experience, but it reaffirmed that he really cared about me. He was hoping to talk me into staying home.

"Lexi, your aunt and I have talked half the night about you. We both think you ought to avoid the funeral. If someone wants to harm you, they may be there. Come and stay with us until this case is solved. Even with your makeup, I can see that you have some bumps and bruises."

Betty had parked the family sedan and was hurrying up the sidewalk. When she reached us, her expression was stressed and pinched with worry. "Lexi, sweetie, we've talked it over and we want you to come and stay with us. Give the police time to solve LL's murder and to find out who tried to hurt you. I can't sleep for worrying about you."

"Aunt Betty, I think I'm safer here than at your place. You're out in the county and your nearest neighbor is a mile away. Uncle Bob's at work during the day. If you and I needed help in a hurry, I'd have a tough time finding any. Here, I'm in a gated community with watchful neighbors and I'm going to have a security system installed in my condo right away. Will that make you feel better?"

I convinced them against their will. Neither of them was totally satisfied. After I locked my front door, we all walked out to where Bob had parked the big Pontiac.

Aunt Betty couldn't resist the opportunity to give one last piece of advice. "Lexi sweetie, you watch that speedometer. That car has too much power and . . . well, you just be careful."

"I promise to be careful. I know this car is special to Uncle Bob."

I climbed in, gave them a wave, and headed for the office. When I pulled up in front, Roger opened the office door, folded his arms across his chest and leaned on the doorframe. He laughed heartily in admiration.

"Wow, that's really a muscle car if I've ever seen one. So this is what's going to replace your Sebring?"

"Temporarily," I responded. As I limped past him and into the office, he gave a low, sympathetic whistle, "Wow. Even under all that makeup, I can see that you look like you took a beating. One of your eyes looks like it has way too much eye shadow. What happened?"

"I guess you could say that both of us—my car and me—took a beating."

"Look, I'm really sorry. I wouldn't have laughed if I had realized that you must be hurting."

"Apology accepted." I put my purse down on the desk. "Did you call Ed Gomes and set up another meeting?"

"His secretary said that he wasn't in and she didn't know when he would be."

"I wonder if he's trying to dodge us to postpone facing the money problem." *Or was he trying to avoid facing me*, I wondered.

Roger just shrugged. "You've got me."

"Maybe we'll see him at the memorial service for LL."

When Roger walked over to the other office an hour later, I dialed the number of the company that installed the security systems in the buildings built by LL Construction. I arranged for a man to be at my house the next morning by eight to give me an estimate on the cost.

Before I left at noon for the memorial service, I put the office telephone on record in case any messages came in while we were gone.

CHAPTER 10

The Veterans' Hall was nearly full for the memorial service. The dais was smothered in floral arrangements. Even though it was supposed to be an intimate group of friends and business associates by invitation only, the word had spread and it gave me a sweet pleasure to see nearly five hundred people there to share in the celebration of the life of that good man.

There were two television vans there to cover the "private" service and to record the presence of any famous attendees for the six o'clock and ten o'clock news. The antenna and satellite dish on each looked as if it could send and receive messages from Saturn.

My aunt and uncle had saved me a seat between them on the front row in the section to the right side of the dais, not far from the exit. Betty patted the seat between them, and as I sat down, Uncle Bob leaned over and whispered, "Give me your purse." I was startled, so he repeated himself. "Give me your purse. I have something to put in it."

I offered him my second-best, large soft leather bag. My best one was demolished during my adventures at the Sunnyville site. He opened it and pulled something from under his suit coat. It was a brown paper bag that was wrapped tightly around something he stuffed into the purse. He closed it and handed it back.

"Keep that close to you at all times," he whispered.

I whispered back, "What is it?"

"We'll talk about it after the funeral."

I reached into the bag and felt it. It wasn't hard to tell that it was a revolver. My expression must have changed. He said again, more forcefully, "We'll talk about it later."

We turned to watch the VIPs as they approached the dais a few minutes before the service was to begin. Tiffany was escorted into the hall by Brandon Corstelli. Looking pale and fragile in a black silk sheath and a black cloche with a little lace veil that came down to the tip of her nose, she held his arm with both hands as he helped her up the stairs to one of the chairs reserved for those who would participate in the service. I could hear the light clink of her silver bracelets when she moved her arms and smoothed her skirt. She smiled up at him and patted the chair next to her inviting him to sit there.

Corstelli was Hollywood handsome, the kind of man whose presence could dominate a roomful of people. If he talked about the weather, people would be spellbound by the authority in his voice. His suit was probably an Armani. The only other time I had chatted with him face to face was about a year ago at the reception held for the opening of the annex to one of the state office buildings, a project that showcased LL Construction Company workmanship at its best.

I looked around for Steve. He entered behind the group that was being seated on the dais, and stood near the wall with some other latecomers, where he could look over the crowd.

On the other side of Tiffany, a rather plain, somewhat overweight woman with long brown hair graying at the temples sat down. Tiffany smiled at her and they squeezed each other's hands. As the other woman smiled back, I could see that they had the same eyes. *So that's the sister that pulled LL into the Sunnyville Estates project.*

During the service, several of the most prominent men in the state praised LL for his community contributions and his sterling work ethic. After the benediction, which was offered by a member of the Interfaith Coalition, the funeral director stood and asked the crowd to remain until those who would be part of the cortege to the cemetery had left the building.

I intended to see LL laid to rest, so after about twenty five people, including some of those on the dais filed out, I rose and said quietly to Uncle Bob, "I'll call you later about the . . . the package." He nodded.

As I neared the exit, Steve stepped up and took my elbow. "I'll follow you to the cemetery," he said quietly.

"Okay."

As we stepped outside into the sunlight, we could see Corstelli assisting both women into the funeral home limousine for the ride to the cemetery. The funeral cortege crept through traffic for the six miles to the All-to-Rest Cemetery. Steve's car stayed behind me all the way. The clouds gathered again while we were driving to the cemetery.

There, the line of cars wound through the lanes and around the circular drive. The cemetery was old, with well-established trees reaching out as if to protect those who rested there. The scene was filled with headstones of weeping or soaring angles, winged cherubs, obelisks, urns, inscribed stone scrolls, and crosses of every style. The mausoleum came into view, its lines of gray stone softened by great clouds of magenta bougainvillea with yellow and pink lantana crowding the edges of the walk to the front entrance.

It started to rain lightly after I parked. I found my umbrella on the passenger seat. I opened the driver's side door and poked it out as I pressed the button that made the umbrella open with a *thunk*. As I stepped out of the car and headed toward the mausoleum, the rain drops against the fabric sounded like corn popping in a pan with the lid on. Steve reached me and took my elbow as I hurried inside. There were folding chairs in four rows of ten in the muted light of the interior. After finding a seat, we all watched Tiffany enter on Corstelli's arm as he held an umbrella over the two of them. The rain had put tiny rhinestones of moisture in her hair that peaked out from under her hat. Roger was the last to enter. He nodded with recognition as he made his way to a seat behind us on the last row.

After a recording of an organ rendition of "In the Garden" had ended, the funeral director helped Tiffany put LL's urn into a little cubicle about head height in a wall of about fifty similar cubicles. Each had a small bronze plaque on the front. A small marble slab was screwed ceremoniously into place and Tiffany was handed a few long-stemmed lilies, which she put in the attached flower holder.

After the funeral director offered a sermonette on the brevity of life, he invited Tiffany to stand near him so each person could offer their condolences as they made their way out of the building. Corstelli stood at her elbow and her sister stood on the other side. I was one of the last ones to reach the three of them. I offered my hand to Tiffany and said again, "I'm here to help in any way. Please let me know if there is anything else I can do."

"You've been a great help already, Lexi." She put a lace handkerchief delicately under her nose.

I watched as Corstelli assisted her into the limousine once more. I wondered if there was more to their relationship than I had originally assumed. I caught Steve's eye and noted that his right eyebrow was lifted in a quizzical expression, which probably mirrored the look on my face.

As the last of the group trickled out of the mausoleum, he stepped over to me. "Hey, you're looking pretty good—considering."

"It took plenty of makeup and patience," I responded.

He nodded toward Tiffany and Corstelli, who were sitting in the limousine. "What do you think?"

"I guess we shouldn't be surprised. I don't suppose she has any male relatives to lean on right now, so the family attorney was undoubtedly willing to offer his services."

Roger stepped up behind us. "Tiffany told me before the services that she wants you and Detective Sutherland to know that you can park around behind her house for the wake. There will be a few parking places there for select people."

I turned to look more directly at him. "That was thoughtful of her."

"Lexi, how are you feeling?"

"I'm doing okay, Roger. Thanks for asking."

We separated and headed for our individual cars and made our way through traffic to the home LL had built for his bride. Roger's Corvette disappeared quickly into the traffic but Steve's car was always in sight. When we arrived, the security gate stood open. The rain had stopped, and the cloud cover had begun to shred, like a gray flannel blanket washed too many times, allowing patches of blue sky to show through. The house was briefly bathed in sunlight, the grounds dappled with shade from the trees, whose branches danced and dripped in an increasing breeze. Tones of sage, deep green, and sand rubbed shoulders, creating a scene like a watercolor until the sun disappeared behind a swath of heavy cumulous clouds that were piling up in the southwest, looking as if they were considering attacking the metro area again.

As others searched for a place to put their vehicles on the street, Steve followed me around to the rear of the impressive residence that almost seemed to rise from the desert, isolated from neighbors by more than a hundred feet on either side. I pulled into a vacant parking place next to Roger's Corvette at the rear of the house. Two were available, just as Roger had said. Steve pulled in next to me.

We looked over the large pool as we climbed the red sandstone steps that rose to the expansive covered patio of the same rock. Despite the event that had brought me there, I had to turn and admire the enclosed garden, and the fountain that splashed into the swimming pool. We entered the house through a rear entrance off the patio, where the sliding glass doors stood open. We moved down the hall past the open door to the library, where I saw Corstelli sitting in a wingback chair with one ankle resting on the other knee, evidently making notes on a yellow legal pad. I recognized several of the people standing in the hall where they were chatting. Many had done business with LL.

Tiffany had wisely arranged to have the event catered. Three pretty, young, dark-haired women were serving, wearing black knee-length dresses with little white caps on their heads. Every few minutes one of them would offer a napkin with one hand, and with the other, thrust a tray full of bacon-wrapped water chestnuts, cucumber sandwiches cut in little triangles, Swedish meatballs skewered with a toothpick, or other such finger food toward each person.

Tiffany sat in a Louis XVI chair with seat and back cushions of white brocade in the conversation grouping at the far end of the sitting room, just a small figure in black against the white background. She had removed her little hat so her silky, blonde hair fell smoothly against her cheeks.

The woman I took to be her sister sat on one of the couches near the fireplace. We had to pass her to approach Tiffany, so I paused and put out my hand and introduced myself. "I'm Lexi Benson. I worked with LL. Are you related to Tiffany?"

"Yes, I'm her sister, Georgia."

"I thought I saw a family resemblance in your eyes."

"Yes, but I'm sure that is the only resemblance you can find." Her words were tinged with bitterness.

Oops, I put my foot in my mouth that time. It was apparent that she felt that she was constantly compared to her sister and came up lacking. The thought suddenly occurred to me that watching the aging process in her sister might be part of the reason Tiffany made so many trips to Bermuda.

I wasn't sure how to respond so I said simply, "May I extend my condolences to you on the death of your brother-in-law? We'll all miss LL."

She smiled stiffly. "Thanks."

She was not making it easy to talk to her, so I tried to end the conversation graciously. "Please excuse me while I offer my condolences to Tiffany." She responded with a small nod and looked away.

I was surprised to see Roger standing behind Tiffany's chair. As I started toward her, he slipped away, and by the time the people in front of me reached her and offered their condolences, he had returned carrying a plate of sliced fruit and other finger food in one hand and a tall, fluted glass of something pink in the other. He offered both to her. She took a small sip of the drink and motioned for him to set both down on the table near her elbow. He returned to standing near her chair. There was something protective about his manner.

Steve tipped his head at me to signal that he wanted to talk in private. I followed him to the patio at the rear of the house. It was raining again, but this was a light, gentle rain, the kind the Apaches called the 'tears of heaven.'

When I reached him, he asked quietly, "Is there any kind of relationship between Roger and Tiffany?"

I hesitated before I answered. "I don't think so."

"What do you make of his solicitous attentions?"

"She's not much older than him, but I think that if she needed a man's shoulder to cry on, Corstelli would be more suited for her. I think Roger's just trying to be considerate."

He was quiet for a minute. "When is the meeting with the managers of the satellite offices going to take place?"

"As soon as the funeral guests have left. I've seen each one of them standing around, waiting for someone to give them the signal. I think Tiffany plans to hold it in LL's den."

"I'd sure like to be present for it, but that might alter the chemistry of the group. I don't suppose you could pass me off as another 'legal counsel'?"

"No, but I have a better idea. LL had closed circuit TV installed when the house was built. I don't think Tiffany will mind if you watch from the security room."

"There's a security room?"

I nodded and signaled him to follow me. "It's in the basement." He looked surprised. "Yes, this place actually has a basement. LL had to have it dug with explosives. It runs under the west half of the house. I'll show you where it is." We made our way through the kitchen, which was full of busy people working for the caterer, taking trays of food from the big, stainless steel refrigerator or from the matching stainless steel oven. I opened the door to the mudroom and Steve followed me to the landing at the top of the stairs. I put up my hand to signal him to stop while I paused and looked at the keys hanging from a board next to the door.

As I examined the keys, I explained. "LL showed me the security room and the closed circuit TV system the first time I was here. He said that Tiffany was nervous about his being gone so much, leaving her alone in the big house." I finally found a key with a little tag that was marked *Sec. Room*.

"I think I've found it. Let's give it a try." I led him down the stairs, talking as we walked. "LL said that there's a remote switch in the kitchen where the cameras can be turned on. LL told me that in one of his previous homes, one of the household help . . . a housekeeper, I think, was evidently light fingered and some very expensive items disappeared, so when he had this home built, he had the system installed and insisted that Tiffany use the cameras on a daily basis for security."

By this time, I had the key in the lock and opened the room. Just as I had hoped, the cameras were running.

CHAPTER 11

W"ow, this is quite a setup," he murmured. "I'm just going to get comfortable and sit here and watch. What a shame it doesn't have sound." He moved over to a chair and sat down while tucking the long end of his tie back inside his sport coat. The screen he faced was divided into four quarters. The upper right was an exterior camera that showed the driveway and entry gate, but the other three were interior views with the lower right camera pointed at the front door and the foyer. The top left scene was of the second floor hall between the bedrooms and the fourth camera showed the living room. For a few minutes, we watched the living room screen as several people offered their condolences to Tiffany and helped themselves to the plentiful trays of hors d'oeuvres.

"Can you point out the satellite office managers?"

"Sure." I stepped up to the quartered screen and pointed to two men talking to one another in the foyer, near the stairs to the second floor. "That somewhat overweight man with that head of white hair is Wilson from the Albuquerque office. That tall, thin man with the gray hair is Conley. He runs the Flagstaff office. As I mentioned earlier, they're in line for retirement, and are looking forward to it." Jack nodded. He was making notes in the little notebook in his hand.

"You can see Rocky Steelman there in the sitting room, talking

97

to Tiffany. He runs the Tucson/Casa Grande office, and he's well qualified to run the company." I paused and looked for Jed Ralston. I finally spotted him exiting the restroom at the back of the foyer, near the kitchen doorway. "There's Ralston. He runs the Vegas office and he's a good, competent project manager." I looked at the screens closely again. "I don't see Stan Bergman at the moment."

I stepped over to look at the control board and noted the cameras were numbered and the feed to each one could be switched to operate in other rooms. I pressed the button on camera three and it changed from the upstairs hallway to LL's den.

I turned and asked with a small bit of pride, "How's that? Now you can see everything that goes on in the meeting."

"Great." He responded with a grin.

I pulled up another chair and we watched the various rooms while I identified the people I recognized. I still hadn't seen Stan. After about ten minutes, I left him there and climbed the stairs back to the mudroom. I crossed the kitchen, dodging two tray-bearing servers. From the hall I could see that some of the guests were collecting their jackets or umbrellas.

The satellite office managers were standing around in desultory conversation. Bergman had joined them and his suit coat was damp. *Maybe he stepped out to smoke, since Tiffany's aversion to tobacco is well known.* I reached the sitting room in time to see the last few guests offering their farewells to the widow. Roger was there, quietly standing to one side. Corstelli was still sitting in the library across the foyer from the living room.

Tiffany followed the last couple to the door and thanked them for their sympathy. The catering crew was cleaning up the remnants of the refreshments and the tall glasses that had been left around the rooms. Corstelli crossed into the foyer and waved to the rest of us to follow him into LL's den. He opened the double doors and entered as if it were his house. Tiffany entered behind the lawyer.

As we clustered at the den doorway, I noted a young man standing across the hallway watching us. He was about my height, and had a shock of sun-bleached hair and the reddish tan from outdoor work that fair-complexioned people often get. He was somewhat familiar, but it took me a moment to come up with his name—Charles Mattingly, who, as I remembered it, preferred to be called Chuck. I had met him about nine or ten months ago when LL, Roger, and I had met at Stan's office for the signing of a contract to build a new elementary school.

I stepped over and put out my hand. "It's Chuck Mattingly, isn't it?"

His smile was filled with surprise. "Yes, it is. I didn't think you'd remember me."

"You're kind of Stan Bergman's right hand man, if I remember right." We shook hands. I noted that his hand was calloused and there was power in his shoulders. *This is a young man accustomed to hard work.*

"You've got a good memory."

"It's good of you to be here to offer your condolences to Tiffany. This has got to be a really hard time for her."

"Roger told me about the wake and said it would be okay for me to attend." He took a searching look around the lower level of the house and added, "And I really wanted to see the place now that it's lived in. This was one of the first projects that I worked on after Bergman hired me. It really turned out great." He paused and looked at his shoes for a moment as if a little embarrassed by his next request. "Roger also told me that there's a meeting with the satellite office managers coming up and since I'm here, I was wondering if it would hurt anything if I sat in on it. I won't draw any attention to myself. That way Stan won't have to tell me later what went on."

"I don't see why not."

I paused and noted that only Rocky Steelman hadn't entered the den yet. Out of courtesy, he seemed to be waiting for me. When he caught my eye, he waved me in ahead of him. I nodded toward the doorway and Chuck followed me, with Rocky bringing up the rear. Chuck took the straight-backed chair nearest the door as if to make his presence as unobtrusive as possible.

After some perfunctory handshaking, Corstelli walked around

the room and turned on every lamp in a proprietary manner before sitting in LL's great, lounger-type chair behind his carved mahogany desk. It was a large room with walnut wood paneling and burgundy leather furniture. Even the tops of the end tables under the lamps were lined in matching leather embossed with a gold border. The carpet was a burgundy area rug with a foot of parquet flooring showing around it. In every way, it was a man's room. The large window allowed in a weak light from the overcast sky.

A maroon leather couch sat against the wall at a ninety-degree angle to LL's desk and another one like it sat about six feet in front of the desk, facing it. I took a place on that couch. Tiffany sat on the other couch at the end nearest the desk. Most of the others seemed to prefer the wing-backed or straight-backed chairs around the edge of the room, some of them sitting forward as if ill at ease. Roger paused and looked around before choosing a spot on the opposite end of the couch where Tiffany was seated.

Corstelli looked at Tiffany for a signal to begin the meeting and she looked at me as if to confirm that everyone was there. It was then that I realized that she didn't know these men, only having shaken their hands as they offered their condolences less than an hour before. I nodded to confirm that everyone was present.

She rose and stood at the side of LL's desk. She spoke almost hesitantly. "I'm sure you're all tired. It's been a long day, but it seemed like a good idea to hold this meeting today, so you can get back to your offices by tomorrow. My husband's death was unexpected and has left some important things undecided since he died intestate."

Frank Conley asked aloud, "What does 'intestate' mean?"

Corstelli intervened and stated, "Please state your name so Tiffany will know who's speaking."

"I'm Frank Conley. I just wanted to make sure I understood what that legal term meant."

"It means that he died without a will, Mr. Conley," Corstelli answered for her.

Stan Bergman responded in a stentorian voice edged with contempt. "If you're such a great lawyer, why'd you let him die without a will?" Everyone's head swiveled to look at Bergman. I was expecting to see a literal chip on his shoulder.

Corstelli said simply, "And your name for the benefit of Mrs. Lattimer?"

"I'm Stan Bergman. I run the local office." He seemed wired, his hands moving up and down his thighs, as if he was full of nervous energy he needed to dissipate.

Tiffany tried to pacify him. "Please, Mr. Bergman, it was by LL's choice. He didn't think he was old enough to need a will." She added quietly, "He didn't expect to be murdered."

In response, Bergman snorted his skepticism as if being murdered was a poor excuse for dying without a will. Seeing an appropriate opening, Corstelli stood and took over the meeting. "As Tiffany's attorney, I have filed a motion with the probate court, and we're waiting for the case to be put on the court calendar. As a courtesy, this meeting was arranged so we could bring you up to date on the present situation."

Clearly relieved, Tiffany returned to her seat on the couch.

"Tiffany is LL's heir, so it's simply a matter of obtaining an official court decision recognizing her legal claim to the estate. Until the court makes that decision, we're moving ahead to keep the company running the way LL would have wanted. I've drafted the necessary documents giving temporary decision-making control to Lexi Benson, whom I'm sure you all know. She has been working closely . . ."

Stan Bergman shot up like he had been seated on a catapult. "So you're really planning on giving control of the company to her?! She wouldn't know which end of a backhoe to use to dig a ditch!" His face quickly became mottled with scarlet patches of anger.

I felt as if a pulse of electricity had jolted me in the chest. Now I knew why he'd been so agitated. The focus of his internalized anger was on me.

Corstelli tried to calm him. "Mr. Bergman, we said this is a temporary arrangement until the probate court . . ."

Bergman cut him off. "You and her," he pointed from Tiffany to me, "you two are trying to lock out any of us who know how to run this company. I could run it—so could Steelman or Ralston. We could run it with one hand tied behind our back. As near retirement as they are, even Wilson or Conley would be a better choice than . . . than her!" His voice was loud and getting louder. "Why would you hand control of this multi-million dollar company to her . . ." his hand was shaking as he jabbed his finger toward me and repeated, "to her? She's just curried LL's favor to get her hands on . . ."

Corstelli's face was almost as red as Bergman's. He stepped over and looked with hard eyes at the angry man. "Mr. Bergman, sit down and shut up, or I believe that I can promise that you will be fired— right here and now." His voice was icy.

Bergman's jaw snapped shut, and he looked from Corstelli to Tiffany to me and dropped back into the chair where he had been sitting. He belligerently folded his arms across his chest.

Corstelli returned to his position behind the desk. "Now, let's get back to what we were discussing. Until the estate has been probated, Lexi will operate the main office exactly the way she believes LL would have run it. In the three years she worked for him, she gained a good working knowledge of how he wanted things done. When the disposition of the estate is complete, then the issue of who will take over the operation of the main office and sit in LL's chair on a more permanent basis, or the alternative choice that Tiffany might want to sell the company, will be revisited."

That brought Bergman to his feet again. "Sell the company! You're out of your mind." Again, he was looking from Corstelli to Tiffany, and then at me. He stepped in front of me, looking down at where I was seated. "Have the two of you women put your heads together and decided to take the money and run?"

His anger had caught me flat-footed. I was still trying to come up with an appropriate response that wouldn't pour gasoline on the fire inside of him when Corstelli interrupted his accusations.

"Stan, we're sorry if this has caught you off guard." The lawyer's voice had become almost oily in his attempt to soothe Bergman.

"I'd say that's the understatement of the decade," Bergman

responded heatedly as he turned his attention back to Corstelli.

But the lawyer had been at least partially successful in his attempt to lessen the man's anger. Bergman seemed to regain some control and sat down again, returning to the same belligerent posture he had adopted earlier.

Wilson interjected a question in an attempt to bring the discussion back to the issue before the group. "So we're to continue all projects as if LL were still running the main office? If we have questions, we call Lexi for instructions? Oh, I'm Bill Wilson, by the way."

I interjected, "Bill, you project managers are the experts in the hands-on part of the business. I respect that fact. I won't give orders so much as tap into your expertise and discuss any issues or questions you may want to talk about."

Corstelli nodded. "Well put, Lexi." He glanced around the room. "If there are no more questions, that about sums it up. It may take a few weeks or even months for the probate court to settle the estate. Until then, continue as you have been." At that, he looked over at Tiffany, obviously to see if she had anything else to add. She shook her head. He looked at me and I shook my head. He started for the doorway and Tiffany rose and followed him. He looked at me as he passed and nodded as if to encourage me to join them for the farewells. The others trickled out of the den, some exchanging comments in low tones.

The three of us gathered at the open front door. Bill Wilson was the first to offer his hand to Corstelli. "Thanks for calling the meeting to keep us in the loop." He took Tiffany's hand in both of his and offered his condolences again.

She leaned toward him and gave him an air kiss on both cheeks. "Thank you for being here and offering your support. I do appreciate it."

He turned to face me. As he shook my hand, he added, "I'm sure we'll be talking by phone in the near future. You've taken on a big job, but I'm sure you're up for it." I think what he really meant was "I *hope* you're up for it."

In quick succession, Ralston, Steelman, and Winston offered similar words and shook our hands. Tiffany gave each of them an air kiss on each cheek. Bergman was slow to reach us, with the scowl still on his face. It was evident that he did not intend to make any socially appropriate comments. He just ducked his head and, with a brief nod in the general direction of Corstelli and Tiffany, he moved rapidly past us.

When Chuck reached us, I looked at him and asked quietly, "Is Stan always so volatile?"

He grinned apologetically. "Some days are worse than others. This was about as explosive as I've ever seen him." He looked at Tiffany. "Let me offer my condolences again on the death of your husband." He turned toward the lawyer. "Mr. Corstelli, thanks for calling the meeting."

"Don't thank me. It was Lexi that felt that it would be a good idea."

He turned back to me. "Thanks, Lexi." He added a little more quietly, "Look, if there are times when talking with Bergman is especially difficult, feel free to use me as a go between—kind of a bridge—if he's not feeling . . . ah, communicative. I have a pretty good working relationship with him."

"Thanks. I'll remember that." And I meant it.

Roger had been standing nearby. Chuck turned to him. "Hey, Roger, give me a call if you want to play nine holes on Saturday."

"Yeah, I'll do that."

He shook hands all around before he left.

Since Steve hadn't appeared, I figured he wasn't planning to interview any of them at that time. When the front door had been closed, I approached Tiffany. "I hope I haven't been out of line, but there wasn't an opportunity to speak to you about the matter when we came from the cemetery. Detective Sutherland wanted to be present for the meeting, but he thought his presence might alter the way the meeting played out. I hope it's okay with you that I took him down to the security room to watch the meeting on camera." I waited for a response.

Corstelli was standing next to her. "I don't think it's a big deal, as long as that's fine with you, Tiffany. After all, it's your house. Now if you'll excuse me, I have some things to attend to at the office."

"Of course, Brandon. You've been indispensable, as always." She leaned up and gave him the same air kiss almost everyone else had received.

As soon as Corstelli was out of the door, Roger turned to Tiffany. "Is there anything I can do, Tiffany?"

"Roger, you've been so thoughtful, but after I settle up with the caterer, I'm going to take a sleeping pill and lie down. I'm just drained. You go on home. We'll all talk again later. You've both been so kind." Her glance included both of us.

"Okay. I hope you get some rest. This must have been a really tough day." He turned to me. "It's got to have been hard on you too, Lexi." I just nodded and took note of the fact that he was apparently not feeling any of the wearying effects of the day. His energy was undiminished.

He turned and made his way down the hall toward the back patio where his car was parked.

"I'll go downstairs and tell Detective Sutherland that the meeting's over." I was sure he had figured that out for himself but I wanted the opportunity to get his feedback on the meeting in private.

She just nodded and turned toward the kitchen. As I walked with her in that direction, I added, "Tiffany, I really meant it when I said you can call on me for anything."

She turned and smiled at me wearily. "I know, and thanks." She paused in the kitchen where the members of the catering staff were cleaning up. I went past her through the mudroom and down to the basement.

When I entered the security room, Steve was sitting with his feet elevated on the chair I had used earlier, still watching the split screen. As I stepped in, he dropped his feet to the floor and grinned. "You don't always have to hear the words to know what's going on."

"At least not if one of those present is Stan Bergman."

"I think I have some questions for Mr. Bergman. We will be having a long talk in the near future."

I was sure my exhaustion was showing. "I'm ready to go. Did you want to ask Tiffany any more questions? If so, it will need to be done right away. As soon as the caterers are through cleaning up, she plans to take a sleeping pill and lie down."

He shook his head. "I'll pass if she's too exhausted. I can call her tomorrow. I'm starved. Are you? How about getting something to eat where we can talk freely?"

"That sounds wonderful." The informality of his suggestion made me feel like I had been taken off the suspect list—if I had ever even been on it. I was so relieved that I must have been beaming. "If you're easily pleased, you can follow me back to my place and I'll pop some frozen waffles into the toaster and scramble some eggs. When I'm tired, I often resort to breakfast in the evening."

"Sounds fine with me. I'll just take a minute to tell Tiffany good-bye. See you at your place."

The rain was coming down steadily by the time I got to the car, making a little river that ran down the sloped driveway. Twilight had turned to dark. The electric eye opened the gate as I approached.

I grinned to myself. I suspected that his suggestion that we get something to eat while we talked was more social than official on his part, and that pleased me greatly. I was humming to myself as I headed out of the subdivision.

After I reached the 101, I checked for Steve's car in the rearview mirror. I couldn't see it, but I figured he'd catch up with me right away.

After I had gone about five or six miles, I noticed a dark SUV about four car lengths behind me. It seemed to stay with me when I changed lanes, so I sped up. It did too. I slowed down, to try to force the vehicle to pass me. It slowed as well. It didn't feel coincidental. I moved across three lanes to the left, high-speed lane and so did he. Now I was getting nervous. The traffic on the road was light but I still couldn't see Steve's car. *Where is he?*

I looked down at my hands, which were holding the steering

wheel so tightly that my knuckles were white. I made a decision. There was a wide shoulder on the right a mile or two ahead where cars in the HOV lane with mechanical problems could pull off. I pressed the gas pedal to the floor and watched the speedometer needle rise to ninety, briefly leaving my pursuer behind.

When I could see him rapidly closing the distance between us, guessing his speed to be near a hundred, I whipped into the HOV lane, braked, and pulled onto the shoulder. My tires slid on the wet blacktop. The SUV flew past but the driver turned away from me and put up a hand to make sure I didn't get a look at him. There was no time to even get a partial license plate number. The only thing I could tell in that brief glimpse was that the vehicle was a Jeep Cherokee.

I waited for my nerves to settle down before I pulled back out onto the highway at a more sedate—and legal—pace. Within a couple of minutes, I recognized Steve's car behind me.

Feeling safer, I picked up speed and watched for the Jeep as I drove. I recognized it as I passed under the overpass of 202. The Jeep was sitting at the top of the exit ramp.

Steve stayed close to my car and followed me through the gate at my condo complex. He parked and was out of his car before I had pulled my keys from the ignition. He pulled my door open. "What on earth was going on? Why did you pull over like that?"

I looked at him, startled by his reaction. "Didn't you see the Jeep Cherokee following me?" I suddenly realized that the two of us were talking much too loudly so I said, "Let's go inside," and slid out of the car. I waved at him to follow me. He slammed my car door and caught up with me.

After we were both inside, having dutifully waved at Mrs. Bolton, I flipped on the floor lamp inside the door, stepped out of my black, strappy heels and dropped my purse onto the table by the door. I looked at my hands, surprised to see them shaking.

He turned me around with both hands on my shoulders and suddenly looked contrite. "I'm sorry if I yelled at you. I was worried. Tell me what happened."

"I need to sit down." I moved over to the couch where he sat beside me. "I thought you would catch up with me right away when I left Tiffany's place, but when I looked in my rearview mirror, you weren't anywhere to be seen."

"Roger was waiting for me outside. He wanted to know if I'd made any progress in the case. I told him not much at this point, and asked him if he had given the matter any thought—if he'd come up with any potential suspects. After I pressed him a little, he said that he thought that Bergman had the best motive, but he didn't really think he was capable of committing murder—despite his temper. Anyway, I didn't get away from him for nearly five minutes. That put me well behind you. Why did you pull off the highway that way?"

"I kept watching for you in the rearview mirror, and after a few miles I noticed an SUV following me. It stayed right behind me, changing lanes, slowing or speeding up just like I did. It never got close enough for me to see the driver. I decided to try to get a look at him, so I sped up to ninety and when he did as well, I pulled over fast and stopped so quickly that he shot past me. He turned away and put his hand up to make sure I couldn't get a good look at him. After I pulled back out onto the highway, I didn't see him until I caught him at the top of an exit ramp." I took a deep breath. "Why has this gotten me so upset? It's not like he aimed a gun at me or anything like that."

Steve took my cold hands in his warm ones. "Lexi, he meant to intimidate you. If he had meant to hurt you or kill you, he would have done more than let you know he was following you." He let go and stood. "Let's get you warm. Do you have a blanket I can get for you?"

"There's a comforter on my bed."

He brought it to me and draped it around my shoulders. He grinned at me. "I'm hungry. I'll fix us some scrambled eggs and waffles."

His grin gave me more warmth than a comforter ever could.

CHAPTER 12

He took off his damp suit coat and hung it over the back of one of the tall stools that faced the island between the living room and the kitchen. He started to roll up his sleeves. "You'll feel better if you eat something. Those finger foods at the wake wouldn't keep a mosquito full for ten minutes."

He pulled out the toaster and searched the refrigerator and freezer. He set a half-gallon of milk, a bottle of syrup, and a butter dish on the serving island. When he had set two places on the snack bar, he broke the eggs into the frying pan one-handed like a chef and mixed them with a fork. In about ten minutes, he stated in a satisfied tone, "Come and get it."

I walked over to one of the tall stools still wrapped in the down comforter. I draped it over the stool back as he set a plate of scrambled eggs in front of me. As I sat down, the toaster popped the waffles up with a cheerfulness that I envied. I was suddenly starved.

As he moved around the island and pulled out the stool next to me, I ate silently, thinking that if he could cook other things as well as he did frozen waffles and scrambled eggs, he had some real hidden talents.

After I had consumed two waffles smothered in blackberry syrup, a glass and a half of cold milk, and at least three scrambled eggs, I put down my fork. "You're right. Eating did help."

He put down his fork and looked at me. "I don't feel good about you being alone and unprotected here at the condo. It would be better if you were out of sight. When you're at the office or on the road, you're especially vulnerable."

I cut him off. "Steve, surely you can understand how I feel. I'm not going to endanger other people by moving in with them—and I refuse to curl up in a ball and withdraw from life. Too many jobs depend on keeping the company running."

"Can't Roger do that?"

I shook my head. "He's nowhere near ready to make decisions of any importance, and I'm not worried when I'm at the office because he's there most of the time, so I'm not alone. There's about a dozen men close by in the other building, and I'm not going to be unprotected here at home. I've arranged for a security system to be installed. The man is coming tomorrow morning to look at my place and give me an estimate." I was rushing my words in order to convince him to agree with me, so I took a breath to slow down. "And Uncle Bob gave me a gun while we were at the funeral. It's in my bag. Between the fence, the gun, the security system, and Mrs. Bolton, I think I'm as safe at my place—or soon will be—as I would be anywhere else." I couldn't tell if I had convinced him or not, but he didn't argue.

He was quiet while he ate until I prodded him. "What are you thinking?"

"I'll need to take a look at that gun before I leave, but getting back to what happened at the meeting at Tiffany's, it's obvious that I need to have a very long talk with Bergman."

I gave a very unladylike groan. "Wow, what fun that meeting was. I sure hope that overseeing the company for the next while doesn't include any more 'little meetings' like that one. If it does, I'll turn in my resignation." I finished the remainder of my milk before I asked again, "Where do you go from here?"

"I did get some additional insight into the situation this afternoon watching the meeting." He stood up and started to gather the dirty dishes. I was glad to let him. I didn't get waited on very often. He stood with his back to me as he ran the water into the sink. Then he gave it a squirt of Joy dish detergent. With the dishcloth in his hand, he turned and looked at me. "What do you know about Bergman—or for that matter, any of the others who were present, including Tiffany?" He momentarily paused. "Do you have job applications or résumés on them? And for that matter, will you get me the job applications on all the employees in the other office—you know, the accountants, architects, the lawyer?"

"Sure, but am I right in guessing it's information on Bergman you want first?" He nodded. "I think LL hired him about five years ago. I've been told that he just walked into the office and threw down some photos of several of the projects he directed while working for one of LL's competitors. LL said he wasn't convinced at the time, but he called around and got a good report on the man—at least on his work. Some folks said he had the personality of an angry badger, but he got things done, done right, and done on time. Somewhere I heard that he spent some time in Iraq doing construction for the Army. Within six months, the local man had retired and Bergman was hired to oversee the projects out of the Phoenix office. LL liked his work, even though there were a few men who walked off the job saying that they wouldn't tolerate the verbal abuse he sometimes heaped on them. LL tried to talk to him a couple of times about being less explosive, but I don't think it made much difference. He was really frustrated that he couldn't polish the edges off Stan."

"Do you think he was considering firing him?"

"It's possible. As far as the other office managers are concerned, they all predate me by several years. Maybe Les Rasmussen, our HR man, would know more about them than I do."

He was quiet for a minute before he asked, "What do you know about Roger?"

"Everything I know about him came from him. He applied for a position in the accounting department. I think LL just took to him—one of those unexplainable things. He's young and confident, and I guess LL saw something there he liked. Ever since he was hired, his mail has come to the office—even his utility bills and his bank statements."

"What's he like to work with?"

"He's usually very upbeat, confident . . . likable."

He turned back to the sink. "What do you know about his personal life?"

"Not much. He once said that he grew up in Colorado and attended ASU on a math scholarship. Another time, he mentioned that he graduated from Stafford University with a double major in business and accounting."

"What do you know about Stafford?"

"Just that it's a small four-year institution that does a lot of correspondence courses. It does have a campus in Kingman. The company built their first on-campus dorms a couple years ago, and LL gave a generous contribution to their endowment fund at the time. The folks in the administration were really appreciative, and both LL and I receive Christmas cards every year from them."

He brushed aside my rambling. "Did Roger ever explain why he started at one university but graduated from another?"

"Something about his mother dying the summer after his freshman year. He apparently had no other family."

"Tell me what you know about Tiffany."

"Almost nothing, other than that she and LL were married about five years ago."

He dried his hands and looked at me with a very serious expression. "It's time I saw that gun your uncle gave you at the funeral."

I got up and located my purse. "I really don't feel comfortable carrying a gun." I pulled the brown paper bag out and handed it to him.

He took the gun out of the crumpled bag and fished out the box of ammunition that was with it. As he sighted down the barrel and opened the cylinder, he talked to me as if I were a fourth grader who needed to understand a difficult story problem. "The incident at Sunnyvale Estates was evidently a crime of opportunity, and we really don't know why you were followed this evening, or by whom.

Perhaps these were acts of opportunity or impulse, for lack of a better term. Maybe there are two people who want to do you harm, maybe only one, but I think you'd better be prepared to defend yourself. This is only a .22 caliber, so it won't have a lot of stopping power, but since someone has taken an unnatural interest in you on two occasions now, I think you need to keep it with you. Do you know how to handle a gun?"

"When I was in college, I dated a guy who thought he was going to make a hunter out of me. He showed me how to use a rifle and took me to a shooting range to show me how to use a revolver as well. He later proposed and suggested that we make his annual deer-hunting trip our honeymoon. When I was less than enthusiastic about that, he made it clear that any girl he married would need to know how to clean a deer. Needless to say, that ended any likelihood of an engagement." Steve chuckled. I looked at him as a new thought occurred to me. "But wouldn't I need to be licensed to carry a gun?"

"That's not necessary in Arizona, as long as you don't have a criminal record, but a concealed weapons permit would be a good idea, in case you ever need to use it. I want you to take the course and get that permit ASAP." He tapped the bullets from the open cylinder into his hand. After examining them, he reloaded the gun. "Will you take the course?"

"Yes, if you say so." I spoke with hesitation. I had always felt that carrying a handgun was an invitation to a mugger to take it away from me and shoot me with it.

"At night, keep this somewhere within easy reach and as soon as you've taken the course, keep it with you during the day."

"Do you think I'm really in danger here at home? Frankly, I think a cell phone is of more value than a gun—usually." I added the last word as the memory of the uselessness of my cell phone out at the Sunnyville Estates nudged my memory.

He handed the revolver back to me. "I'm going to take you out to a gun range just off I-17 and Carefree Highway on Saturday morning." He paused and looked at me as if it had just occurred to him that I might have some other idea of what to do with my

Saturday morning. "Will that work for you?" I nodded. "I'll pick you up at seven thirty. They have the best qualifying course in the state. The course is four hours long but it will require some extra time for filling out paperwork and having your fingerprints taken. By the time it's over, you'll have qualified—unless you can't hit the broadside of a barn," he teased with a grin. He became serious again. "Be sure to take your gun and ammo. They'll furnish you with anything else you'll need. I'm serious when I tell you that I want you carrying this as soon as you finish that course."

As he rose to leave, he put out his hand. "Give me your cell for a minute." I pulled it from my bag and handed it to him. He opened the back of it like he knew what he was doing and pulled out the SIM card. He studied it for a second, and then put it back together. He took the notebook and pen out of his shirt pocket and made a note.

He looked up at me and grinned. "Now, no matter where you're using your cell phone, I can find you."

"As long as there's cell service." I added, with a bit of skepticism.

"Lock your doors. And hey, do you have my number programmed into your cell?"

"Yes, I do now."

With a wave, he was gone. I dutifully locked the door and put on the chain. I was tired with an exhaustion that permeated my bones. I pulled off my dress and put on my pajamas, fuzzy robe, and slippers, and stretched out on the couch wrapped in my comforter cocoon.

As I drifted off to sleep, I saw the bulldozer come at me. In frustration, I sat up and tried to shake that mental picture when someone knocked.

I head Mrs. Bolton's voice through the door. "Lexi, come meet our new night watchman."

I opened the door and there stood a giant of a man. He must have been 300 pounds, but I wouldn't have described him as obese. He carried some extra weight, but he was so tall I almost got a crick in my neck looking up at him. He looked about twenty-five.

"This is Tommy, my granddaughter's husband. You can sleep better tonight."

I put out my hand. "I really appreciate your willingness to give up your nights to keep us safe, Tommy."

"Glad to help out, at least until I get another job." His voice rumbled up from his shoes.

When I closed the door, I leaned on it and chuckled. If someone tried to come over the fence or in through the gate without permission, the sight of Tommy might cause a heart attack.

I gave up on sleep and moved into my second bedroom where I sat at my computer, still wrapped in my comforter.

If I ever had guests, I would be hard pressed to give them a bed to sleep in since the smaller of the two bedrooms was home to my computer desk and printer, my quilt frame, and the nearly completed baby quilt for Percy's next baby spread out on it. I had a six-foot folding table against one wall that was cluttered with binders full of family history, my favorite hobby. In the corner was an easel where I had a desert landscape awaiting my return to finish it.

One wall in that room was covered by two very large bookcases, which were filled with my printed treasures. I was an omnivorous reader, so the books covered a multitude of subjects: fiction, nonfiction, history, and religion.

Sitting at the computer, an idea tapped me on the shoulder. Responding to that prompting, I sent an email to a friend from my college days, Diana Fieldstone, an administrative assistant to the chancellor at ASU. We had formed a firm friendship while she was an instructor and I was an undergraduate student there.

Then I sent another one to Stafford University, addressed to Joseph Landgrave, PhD, the head of the department that handled endowments and gifts. I knew him from the dorm project and LL's gift to their endowment fund. LL never liked a lot of pomp and fuss, so he let me present the check. That had given me the chance to meet Landgrave a couple of times, so I was fairly sure he'd remember me.

Just before midnight, I finally decided to climb into bed. The rain began to lash at the windows like someone was spraying the structure with a power washer. I hoped Tommy was sitting in a car near the gate. The lightning flickered a blue light through my interior shutters, but even that ruckus couldn't keep me awake any longer.

Chapter 13

The next morning I labored to get out of bed, trying not to make my bruises and sore spots slow me down too much. I had just finished my bowl of instant oatmeal and my glass of orange juice when the man from the security company arrived. His name was Ralph, according to the blue uniform shirt he wore. He walked through my place, looking at the exterior doors and windows and asking questions. He finally seemed satisfied.

"We'll wire your place so that any attempt to force a door or a window will set off a call to the local police department."

"What if someone breaks a window?" I asked.

"Same thing will happen. We'll mount a keypad on the wall by the living room door and when you use your key to come in, you'll have forty-five seconds to put your code into it. That should give you time to put down your groceries or packages. If you take longer, a loud alarm bell will ring and disturb your neighbors. If, after fifteen more seconds, you haven't punched in the code, a call goes to the police department. You want me to schedule the installation?"

I nodded. "As soon as possible."

"My boss says we do a lot of work for the company you work for, so I'm supposed to give you a ten percent discount and really good treatment. I can do it in the morning if that's okay."

"How long will it take you and when can you get here? I have a seven thirty appointment."

"It'll take about an hour with two men, and we can come as early as you want."

"Six o'clock?"

"Six o'clock it is." We shook hands before he left.

• • •

When I got to work, the office was dark, which was not surprising. I often arrived before Roger. As I pushed the door open, I spotted an envelope on the floor, apparently slid under the door.

I put my bag down on my desk and picked up a letter opener. I pulled out the single sheet folded twice and was surprised to find it hand written, or more accurately, hand printed in big block letters. It read: "Benson, Go and get married. Raise some kids. Let men run the business world—or face the consequences." The last four words were underlined. *So this is another part in a scare campaign.* I was determined not to let the letter bother me, but it did—more than I wanted to admit.

I put it back into the envelope and stuck it in my bag. I moved over to the four-drawer file cabinet next to LL's desk and opened the drawer marked *Personnel.* I thumbed through the files and pulled out almost all of them. The ones I left in the drawer belonged to a few retired employees. I carried them over to the copy machine where I pulled the applications and the résumés. When I had finished copying each one, I put the copies into a brown envelope for Steve. I realized that I didn't have anything on Roger, and all I had on Stan Bergman was his W-4 withholding form. I wasn't concerned about Roger. His application was probably filed in the other office, since he had been hired initially for a position there, but the lack of anything on Bergman made me wonder.

I walked the distance to the other office and asked our personnel man, Les Rasmussen, if he had a job application for Roger or Bergman. "I'm sure I do," he cheerfully responded.

After searching his files, he came up with the application each had filled out at the time of his hiring. The information on each was skimpy at best, but at least I could include it in the packet I had ready for Steve.

I called him. "I have copies of all the job applications you wanted."

"Can I pick you up for lunch? We'll go somewhere where I can take a few minutes to look at them and you can add anything you think might be useful."

"Okay." My heart leapt and then almost immediately dropped. *He wants to take me to lunch—or maybe it will be just a working lunch. I hope that there's a social reason as much as a professional one for him to want to go to lunch with me. Something about him makes me feel safe . . . and . . .* I didn't let my thoughts go any further than that.

"Did Roger come into the office this morning? I've got a question or two for him."

"No, and he hasn't called. Do you want me to tell him to give you a call when I see him?"

"I'd appreciate it."

I had some time to return phone calls, but as I reached for the phone, it rang, making me jump.

It was Bergman. "Look, Lexi, I'm embarrassed about the way I acted at Tiffany's. I was caught off guard. I hope you'll accept my apology."

I was stunned. This man really could run hot and cold. I took a deep breath and tried to be gracious in my acceptance of the apology. "That's somewhat understandable, Stan. I'm sorry you were blindsided."

"I've been thinking about the Sunnyville project, and I thought I would just offer my advice."

My thoughts were running in overdrive. *This is one guy I should keep at arm's length in the future . . . or . . .* A new thought hit me. *Or perhaps it would be wiser to cultivate a friendship with him.*

I decided to try the second approach. *You can draw more flies with honey than with vinegar,* Aunt Betty often said. "Look, Stan, I'll come over to your office so we can talk about your concerns in person. Give me about thirty minutes to get through traffic."

He seemed genuinely pleased that I was willing to make the effort to meet with him on his own turf. I called Steve and left a message that I would call him after my meeting with Bergman.

The yard of the local Phoenix area office of LL Construction was paved with battered asphalt, where at least a dozen trucks, pickups, concrete pumpers, skip loaders, and pavers sat, all painted white with the vivid green logo of LL Construction on their sides. A large portion of the lot was given over to the massive machinery where broken concrete and asphalt were crushed, recycled, and mixed into road base that would meet state and federal specifications.

In the far southeast corner of the lot was a two-story, corrugated metal garage filled with well-used maintenance and service equipment for the company vehicles. Gas pumps stood next to the building, and on the far side of it were three bright yellow caterpillars and a John Deere crawler 'dozer. I stopped the first man that I met in a hard hat and a denim shirt and jeans. It was Chuck.

"Hi, Lexi. You come to meet with Stan?"

"Yes, you might say I'm hoping to soothe his ruffled feathers. Has he moved his office? I remember it used to be in a big trailer near the fence."

"He did a big remodel job a few months ago." He pointed to the metal warehouse. "His new office is over there, just behind that dump truck that I'm going to move in just a minute. He's been downright congenial today. He must have taken a tranquilizer this morning."

"Thanks." I walked around the front end of the big truck with the grumbling engine. The sign that read *office* couldn't be seen until I was nearly on top of it. I pushed open the door, expecting anything but what I found. Bergman's office was large, and paneled in glossy walnut with dark blue indoor-outdoor carpet. It had gray file cabinets and four dark walnut desks. It was an office appropriate for an executive.

Wow, this is so much nicer than the corporate office. Three men were talking in a corner, hunched over a set of blueprints spread out on a long table. They wore the same unofficial uniform that LL had usually worn: white short-sleeved shirts, ties, tan slacks, and high-topped, leather lace-up shoes with crepe soles for walking over rough building sites.

Stan rose from behind his desk as he completed a phone conversation and put the receiver into the cradle. He waved me over.

"Lexi, I can call you that, can't I?" He didn't wait for an answer. "Come over and have a chair here by my desk. I want to show you the architectural drawings for the finished Sunnyville project. It'll help you 'get the vision,' so to speak."

I had already seen the drawings and the blueprints for many of the homes and the clubhouse, but I was glad to see him calmer than the previous day. He spread the plans and drawings out on his desk and pointed with a pen. "See the sweep of the golf course and the patio and pool right there next to the clubhouse? This will be a premier course in the metro area. You've got to cut Ed Gomes some slack. He'll get the money together."

He rambled on for at least ten minutes without my saying anything. I wasn't sure whether his rambling was due to emotional commitment to the project or because he was uncomfortable with me. Some people tend to talk too much when they're ill at ease.

I made myself focus on what he was saying. "Even if Ed took out bankruptcy, which isn't going to happen, the bank would put the property on the auction block, and I'm just suggesting that you seriously consider bidding on it, if something like that happens. Sunnyville Estates will be a first-class financial success if we just wait for the economy to turn around." The intensity in his voice showed me that his strong feelings were rising to the surface.

I responded and tried to show him I was willing to listen. "I can appreciate your viewpoint, Stan. I'll certainly give your suggestion serious consideration. Thanks for your . . . um, recommendation in the matter."

We talked for nearly an hour about the other projects in the metro area that were either just getting started or nearing completion. He was much more relaxed than he had been at the wake. He even laughed a time or two before we shook hands and I took my leave.

A thought took shape as I walked to my car. I dialed Ted

Jorgenson, our head accountant. It took four rings for him to pick up. "Ted, this is Lexi. I need to ask a special favor."

"Sure, what can I do for you?"

"Will you run an audit on the Sunnyville Estates project and . . . and Hebestreet's loft project for me?" *Might as well take a close look at both.*

"No problem. When do you need them?"

"ASAP, and keep it quiet."

"OK. Anything else?"

"Yes, and again, it's very important that you keep it quiet. I want a full audit of every project Roger has handled. I'm genuinely concerned about his record keeping. He hasn't been keeping the Sunnyville account up to date. I'm worried about the other accounts he is responsible for. Go back to the date of his hire."

"That'll take some time."

"Just do it as soon as you can. Thanks, Ted."

When I got back to the office, the phone rang as I was sitting down. The voice on the other end was full of synthetic friendship and bravado. "Hi, Lexi, this is Bud Hebestreet. I've had a little chat with Tiffany this morning about a contribution for a congressional candidate I'm supporting. We're getting a head start on the fundraising for the election even though it's two years down the road. She said that she would certainly be willing to make a sizable contribution to his campaign in LL's memory."

All my defenses went up. "What's this guy's name, Bud?"

"Tony Blankenship." Before I could say anything, he hurried on. "I've been working with him for several months, and he's really a sharp candidate. We're getting a jump on the fundraising so he'll be out in front in the next election. He's a good businessman and presents himself to the public in a first-rate manner. He'll be a real help in DC for our state and . . ."

I plunged in. "Bud, I hate to disappoint you, but a couple of months ago, LL refused to make a contribution to this man's campaign. He made it clear that he felt this guy was . . ." I reached for some tactful words, "of less than sterling character, and had been involved in some very questionable business deals. He has at least three former business partners who have lined up to take him to court. LL wasn't willing to give him a dime."

"Lexi, LL didn't really mean it. I just caught him on a bad day. Tiffany says that you can cut a check . . ."

"I'm sorry to upset you, Bud, but I've been charged with continuing to operate this office in the same way LL would if he were here. I'm not going to go against his wishes to give you a big contribution for a candidate LL wouldn't support."

"Lexi, you're making a big mistake. If I can get this guy elected, I can get you a position in his office—in Washington, DC, or in some place like the State Department, if you want. Wouldn't that be a big step up from what you're doing now?"

"Bud, the matter isn't open to further discussion."

"Look, don't hang me out to dry on this." His voice was gaining a note of panic. "I've made promises that I've got to keep. You'll really be glad you were in his corner when he's a big shot in Washington."

"I'm sorry, Bud, but I've got to do what LL would have done." To pull him off the subject, I asked, "Are the suspended ceilings in your loft project on track?"

He inhaled deeply and then exhaled more slowly. "Yeah, but there's some problems with the units on the top floor. I told the workmen to stop until we can find a solution and get the problems solved. You'll need to see that they're fixed before we talk payment."

"We'll do that, Bud. When do you want to have a walk-through?" He was one unhappy man. *I'll bet he can find a whole list of "problems" to be fixed before he'll pay, now that I've turned down his favorite candidate.*

"I'll give you a call." He said tersely before he hung up.

I rubbed my temples for about a minute. Maybe that increased the blood flow to my brain, because a new thought occurred to me. I picked up the phone and dialed the Washington office of Congressman Skidmore. When the receptionist answered, I asked to speak to the legislative assistant over military matters for the congressman. LL and I had supported Skidmore in his first election and I had encouraged the guy who now filled that position to apply, so I felt it was a good time to call in a favor.

"This is Nate Wade." He had a young voice, full of self-confidence.

"Hi, Nate. This is Lexi Benson. How's everything going in DC?"

"Hi, Lexi. It's crazy as usual. How can I help you?"

"I imagine you heard about the death of Lawrence Lattimer? I know he was a friend of your boss."

"We not only heard about it, we heard that it was murder. Is that true?" His voice reflected his amazement.

"Yes, it's true, and I need to call in a favor. One of the men who has been acting like he expected to take his place as head of the company has drawn some attention. I heard that he did some building in Iraq for the Army. I don't know if he was enlisted, served as a career officer, or worked for a private company under contract to the military. If I give you what I have, will you call someone over in the Pentagon and find out anything you can about him?"

He hesitated for a moment but finally responded. "Yes, I can do that. You say this is important?"

"Yes, Nate, it's very important."

"All right, I'll make some phone calls. Give me a number where I can get back to you if—and I do mean *if*—I find anything."

I gave him Bergman's full name, birth date, and social security number as listed on his W-4 form. With that much information, any American on the face of the earth can usually be located and his life story uncovered within twenty-four hours. I repeated my cell phone number and my email address. "Thanks, Nate. You're a real asset to Skidmore." I hung up.

The dial tone was breaking, telling me that I had a waiting message. At eleven, Steve had called to tell me that something had come up and we would have to postpone our talk until he picked me up to take me out to the shooting range in the morning.

When I hung up the phone, it rang again. It was Percy. "Lexi, Richard got home this morning from a business trip to LA. He's only been gone a couple of days, but I told him that if he doesn't take me out to lunch, he's in big trouble. I need some quiet time and some adult conversation. Can you watch the kids for a couple of hours?"

"Sure, sis. I need some time away from the office. Be there in about a half hour." I responded to her request with mixed feelings. I loved my four nieces, but two hours with them equaled three hours of hard work at a gym. There was no one around to complain if I took a few hours off.

When I arrived at the rambling, Spanish-style house built in the suburb of Gilbert, south of the metro area, I smiled at the mass of wheeled children's toys in the driveway. I pulled up behind Percy's minivan, which was parked on the street. The house had been built to look like a Mexican adobe with a flat roof. The front yard was gravel, like the others on the street but there was a lawn of grass in the back for the children to play on. As I got out of my car, the three oldest children ran toward me from the open front door like a trio of Union officers attacking a defenseless Confederate private. Their battle cry was "Aunt Lexi's here, Aunt Lexi's here."

I stooped and wrapped the three of them in my arms as the fourth toddled toward me unsteadily. Pamela was nearly eight, McKenzie was five and a half, and Olivia was three. The youngest, Lily, was about twenty months old. I dreamed someday of teaching them to sing together and making them as famous as the Osmonds. Then I'd retire from the construction business and become their agent—or even better, I'd find the right guy and produce my own little brood of musicians. At that thought, Steve's face popped into my mind. I closed that picture firmly. *Why did his face come to mind?* I scolded myself.

As I stood with the clinging, blood-related offspring hampering my movement, Percy and her tired-looking husband, Richard, followed the children out of the house but headed straight for the minivan at the curb. Percy was holding her belly the way women near their full term often do. She looked like she had an enormous watermelon under her A-line dress.

As Richard held the car door open for her, she called to me, "Thanks, Lexi. We can talk when I get back." They drove off to some quiet, climate-controlled restaurant where the two of them could talk, without interruption, about adult things in words of more than one syllable.

When they were gone, I fixed all the girls toasted cheese sandwiches and cups of tomato soup, just like the TV commercial. They liked that, especially Lily, who squeezed pieces of the sandwich in her hands until the cheese squished out between her fingers.

We played Barbie dolls, which I utterly hate, but the girls love. I'm afraid the Barbie doll will lead my nieces to believe that real women are shaped like that.

When my sister and her husband returned home about two, I proudly announced that the three youngest girls were down for their nap and Pamela was playing in the playhouse out back. As I picked up my purse and the umbrella I hadn't needed that day, my brother-in-law excused himself, heading for a nap like his girls, but Percy had something on her mind.

"Lexi, sit down. We need to talk."

Uh oh, I know what's coming. That sisterly communication was at work. I remained standing while she sat on the couch.

"Lexi, worrying isn't just a hobby with me where you're concerned. I'm frantic about your safety." Tears started down her cheeks. She brushed them away with the back of her hand.

I suspected that the conversation at lunch had been focused on me and my situation. "You've got to quit that job. Your boss is dead and someone tried to kill you!" Her voice was rising, so I put my finger to my lips to remind her of the sleeping children. She lowered her voice. "Please quit and come and stay with us until this mess is solved."

"Percy, I've told you before that I can't put you and your little girls in danger. That would be crazy," I whispered forcefully.

"Oh, Lexi," it was a quiet wail. "I wish you had married Jimmy when you were in college. Do you know he and his wife have three children, and he has his own auto body shop now?"

"Percy, we're not going to have this talk again, are we? You know he and I had almost nothing in common. We dated for a couple of years, but we weren't in love—or at least I wasn't."

"Then what about that guy, Rick, you were dating a year ago? You seemed to be getting serious about him and then all of a sudden, it was over. Isn't anyone ever going to be good enough for you to marry?"

"Rick didn't propose. He asked me to move in with him and 'play house' so he could decide if he wanted to propose—and he wasn't interested in the Church. He thought organized religion was for weaklings."

"I'm sorry. You never said anything about why you broke up. I really don't mean to pry, but when we were little and played dolls almost every day, we promised each other that we'd get married and have lots of babies and live next door to each other," she paused to get a breath. "But look at us now. I've got a house full of little girls and all you have is a job—and someone wants you dead! I think I got the better part of the deal." Her voice was rising again.

I helped her up from the couch and put my arms around her. We stood like that until she controlled her tears.

"Percy, I have a satisfying life. Perhaps it's not exactly what we anticipated it would be when we were kids, but I have no bones to pick with God for not giving me that family I always wanted. I'll admit that this is a road that just happened. Like a lot of women, I didn't make a conscious decision to be single and childless. I still hope to find the right man and eventually have a house full of children, but maybe that isn't going to happen . . ."

She pulled away from me, clearly frustrated with my answer and halting my rambling. "Okay, if you won't stay with us, what are you doing to protect yourself? How about moving in with Uncle Bob and Aunt Betty?"

"Surely you know I can't put them in danger. I don't want to put anyone in danger, if I can help it. Mrs. Bolton hired her granddaughter's husband to serve as a night watchman and I'm having a security system put in tomorrow morning." I decided not to mention that Steve was taking me out to the gun range in the morning to learn to shoot. That was something else for her to worry about. "So you see, I'm being careful."

"Oh, I give up." She put her hands on her hips. "Lexi, you *are* a problem. I don't know what to do with you."

"But I'm not *your* problem. I'm just your sister. Now I'm going back to the office and I don't want you to worry about me anymore."

After another quick hug, I hurried out to the car. Remembering my experience on the way home from the meeting at Tiffany's, I checked my rearview mirror often. Traffic was heavy enough, though, that I would have found it difficult to spot a following car, even if there had been one.

I decided to follow an impulse and diverted to the main county government center, where I parked out in the back parking lot. When I entered the marble halls, I paused and checked the directory in the main lobby and located the office that issued business licenses. There, a woman wearing good sturdy shoes, navy blue slacks, and a prim white blouse approached me. She didn't wear a nametag, but in my mind I dubbed her Miss Efficiency.

"I'm seeking information on the original business license granted to the company doing business locally as LL Construction."

She beamed and sat down at a computer screen. "Is it publicly or privately held?"

"It's privately held."

"Give me the name of the principal owner and the address of the central office or primary location of the business."

I did, and within three minutes of pushing and clicking the mouse over the pad, she swiveled the computer screen and showed me what she had found. She said proudly, "We recently digitalized our records all the way back to 1965. You can see how complete they are."

She pointed. "See, right there is a change in the DBA name and here you can see where the name of one of the joint owners—it looks like it may have been a wife—was removed. Here's the link to the assessor's office, in case you want to obtain a listing of properties owned by the corporation. Would you like a copy of what's on the screen? It will cost you two dollars."

I nodded, and she hit the print button. I stuffed the copy in my bag and hurried out of the building. A chill wind moved the palms and the branches of the mesquite trees bordering the parking lot, making them restlessly bend and wave their filmy branches in the wind, like a woman's hair. The creak and rustle of palm fronds was accented by one that had broken loose and was being swept along the sidewalk. The unseasonable rain was going to return soon.

As I inserted the key in the driver's side door, a clerk from the license office who had been sitting at a desk while Miss Efficiency assisted me reached the car next to mine, and took out her car keys. "You must have Triple A," she said.

I paused, and said with some confusion, "I . . . what do you mean? Do I need Triple A?"

"Well, when I came out to get my umbrella about an hour ago, a man was busy working on your car. I figured he was from Triple A or some other auto repair you had called."

I froze for a moment. "Did you get a good look at him?" I tried not to let my alarm show in my voice.

"No, he was kneeling by the open driver's side door, and wore mechanics coveralls and a baseball cap. I spoke to him as I stepped over his feet, but I guess he didn't hear me."

Something prompted me to remove the key from the door lock. "I've just remembered something I need to do before I go home."

I don't know why I was trying to sound so casual. Social norms seem to make us want to avoid upsetting other people, especially strangers, even in what might be a personal crisis.

As the clerk pulled out of the lot, I dashed up the stairs and into the little foyer at the rear building entrance. I found a corner where I thought I wouldn't draw attention and hit the speed dial for Steve's number. I swallowed to steady my voice. I got his voicemail. "Steve, I'm down at the county government center. I parked and left my car unattended while I did some research here. When I was going to get into it, a woman getting into the car next to mine said that a man had been working on it while I was inside. I'm wondering what's going on. Maybe I'm just being a bit nervous about it, but I'm going to wait here until I hear from you."

In the time I stood and waited for his response, a dozen county employees exited and drove out of the parking lot. I began to feel foolish. I stood around checking my watch every two or three minutes. When my cell phone rang, I put it to my ear and Steve yelled at me, "Don't touch the car. I'm on the way." I didn't get an opportunity to respond. Within a few minutes, I saw red and blue lights flashing in the grill of his car as he pulled into the parking lot. I pushed through the door and hurried down the stairs to meet him.

"Why didn't you call 911?" Steve barked as he rushed over to me. He didn't wait for an answer. "Where's your car?"

I pointed at the big Pontiac in the second row from the door about the time he spotted it. "I hope I don't have to answer to the insurance company about it." I smiled weakly, wondering if I was being foolish.

"Go back inside. Don't let anyone else use that exit until I tell you it's okay."

I did as I was told and within the next few minutes, three black and whites pulled up with lights flashing and sirens wailing. The first uniformed officer climbed the stairs and stood at the double doors, not allowing anyone out. Within another five minutes, a big white van pulled into the lot with black printing on the side that caught my eye. The printing read *M.C.P.D. Bomb Squad.*

CHAPTER 14

From where I was located behind the heavy Plexiglas doors, I could see what was going on. I stood there and watched, along with about a half-dozen remaining county employees waiting to go home. I saw two men climb out of the van and approach the car. They were wearing bulky, padded blue suits with transparent face covers attached to their helmets. One stretched out on the ground and, with a flashlight, looked over the underside. The other one examined the outside of the grill and hood. With great care, they opened the driver's side door and examined the underside of the driver's seat.

After about twenty minutes, they both waved the police and spectators further away from the vehicle. The spectators that had gathered were moved out of sight, probably around to the side of the building.

When that had been done, one of the bomb squad men squatted and the other knelt, holding the flashlight. The first worked carefully under the seat, finally removing something that from where I stood looked like a small, light-colored square of putty. Several short wires or chords appeared to be attached to it. The other man took it, handling it as carefully as if it were a fragile and valuable Fabergé egg.

He carried it gingerly to a converted, reinforced, fifty-five-gallon drum on wheels that had been removed from the back of the white van. The little package was carefully put into it and the lid was tightened down. One of the men in the bomb squad uniforms pushed it about four hundred feet to the back of an empty adjoining parking lot that belonged to a darkened office building.

The drum had been pushed so far back that I could just barely see it, but after the bomb experts returned to stand by the police cars near the front of the lot, we heard a loud *whump* as they set off whatever was in the big barrel, making it jump about twenty feet into the air. That was followed by a loud thud as it returned to earth and hit the pavement.

After another five minutes, the uniformed officer received a signal that it was okay for us to exit the building. As I and the others who were waiting to leave stepped out, the faint smell of burning chemicals reached us. I approached the cluster of police officers, including Steve, who had gathered around the two bomb squad officers. Bits and pieces of the conversation reached me. "C4 primed with def cord and a blasting cap connected to a compression switch. If she'd sat down on that seat, or even just dropped her purse . . ." The officer looked up when he saw me coming and stopped speaking.

Steve turned and saw me. "You said someone saw a man working on the car?"

"Yes, one of the county clerks. She drove off before you got here, but I imagine she'll be back to work Monday. She wore a nametag that said her name was Dottie."

"We'll have someone talk to her. In the meantime, I think it's time for you to go home, lock your doors, and stay there."

"Can I drive the GTO?"

"No, it'll be taken to the garage where the CSI team will go over it. If you'll wait a few more minutes, I'll drive you home."

While I waited for him to finish his conversations with the other officers, I sat on the top step near the front door of the building, noticing that I was soaked with nervous perspiration. He finally waved me over to his car and we headed for my condo. After a few minutes he spoke. "I'll bet you're as hungry as I am. What do you want, pizza or Chinese?"

"I've got a supreme pizza in my freezer."

"That'll work just fine."

We drove the rest of the way in silence. I could see he was thinking hard, and whenever my dad had looked that way when I was a child, I knew better than to bother him.

He parked in my vacant spot and as we walked toward my front door, I waved at Mrs. Bolton. So did he.

In my little kitchen, I turned on the oven. "There's a TV tray between the fridge and the wall that we can use to eat in the living room. I'm going to trust you to put the pizza in the oven. It's in the freezer section of my refrigerator. Give me a minute to change out of these shoes."

On my way to my bedroom, I paused to turn on my computer. With fuzzy slippers on my feet, I returned and sat down to check my email. I could hear Steve getting in the cupboard. He called out, "Got any napkins?"

"No. We'll have to use paper towels."

"What've you got to drink? Soda?"

"Never in my house. There's milk, orange, and apple juice in the fridge, and there's always that unusual drink called ice water. I'd like some apple juice."

"Will do." The oven pinged and I heard him slide the pizza into it.

Nate had sent me something with an attachment. His email simply said, "Hope this is what you wanted."

I opened the attachment and hit print. The printer started to hum and as the sheets of paper fed out, I read the first page on the screen. On US Government letterhead, I saw the words *United States Army vs. M/Sgt Stanley Hardy Bergman*. The court case was eight years old. It had involved the theft of explosives of various descriptions and amounts, including dynamite, Symtex, and RDX from a warehouse in Kandahar Province in Iraq. The disposition of the case: *Defendant pled guilty. Sentence: time served (254 days), a fine of ten thousand dollars, dishonorable discharge, and loss of all veterans' benefits.*

I picked up the copy and returned to the living room. Steve

carried in the TV tray with two glasses of apple juice and a roll of paper towels on it and put it near the couch. I handed him the email attachment from Nate and crossed to my purse, where I retrieved the information from the government center. Seeing the envelope that had been pushed under the door of the office that morning, I picked it up as well and brought it over to where he sat.

He read the case of *Army v. Bergman* twice before he chuckled cynically, and shook his head. "So our boy knows how to handle explosives. That adds considerable interest to the case."

The timer dinged and I rose to retrieve the pizza. When it had cooled, we both picked up a triangle of cheesy, heavily loaded pizza to eat.

"Mmmm," he said under his breath. "What else have you found?" I laid my piece of pizza down on a paper towel, wiped my hands, and offered him the printout of the history of LL's company. He spread it out on the coffee table and ran his finger down the page. We noted the original business license was issued thirty years earlier with the co-owners listed as Lawrence and Louise Lattimer doing business as Triple L Construction. Then five years later, her name was removed, and the name of the company was changed to LL Construction, with the sole owner listed as Lawrence Lattimer.

Steve looked up at me. "Just where is all this going?"

"Maybe nowhere, but I found it interesting. At least now we know that LL's first wife was named Louise."

He shook his head. "I doubt that any of this is pertinent to the case."

"You're probably right. Has anyone interviewed the names on the list of clients I gave you?"

He nodded. "I've got a team doing the interviews. Nothing of any real use has come to light yet. I sent the other team working on this case out to the state pen yesterday to interview the cellmate of Chet Huddleston again. Since the cellmate's parole date is coming up fast, I hoped that would motivate him to talk freely. I'm waiting for a report on that interview. I asked around headquarters about some of the clients on the list and I've heard some rumors that Hebestreet may have some really old and dirty connections to a drug cartel figure from Juarez, but so far it's just rumor. I did take the time to run his name through police records and he comes up clean."

I sat upright in amazement. "Who made the connection?"

"Glade Schmidt remembers something about it, but since nothing shows up in federal or state arrest records, I think Schmidt's mixing memories. He's been around a long time."

But an idea had gone off in my head. "If any of what Schmidt thinks about Bud is true, maybe the *Federales* would have something on him."

"I've got a request in to their central law enforcement agency in Mexico City through all the proper embassy channels for a records search on him, but with the chaos going on down there, I might never hear back from them. Let's face it, they have their hands full with the drug war going on."

I got up from the couch, put the last bite of pizza in my mouth, and wiped off my hands one more time. I pulled a small book of telephone listings from my desk drawer that listed connections that LL had made through his construction work as well as some of his old friends. I always called it my "magic book" because many private numbers of important people were in it. Some of the numbers were nearly three years old, but might still get me what I wanted.

I dialed the area code for Matamoros, Mexico. When the female voice answered, I stated, "*Comandante Luis García, por favor.*"

"*Un momento.*"

A heavy masculine voice came on, and spoke rapidly in Spanish, asking the purpose of the call. I asked, "Do you speak English?"

"*Sí*, I speak English."

"This is Lexi Benson, executive assistant to Lawrence Lattimer, a good friend of Comandante García. I need to speak to the Comandante."

The man grunted and I heard some fast Spanish as he covered the receiver with his hand. He returned and said, "*Un momento.*"

A familiar voice came on. "Lexi, it's good to hear from you." His voice was so warm and gracious, I felt as if I had wrapped my comforter around my shoulders again. "How is LL?"

"That's what I'm calling you about, Luis . . . I . . . I hate to give you bad news, but LL was murdered several days ago and we need some help up here with a matter that bears on the case. It may take forever if we use formal channels. I thought of you as the most efficient source of information, if you can help us out."

He exhaled slowly. "Lexi, I am so sorry to hear about his death. He was a good man. You know I will help if I can." His voice was filled with genuine regret. Then his hand went over the receiver as he gave someone instructions to exit and close the door.

"We have a need for information on someone your law enforcement officials may have dealt with in the past." I gave him Hebestreet's name, spelled it, and included his approximate age. "It's rumored that he might have some connections to a drug cartel." I could hear the scratch of pen on paper as he wrote it down.

"Bud Hebestreet," he repeated. "The name means nothing to me and I am familiar with the name of every drug connection in the Sinaloa Cartel going back to its early years, but if you want me to, I will make a few calls and see what I can find."

"That would be great. Luis, God bless you. You're a real friend." I breathed a sigh of relief. Surely Luis would know if Bud was involved with anything shady.

His laughter was tinged with sadness. "I know, I know, and if things get any hotter down here in this drug war, I'll need all the blessings you can call down from heaven. If you hear about my funeral, please offer prayers on my behalf." It was said lightly, but I knew he meant it. "I have lost many friends in the war against crime here in Mexico, but I never expected to lose my friend LL. He was my best friend while we were at university and we enjoyed our fishing trips together for many years. I will miss him." He ended the call.

When I looked up at Steve, he was grinning in a funny, crooked way. "We get years of training on how to follow procedures, and you can get more done with a phone call than the entire department could in six months. With your connections, I think you should give up running LL Construction and become a private investigator."

The suggestion really struck my funny bone. I started to laugh, and I couldn't quit until I was wiping my eyes. What a wonderful tension release the laugh provided. "It's good to know that I have a fallback position if I ever decide to quit the company." I took a breath. "Comandante García didn't know anything about Hebestreet, but he's going to look into it. Now where do we go from here?" He was quiet for so long that I asked, "Were there any fingerprints on the bulldozer?"

He shook his head. "Just smudges. The guy wore gloves. If we're really lucky, maybe the CSI people will turn up something on the Pontiac, but I really doubt it."

"When can I have it back? I'm without transportation right now, and I hate to rent a car if I can get that one back right away."

"They'll probably be through with it by Tuesday. You won't be needing it while you're qualifying for your carry permit." He stood to leave.

"I'm having a security system installed early tomorrow morning. Hopefully the job will be complete by the time you arrive. If not, we may have to wait for a little while before we can leave."

"Good. A security system should give us both some peace of mind." He started for the door.

"Wait a minute. I have something else you might find interesting." I handed him the envelope. "I found it shoved under the office door. I'm guessing that it was put there during LL's funeral, when the office was closed."

He read it, put it up to the light, and then reread it. "Not exactly a death threat, but definitely not something to be ignored. I'll have the lab look at it. Maybe they'll find something."

He shrugged on his jacket, tucking the letter into an inside pocket. He bent and picked up the copies of the printouts we had been studying. "You lock the door, and keep the gun and your phone by your bed." He put his hands on my shoulders and looked at me very seriously, raising both eyebrows signifying that he meant it. I nodded. He turned and headed out the door.

His concern seemed genuine and made me feel warm all over.

CHAPTER 15

As I cleaned up the paper towels and pizza crusts, my cell phone rang. "Lexi, this is Hebestreet. Can you come over to take a look at the ceilings in the loft project tonight? I know this is an imposition, but I have a buyer lined up for the building. He's offering a good price. He wants a walk-through in the morning. This would be a real favor for me, but it will benefit the company too, since I can pay what I owe right away if this guy signs the purchase contract." I didn't respond immediately, so he added with a pleading tone, "It would be mutually beneficial for both of us."

"Tonight? You're sure this can't wait?" I looked at my watch. It was a quarter after seven.

"Lexi, if you'll do this for me, I'll promise not to press you for any more contributions for the candidates I'm supporting. If I can sell the lofts right away, I'll be able to make a personal contribution big enough to keep my man happy."

I was too tired to argue. The relief at learning from Luis García that he had never heard of Bud and getting his promise not to coax me for future campaign contributions made his request worth considering. *Let's face it; I've done him an injustice by calling Luis. Glade Schmidt was confusing him with someone else, and tasks like this go with the job.* Bud had certainly never done anything to make me feel threatened.

With a long exhale, I responded, "I don't see how I could get there before eight. Oh, wait. I don't have a car. Let's make it another time—like tomorrow afternoon."

"Lexi, this buyer wants to see it early tomorrow morning. I need to be able to promise him that any little problems can be easily fixed. I'll pick you up. Give me the address. I'll get there by a quarter to eight."

I repeated the address while he wrote it down. "I'll wait for you at the gate, unless it starts to rain. If it starts to rain, we'll have to make it another time. As I mentioned, it's been a long day."

"Thanks, Lexi. I really appreciate this."

I hope so. While I waited, I called Steve's cell phone. It went to record. "Steve, I'm going over to the warehouse project in Tempe as a favor to Hebestreet. He wants me to meet him there. I think you know where it is—just a couple of blocks off University Avenue near ASU. I'll call you when I get home."

I waited until twenty to eight, and then walked down to the gate with my bag and umbrella under my arm. The sky was overcast, and a wind was stirring. I was really, *really* dreading riding with him for fear that he would forget his promise and get on me about the contribution to Blankenship. *I really should not have agreed to this,* I scolded myself.

He pulled up within five minutes in a big black Ford F-450 XLT pickup. It was the kind of vehicle a man would choose if he wanted it to show the world that he was a success. I was glad I was in jeans since I had to climb into the passenger's seat like I was climbing onto a very large boat. At least it was steadier than a boat.

When I settled myself and clicked the seat belt, he said again, "I really appreciate this, Lexi."

"It won't take long, will it? I'm really worn out tonight."

"Just give me a half hour and I'll have you back home by nine."

On the ride downtown, we chatted about the project. If he was still upset with me about my refusal to make that big contribution to his candidate, it wasn't showing. But I was still feeling foolish about my willingness to do this kind of an inspection at night. A morning, any morning, in the daylight would have been much better. I'd been there twice with LL during the renovation and remodeling process and remembered that there were about six parking spots in the front for guests. About a dozen more slots were located around back, but it was in a part of town where street lighting was less than adequate.

When we got there, I noted the stacks of ceiling tiles still wrapped in waterproof plastic and piles of suspension bars and bunches of wires waiting for installation sitting in the parking lot. He had planted some evergreens and even had some ivy plants that had started to climb the bricks of the old building, softening its otherwise harsh lines.

He pulled down the narrow driveway at the side of the building and parked in the rear, where I noted with approval that the rear loading dock had been converted into a covered patio. It wouldn't be used much, but it increased the curb appeal, if a converted warehouse has such a thing. I couldn't help but notice the darkness of the neighborhood. There wasn't a streetlight for more than a block in any direction.

"Are you going to put in some dusk-to-dawn lighting, Bud?" I asked as we approached the back entrance. "This parking lot will be a haven for muggers without it."

He nodded. "It's in the works."

The rear entrance was a heavy set of double doors about ten feet high and eight feet wide, the kind commonly found on warehouses built in the thirties, probably original to the building. Its big hinges permitted each half to swing open easily. Bud pulled the right side open and when we stepped inside, the darkness of the interior hallway was so intense than I could almost feel it in my lungs.

"Hang on while I turn on the lights from the main breaker box." He turned on a flashlight and I stood by the open door while I watched the beam move down the long, dark hallway and disappear down a flight of stairs at the other end. When the units had been sold or leased, it was obvious that the hall lights would need to be kept on twenty-four/seven, so they were probably controlled by a master switch somewhere.

As I stood there, they suddenly came on—four banks of florescent light fixtures that made it as bright as a sunny day at noon. The hall was about twelve feet wide and was carpeted in coarse sisal carpeting in a rust color. From where I stood, I could see four large doors to the units on that floor. Each one slid sideways on rollers, and furnished a large splash of a color reflecting hues from the local desert landscape: taupe, red adobe, warm tan, and sage green. In the four end corners of the hundred and twenty-five–foot long hall were artificial ficus trees in terra-cotta pots. The walls were a light buff above blonde wood-grain Masonite wainscoting. Overall, the decor produced a pleasing effect.

I released the breath I had been holding and stepped inside, allowing the door behind me to close. From the far end of the hallway, I saw Bud's head bob into view as he climbed back to the main floor.

"Now what do you think about what we've done to the place?" It was apparent that he was genuinely pleased.

I responded, "It looks great, ready for any serious buyer."

"It is, almost. Let's go up to the fourth floor where I'll show you my problem with some of the new ceilings. I won't give the go-ahead to do the other floors until you can assure me that my problem can be fixed."

He pointed to a large freight elevator centrally located in the long hallway. When he pushed the button, the exterior doors slid open. They had been finished with the same Masonite veneer as the wainscoting in the hallway. The opening doors exposed the two interior doors, which opened like a wide carnivore's mouth, separating in the middle so the top slid up and bottom slid down. They were made of wooden slats that reminded me of the yellow teeth of a tiger. I followed him inside, and with a light tug on the bottom half of the horizontal door, they closed as if the tiger had us in its mouth. The interior of the elevator was clean and light with a framed inspector's certificate on the wall next to the door. He punched the button for the fourth floor and the elevator began to rise.

As was to be expected, the elevator didn't break any speed records. We stepped off on the fourth floor, which looked identical to the first except for small, multi-paned windows high in the walls at each end of the long hallway. Because it was dark outside, they didn't have any light to let in. That made me even more grateful for the brightness of the florescent ceiling lights.

He waved at me to follow him and we turned to the left, walking about thirty feet down the hall. He put a master key in the lock of the big door that had been painted adobe red. He pushed the door to the right. It opened into a large, finished apartment of more than two thousand square feet. He reached out with his right hand and flipped on the light switches on the front wall.

Space is expensive. Money buys light and high ceilings. The unit had five large multi-paned windows that I could see from where we stood. The ceiling on this floor had been hung about ten feet high, which was about two feet above the upper frame of the windows. The windows had plantation shutters, which could be tipped shut to keep out the sun. The interior walls separating the kitchen from the great room and the bedrooms extended up to a height of eight feet, giving the place a feeling of privacy and openness at the same time.

The original wood floors had been resurfaced. The kitchen had a ceramic tile floor and matching countertops with stainless steel appliances. It was a dream of an apartment, if you wanted space and light on a sunny day, but in the heat of summer, with that suspended ceiling holding the heat down, it would be expensive to air condition.

He led me over to the outside wall where the support rails for the ceiling tiles were attached. He pointed. "See, Lexi, the support rails leave an ugly gap along the wall. What can we do to fix that?"

I squinted and could just make out a gap of about a half-inch to an inch in irregular places where the aging brick of the wall was less than perfectly straight.

"Well, Bud, I think you may be making more of this than is necessary. It takes an eagle eye to see it, but if you want me to, I'll have Bergman get a man good with silicone caulk and have him fill that gap."

"Yeah, that might work, if he's careful not to get the caulk on the brick."

At that point, the lights suddenly went out. With the overcast night sky, there was so little ambient light coming in the windows that for a few seconds I was blind.

Bud muttered, "What the devil? Just wait here and I'll go back down to the mechanical room. Something has thrown the circuit breaker for the entire building." He turned on his flashlight and hurried out of the doorway. I stood still, waiting for my vision to adjust.

Suddenly I heard Bud yell—just an inarticulate "Ahhh!" followed by a heavy thud and a clatter, probably the flashlight falling and hitting the stairs. I hurried out of the doorway, with my hands extended in front of me. When I reached the hallway, I moved toward the stairs with the fingers of my left hand moving along the wall. I could see the stairwell in the indirect light from Bud's flashlight. The beam was bouncing off the wall of the stairwell somewhere below the landing on the descending flight. I rushed down the stairs in the distorted light and saw Bud lying at the bottom of the flight on the floor of the third level.

"Bud! Bud, are you hurt?" I was yelling in alarm.

He was on his side with his knees bent and his right arm splayed out. The flashlight was glowing about four feet from his hand, the glass face cracked. I hurried to him and, kneeling, put my fingers gently against his throat. His pulse was strong and steady.

As I fumbled in my bag for my cell, his flashlight went out. Well, what did I expect when it had been dropped down the stairs? Murphy's Law was in full application this evening: what can go wrong will go wrong. I found the cell and pressed 911 when something hit my shoulder hard from the rear, and my cell flew from my hand. It slid across the rough carpet and hit the wall. A woman's voice answered, "911, what is your emergency?" Her voice was halted as someone terminated the call. Then I heard the cell hit the wall further down the hallway.

In a flash, I realized that this had been a trap. Was Bud in on it or had he mentioned our meeting to someone he shouldn't have?

I threw myself to the left and rolled toward the stairs, expecting another blow to come out of the darkness. My shoulder was throbbing. When I felt the first stair tread, I held my purse against my chest, swung my feet around in front of me, and slid on my backside like a little kid on an uneven, snowy hill, bumping down the stairs, accepting potential new bruises on top of old ones as an easy alternative to whatever my attacker had in mind.

I felt the vibration of heavy feet on the stairs behind me so I stood and took a flying leap in the dark toward the landing below. When my feet hit the floor, my momentum carried me into the wall. I dropped onto my hands and knees and scrabbled like a crab across the landing toward the descending half of the stairs, feeling in front of me for that first step. My purse was dragging on the floor. I started down that flight on my backside as fast as I could.

When I had reached what I hoped was the midpoint of that flight, I stood, and took another flying leap into the darkness. When my feet hit the hall floor, I bent my knees and rolled. Standing unsteadily, I noted that I could see some differentiation between the black of the stairs behind me and the lighter walls of the hallway. I noted a darker square where the door of the first apartment unit was slightly recessed into the wall. I rushed to it and flattened my body against it just inside the doorframe. I tried to will my heart to slow down. Above its pounding, I could hear someone breathing. I realized it was me. I tried to hold my breath and stifle the urge to inhale but was unsuccessful. The blood surging through my veins was draining the oxygen from my lungs so fast that I had to inhale again. I tried to do it slowly and quietly.

Above my noisy heartbeat, I could just barely make out the sound of a shoe against the carpeting. It was nearly inaudible, made by the slight friction of the two surfaces touching. Then it stopped. Whoever it was had paused to reconnoiter. This time I managed to hold my breath. I heard him take another step. He was just the faintest figure of dark gray against the slightly lighter gray of the walls.

Think, Lexi, think! Anxiety made my thoughts as sluggish as industrial sludge. After two slow, deliberate breaths, my thinking began to clear. I'd left my umbrella in the truck. It might have been useful. I remembered the revolver and I wished fervently I had put it in my purse before I left home. But my attacker didn't need to know it was home next to my bed.

I said with as much firmness as I could muster, "I have a gun and I'll shoot."

I heard a sharp intake of breath, and then I could hear some kind of a racket on the floor above. It sounded like Bud was shaking the flashlight. I yelled, "Bud, there's someone here who wants to hurt us. Call 911 or I'll have to shoot him."

His voice came down to me. "I'm calling right now. For crying out loud, Lexi, don't shoot anyone or anything."

The faint figure began to move toward the stairs that descended to the entrance doors. He was sufficiently familiar with the building that the dark didn't seem to present a problem.

"Bud, are you making the call?" I called nervously.

"Yes, yes, police are on the way. Are you okay?"

"Yes, I'm fine," *except for a real case of nerves and some new bruises.*

In the darkness, I recognized the sound of the big door at the rear of the building as it opened and closed, and then I heard what sounded like a lightweight motorcycle, probably a road bike, as its ignition caught and then the sound steadily diminished as it was ridden away.

It took the first patrol car almost ten minutes to arrive. By that time Bud had made his way down the stairs to the mechanical room and managed to get the lights on. I had climbed back up the stairs and located my cell phone where it had been tossed in the darkness by my attacker. It was still working so I called Steve.

He yelled into the phone, "You didn't give me an address when you left your message so I couldn't find the warehouse!"

He arrived at the same time as the uniformed officers. He rushed in and grabbed me by both arms. "I didn't have an address until Hebestreet called 911. What are you doing here at night?"

I explained in as much detail as I could and ended by stating, "I think whoever it was wanted to kill me, Steve, and maybe Bud too.

If I hadn't told him I had the gun and that I would shoot, I think he would've tried." I laughed nervously. "Bud begged me not to shoot anyone."

Bud looked defensive. He was holding a folded handkerchief against a cut above his right eye. "Lexi, I think it was just someone trespassing. He didn't mean to hurt us. I should've locked the big door behind us when we came in. Look, I'm glad you weren't hurt, but you got to know how much damage a bunch of bullets would do to the walls and ceiling."

Steve looked hard at Bud and asked gruffly, "Are you all right?" Bud nodded and looked at the blood on the handkerchief before pressing it back to his forehead. Steve looked back at me. "How did you get here?"

"Bud gave me a ride."

"Come with me. I'll give you a lift home." He took me by the arm and guided me firmly to his car. After we got in, he shook his head as he turned the key in the ignition, "I can't leave you alone, even for a minute." He sounded like a frustrated parent.

As we drove, he asked, "Hebestreet said that he had a buyer for the warehouse project?"

"Yes, he said if I could promise to satisfactorily fix the problem with the gaps where the support braces for the suspended ceilings meet the brick outer walls, then he had a deal in the works. Do you doubt his credibility?"

"Maybe. I'm going to have a talk with him and get the name of that potential buyer."

When we arrived at the condo, Tommy was on duty. His big frame appeared out of the darkness and he insisted on seeing Steve's badge and ID before he would open the gate.

"Tommy, he's with me and he's a policeman."

"I'm supposed to check everyone who comes through the gate after dark."

"I appreciate Mrs. Bolton's concern. Thank her for me."

Steve parked his car and walked me to my door. There, he insisted on checking the place before he would leave. It took all of three minutes. Before he left, he said, "I'm glad to see a night watchman on site, but keep the door locked and the gun and your cell within reach."

As I closed the door and put on the chain, my phone rang. "Lexi, who's that man that just left your unit?" It was Mrs. Bolton.

"That's the policeman I told you about, Detective Sutherland."

"Is everything all right?"

Much as she would have liked being told every detail of my latest adventure, I simply responded, "Yes, he just gave me a lift home."

"Well, don't hesitate to call on me anytime. You know I'm always here."

Though I went to bed, I didn't get much sleep. I spent most of the night mentally examining scenarios to explain the events that were making me feel threatened at every turn. In the morning I felt like I was ready for a very long vacation.

• • •

I forgot about the guys who were going to install the security system until they rang my bell at six a.m. I jumped out of bed and threw on my fuzzy robe. While I dressed in the bathroom, they worked. By seven fifteen, they were prepared to show me how to put a combination into the keypad that had been installed near the front door.

Ralph had me step outside, and after he closed the door, he told me to open it with my key. When I got inside, I punched the combination into the keypad and it was automatically reset. When I opened the back door, Ralph put out his arm and blocked me from entering.

"What are you doing?" I asked.

"I just want you to know what to expect if you forget to punch the code into the keypad."

It took about 30 more seconds before the high-pitched alarm almost split my eardrums.

"Now punch in the combination or you'll have the cops here in a few minutes. You've only got 15 seconds from the time the alarm goes off." I did.

Steve arrived as they were leaving. The sky was filled with scudding clouds left over from the recent rains and the wind penetrated my jacket. I hurried out to the car.

"The course begins at eight thirty and I've called and had a place reserved for you."

"Thanks."

I figured we had at least forty-five minutes of conversation time. I was looking forward to having some time to talk with him socially. What I knew of him I liked, but I really didn't know much about him.

I primed him with questions and he admitted that other than work, he had two long-standing interests: handball for exercise and playing the piano for relaxation. Talking about himself clearly made him a little self-conscious but he admitted with an engaging grin, "Yeah, I play for church meetings. When I'm on duty through the weekend, I've got a good assistant who covers for me."

I was startled. "You go to church? In your job, I find that surprising."

"Whenever the job doesn't prevent it." He continued a bit sheepishly. "I also love a good symphony or a piano concert."

It occurred to me that there would be several in the upcoming Christmas season. I would love to attend a few with him, but of course, I wasn't about to say anything. How obvious would that be? I had no way of knowing how much—or even if—he really liked me. I really wanted to ask what denomination he attended but felt that that might be a bit pushy.

He seemed to be finding it easier to talk about himself. "In high school I wanted to become a concert pianist, but my height got me a college basketball scholarship. I lost it when I accepted a call to serve a mission for my church."

I found it impressive that he had been willing to forfeit his scholarship for service to others. In my experience, many young men at that age seemed to be self-absorbed. I found my approval of him steadily increasing.

"When I finished my mission in Taiwan, I signed up with the

148

Army to obtain G.I. Bill benefits so I could finish my college degree. While I was in the army, I was trained as an M.P. and that led me into police work when I had finished my college days."

I kept prodding. "Do you like police work? Is it a good fit, or did you just fall into it because of your military experience?"

"In the beginning, after I got over the nervousness of being a rookie, I really ate up the idea of being a white knight riding to the rescue of innocent people and catching the bad guys. For about four years, I was an adrenaline junkie. A racing heart made me happy. It told me I was alive. But after more than a hundred arrests and the twenty-fifth body, I began to wonder if there wasn't a better way to see life. It can pull you down, if you don't have some kind of balance. That's where my faith, handball, and music come in."

I took a deep breath. "I know what you mean. I'm glad your faith is important to you. Mine is a very important part of my life too. Maybe that's why I feel that God will see me through this situation. I keep remembering that scripture that says 'All these things shall give thee experience and be for thy good.'"

"But don't let that feeling make you careless. If it makes you overconfident . . ." He let the sentence dangle and I knew he was referring to last night.

If he was waiting for a response to his warning, he wasn't going to get one. I changed the subject. "Are you married? Or am I out of line in asking? Maybe you are, and it's none of my business."

He was quiet for a few seconds before he said, "I got a 'Dear John' letter on my mission. She's married now with three kids, and I've just never had the time to get serious about looking for someone else. I've dated a couple of nice women, but they were turned off by the demands of my job."

His answer made me smile with satisfaction. *He was available!* Then I scolded myself. *Good grief, Lexi, you hardly know the man. Don't start planning a future with him.*

About twenty minutes into the ride, he ended the discussion of his personal life to return to the progress of the investigation. "I got a call from the warden at the state pen this morning as I was leaving my place to pick you up." That got my full attention. "It seems that our friend Chet Huddleston may potentially be coming into some money. His ex-wife died in a car crash three weeks ago. She was T-boned at an intersection by a hit-and-run up in Prescott, where she had moved after the divorce. The warden found out that a few days after her death, Chet received a visit from an attorney—the same one that handled the divorce for his wife—telling him that she had come into some money on the death of her mother a few months earlier. Being a woman in her forties, it wasn't a surprise that she died without a will. Since she and Chet had no children and her brothers were both dead, she had no heirs. This attorney—a guy by the name of Foxworthy—was offering his services to Chet and encouraging him to make legal application to the probate court as the nearest thing to a relative she had and that way, he could claim the estate."

"That seems crass. Why would an attorney do something like that?"

"My guess is that he would ask for a substantial fee for his legal services if Chet's claim were successful. He might even insist on splitting the estate fifty-fifty."

"Aren't attorney-client conversations privileged at the prison? How did the warden find out all this?"

Steve was suddenly very serious. "I don't mean to scare you but it seems that Chet told his cellmate about the possible windfall and tried to hire him to take out a contract when he was released. The contract . . . ," he paused, "was on you, Lexi, since LL is already dead. We know about this because his cellmate was caught with some contraband a few days ago and was facing the revocation of his parole, so he traded the information to the warden so he could keep his release date."

I felt as if my heart had dropped a couple of inches in my chest. "So our presumption that Chet wasn't in a position to be a threat might be all wrong. But if he didn't kill LL, why the sudden interest in me? My testimony at his trial was of secondary importance. There were more than a dozen other prosecution witnesses."

"He may have a list of people he wants to pay back, and you're near the top."

When we arrived at the gun range, he stopped in front of the office. "I don't think you'll be in any danger here since no one knows where you are." He pointed to the office. "Check in with the guy in there. He'll want to see your weapon. You remembered your ammunition?" I nodded and patted my purse. "You'll sit through about three hours of classes and spend about an hour on the range using your weapon. I'll pick you up at one." I slid out and with a wave, he drove off.

This new information made me feel that there were increasing reasons to keep the gun with me.

CHAPTER 16

The man behind the check-in counter wore jeans and a western cut shirt with cowboy boots. It was the look on his face when he stepped up to take my credit card for the $89 fee that made me remember that I hadn't made any effort to hide the bruises on my face that morning. The guy probably thought I was getting a carry permit to keep an abusive boyfriend or husband in line.

After I paid my fee, I was pointed to the large classroom where the others present appeared to include a few guys who would be great cast members of the TV show *Duck Dynasty*. Those beards were really something. There were two women who looked like they wouldn't need a gun to handle a mugger. There was a kid who looked twenty-one plus a day. Three of the others looked like bank employees and each appeared a little ill at ease, about like I felt.

I made it through the gun safety classes and the demonstration of the proper handling, storage, and cleaning of weapons of all sizes, including shotguns, rifles, and handguns. We were also taught the provisions of the state gun laws during which I did plenty of fidgeting in the seat due to the bruises gained the previous evening. I had to concentrate to keep my mind from wandering back to Chet Huddleston and his potential windfall.

As a group, we were walked to the range single file where we women were offered a small locker for our purses. We were each handed protection goggles and ear protectors. By the time I had used about $100 worth of ammunition, I felt that I was getting the hang of it.

The instructor repeated his mantra: squeeze, don't pull the trigger, aim for the biggest part of the body, don't try to wound, because your attacker might get up and kill you—that kind of stuff. By the end of the hands-on training, we were told to return to the classroom where every member of the group was handed several forms in which each one of us stated under penalty of law that we were at least twenty-one years of age, had never been found guilty of a felony, nor were we in the country illegally, and that we had never been found mentally ill. I signed on the bottom line, which gave the State of Arizona permission to run a check of any criminal record I might have.

When each person finished with the forms, he or she was pointed toward the table at the rear of the room, where we were each fingerprinted. We were then handed a Certificate of Completion that qualified us to receive the Arizona Concealed Weapons Permit, which would be forthcoming once the State had run a background check on each applicant. I was as proud as if I had won the Miss America beauty pageant.

Those who wanted to could return to the range and take a few more practice shots, which I did. As I was "squeezing" off some last shots at the silhouette on the paper target, I felt two long arms wrap around me. Startled, I turned to see Steve.

He pulled off my earphones and laughed. "I'm sorry if I startled you, but if you hold the gun with both hands like this, it will be steadier." He demonstrated before he dropped his arms. I fleetingly wished he hadn't.

I did as he had shown me; putting my left palm under the grip as he suggested. My final score was the best of the day. As we walked to his car, I was grinning as if I had received a trophy for winning a marathon. I was not encumbered with even a little bit of humility. I was as good as Annie Oakley—at least in my own mind.

The ride back was as comfortable for me as it would have been with a longtime friend. I wondered if he enjoyed my company half as much as I was enjoying his.

After a few minutes, he asked, "Now that you'll soon have a license to carry a gun, do you think you could use it?" When I didn't answer immediately, he added, "It looks easy on TV and in the movies, and life looks cheap, especially the bad guys, but in real life, there are ramifications that need to be thought through before you ever use a weapon. You've got to have your mental attitude set. Don't wait until you need to use a gun to start to evaluate the situation."

"What do you mean?"

"There are moral implications involved in using a weapon. You need to determine under what circumstances you would use it and then hold to your pre-established rules. Then, when push comes to shove, don't second guess yourself."

"For example?"

"Ask yourself what you would be willing to do if a burglar entered your house while you were home. Would you be willing to shoot him even if he were unarmed? Or would you need to wait until he threatened your life with a weapon? Do you see what I mean? There are different conditions to consider." He paused while I thought about what he was saying. "No matter what the circumstances, there is an emotional toll on anyone that takes the life of another person, no matter how urgent the situation . . . and if there is a question about your judgment—that maybe you shouldn't have fired—there can be legal ramifications."

"I see what you're saying. I need to think it through, so if the crisis arises, I'll know what I'm willing to do—and then I'll pray fervently that I never find myself in a situation where I need to do it."

"You're getting the idea."

I was quiet for several minutes while I thought about what he had said. He broke into my thoughts. "Tell me about your family. You've never mentioned your parents. Was that who you were sitting with at the memorial service for LL?"

I remained silent so long that he said apologetically, "I'm sorry if I'm asking questions that are too personal."

"No, no your questions aren't too personal. My parents are both dead. I was sitting with my Uncle Bob and Aunt Betty."

I found myself telling him about Percy and our unusually close relationship. He was so easy to talk to that I even found myself telling him about the night my parents died. I hadn't spoken of that night to anyone, not even Percy, since it had happened.

"I got the call from the hospital at about four a.m. telling me that there had been a car crash and it fell to me to call Percy and Aunt Betty, Mom's sister. I rushed to the hospital where it was confirmed that my dad had been killed on impact. My mother was semi-conscious in the ICU. They let me sit with her. I had called Percy before I left for the hospital, and since it was the middle of the night and Richard was out of town, she had some difficulty finding a babysitter.

"Even though she was doped up on morphine, Mom knew I was there. I held her hand and watched the sky lighten in the east. By the time the sun was up, I was emotionally exhausted, so I laid my head down on the bed that was raised as high as it would go. She lifted her hand and laid it on my hair. She whispered, 'Alexis Aurelia, my joy. Thank you for being here.'"

My voice caught. I swallowed to get control of it again. "Then she was gone. I didn't move, hoping that the heart monitor would begin beeping again to tell me that she wasn't really gone, but the nurse came into the room and one of the staff doctors followed her. They disconnected the monitors and the doctor expressed his sympathy and explained that while Mom had been conscious in the emergency room, she insisted that she wasn't to be resuscitated if her heart stopped. She told the doctor there that she would rather go with my father. They let me sit with her for a while longer. I was twenty-two and an orphan. I felt as lost as if I were six."

Steve was quiet while I got a tissue from my bag. When I fully regained my composure, he asked quietly, "When did your sister or your aunt get there?"

"Percy got there about twenty minutes after Mom died and Aunt Betty and Uncle Bob arrived about five minutes after her. Since that time, my aunt and uncle have played a large part in my life—and in Percy's—as kind of surrogate parents. They had no children of their own so we became their family. Percy had married two years after high school graduation, so she had Richard, and they had a new baby. That helped her fill the emptiness in her life."

"What about you? What did you do to fill the void?"

"I landed a job at a bank a week after the double funeral and I tried to make that work. But a job can't really take the place of people. Maybe that's why LL's death hit me so hard."

He finally asked the question I think he had been leading up to. "Who do you think is behind the attempts on your life? Do you think it's the same person who killed LL?"

"As far as the death of LL is concerned, I can see a motive for just about anybody on the radar. I'm trying not to jump to conclusions because it would be so easy to focus all my suspicion on the person I dislike the most. Right now that's a toss-up between Stan Bergman and Ed Gomes. I'm so ticked off at Ed. He's disappeared and I can only guess that he's trying to hold off making the payments he owes."

I cleared my throat and asked the questions that had been nibbling at the back of my mind for several days. "Steve, I don't know how to say this but . . . but it seems to me that you've made a major effort to cultivate my friendship. You didn't need to drive me out to the weapons course. You could've just told me that I needed to take it. I could have gotten myself out there." I plunged ahead. "Am I a suspect in LL's death? Is that why you have been so . . . so ever present?"

I glanced at him from the corner of my eye and noted that he was grinning a bit guiltily. "Maybe the thought crossed my mind in the beginning, but when I saw how green you got at the M.E.'s office, I doubted it, and after someone tried to bury you with a bulldozer, I gave up that idea completely. If I seem to have intruded into your life, it's because you seem to be central to this investigation. You know every one of the suspects and can give me insights that I can't get from anyone else." He cleared his throat. "And to be honest, I like your company. You've got a good mind, and since I don't have a partner right now, you seem to fit the bill to some degree."

"Oh, is that it?" I felt relieved, but also a teensy bit disappointed. *But what did I expect him to say? "I'm crazy about you"? Get your head on straight, Lexi.*

He took a deep breath. "There's more to it than that. It's unprofessional of me to admit it, but I enjoy your company more than I've enjoyed anyone else's for . . . for a long time."

I was suddenly so thoroughly pleased that I probably glowed. I looked up at him. "I'm really glad to know that. I'm really flattered— and frankly, even if there wasn't someone trying to kill me, I'd be glad to have you around." At that, I leaned back and closed my eyes. I'm sure I was smiling.

I'm still young enough that I don't usually pay much attention to the passing of time, but while we rode quietly, for some reason I couldn't explain, I began to take a good, hard look at my life. I was basically alone, my twenty-ninth birthday was fast approaching, and it suddenly wasn't enough to have a good job and some pleasant, useful hobbies. Since the death of LL, I felt that dark forces were gaining ground in my world.

I realized that I was tired of living alone. I felt a yearning for continuing contact, for friendship and shared laughter. As we rode in comfortable silence, I reminded myself that most people have hotly held opinions, habits, and mannerisms that can irritate. They have views on art, music, not to mention food likes and dislikes, moods, messy hobbies, allergies, emotional fixations, and attitudes that in no way parallel my own. But despite all these known facts, I wanted someone to share a batch of chocolate chip cookies with me, to laugh with me at a TV show, to hold hands on a walk. I wanted the simple comfort of companionship, someone to discuss my day with, and someone who'd commiserate with me if I caught a cold or who'd celebrate a raise with me. I wanted someone to reach out to touch in the night, and know that I was as important to him as he was to me. I wanted to be in love.

I wondered if Steve had ever felt that way—but I decided that I sure wasn't going to ask him. There was no way I'd ask him that. At least, not yet.

Hoping that I wasn't attempting to move this budding relationship along too fast, I decided there was something I could ask him. "Steve, next week is Thanksgiving. Do you have any plans?"

It took him a fraction of a second to respond. "Well . . . I was planning on volunteering to work so someone with a family wouldn't have to. I usually do that every year."

"You don't have family close?"

"My oldest brother lives with his family in Tampa. He's a good deal older than I am, and his kids live close by, so holidays are a big deal to them. My next oldest brother is in Lancaster, Pennsylvania, where he's a dairy farmer. His oldest sons help him run the place and he seldom gets away from it. My other brother is in Tacoma, Washington, and he has four teenagers. That leaves me pretty much alone with time on my hands during the holidays."

"So you're the baby of the family."

"I am now. My younger brother Chad was a member of the US Olympic Track and Field Team for the Beijing Olympics, but last year while he was out running with a couple of friends to prepare for a local marathon, the three of them were hit by a driver who was later arrested on a DUI. Chad was killed, his buddy died a few days later, and the third man is still in a wheelchair." I could hear his voice tighten as he talked.

"The driver was drunk?"

"It was seven o'clock in the morning, but the driver had been smoking pot for most of the night. He was driving home when he hit Chad and his friends." His voice was full of bitterness.

"I'm so sorry. What a terrible waste of innocent life." After a couple of minutes, I tried to brighten my voice to change the direction of his thoughts. "Look, I don't want to coerce you into this, but if you'll say yes, you're invited to join my family for Thanksgiving in my Aunt Betty's big family room. Of course, Percy and Richard will be there with their brood. Can you handle four little girls for a few hours?"

"I can not only handle them, I can enjoy them at the same time. I really like kids."

My heart jumped. *Oh, that is good news.*

When Steve dropped me off at my apartment, he grinned. "Congratulations on qualifying for a concealed weapons carry permit." He didn't say it but his manner suggested that he was proud of me.

"Thanks for arranging it for me—and for the ride. You didn't have to do that. It must have taken a big part of your day."

"That's okay. I was glad to do it." We shook hands before I got out of the car, but I noticed that it turned into more of a hand holding than a hand shaking.

• • •

I planned on retiring early that evening, but Mother Nature had other things in store for me—and for Percy. At nine p.m. my cell phone rang. "Lexi, my water broke. We need you here at the house to watch the girls."

"I'm on my way."

I was out of the door before I remembered that I didn't have a car. It took me about two seconds to decide to ask Mrs. Bolton to lend me hers. I climbed the stairs and knocked hard on her door.

"Lexi, what's the matter? Do I need to call Tommy?"

"No, Mrs. Bolton. My sister's baby is coming and she needs me to take care of her kids while her husband takes her to the hospital, but I don't have a car right now. Can I borrow yours?"

"Of course, of course, my dear. Just let me get my car keys." She moved across the room and rooted around in her purse for a minute before she came up with them. "Here you go. I don't know how much gas it has in it. I haven't driven it in nearly a week."

I grabbed the keys. "That's okay. I'll put some gas in it if I need to. Thanks."

I dashed out to the parking lot and opened her 1996 Olds Cutlass and slid in behind the wheel. It started up right away and I hurried out to the highway, before I even thought about the likelihood of someone following me. That sent a sudden chill up my spine, and I

159

watched behind me in the rearview mirror. No one seemed to have an interest in me, but then I was driving a different car.

I drove much too fast to get to Percy's home. Before I was out of my car, she and Richard were into theirs and on their way to the hospital.

The night hours were quiet while the girls were sleeping, but the next day dragged on, with me feeding four little girls' appetites for food, fun, and games. I had finally put them to bed that evening at eight thirty and was lying on the couch half asleep when I received the phone call that the girls now had a baby brother, not the baby sister they had expected. I laughed out loud. *Oh, that poor kid. Four older sisters? The two oldest girls will have to be married before he ever gets the chance to use the bathroom.*

Richard arrived home at eleven and released me from duty.

"This delivery should have been a cinch, but I guess boys require more labor that girls—at least in this case. Can you imagine 24 hours of labor?" Richard looked exhausted. I could only guess how tired my sister was.

"Is Percy okay?"

"Yes, she's fine, just really tired."

"Do you need me tomorrow? Who will stay with the girls when you go to visit Percy?"

"My mother will be here in the morning. She's a good grandma."

As I picked up my purse, I asked, "What are you going to name him?"

"What else? Richard—after me."

I left feeling greatly relieved and made my way home at a much slower pace. When I reached the front gate, it was standing open. That was worrisome, and as I drove through it, I quickly caught the reflection of red and blue lights as I neared the parking lot. There were two black and whites with lights ablaze parked there and I could hear the alarm in my condo trying to wake the dead.

I ran toward my unit where I could see a crowd of my neighbors standing around, many in bathrobes and slippers. As I paused to look around to see the cause of the fuss, Mrs. Bolton grabbed my arm.

"Lexi, we had a prowler less than an hour ago. I think he was scared away when your alarm went off. I called 911 before I rushed out with a flashlight to see what was going on. I saw someone in black running toward the fence where he nearly made it over with one bound. The police got here in about four minutes."

"Did he get inside? Did he take anything? Where was Tommy?"

She suddenly looked extremely contrite. "Tommy came up to my place to use the bathroom and I insisted that he stay long enough to have a sandwich. He was just finishing when we heard the burglar alarm at your place."

At this point, a uniformed officer came around the end of the building. Mrs. Bolton waved him over. "Officer Martinez, this is my neighbor, Lexi Benson. She owns this condo."

"Miss Benson, can you get the alarm turned off?"

"Sure." I pulled my keys from my purse and opened the front door. I punched the combination into the keypad and the noise stopped.

Martinez followed me inside. "Neither my partner nor I could see any damage other than some splintered wood on the rear door and doorjamb. I don't think he got inside, but if you'd like us to, we'll check it out before we leave."

"Thanks, I'd appreciate that very much."

Martinez and his partner checked every room, even the closets to make sure no one was in there.

"The door is okay. It's a solid core door and the lock doesn't seem to have been damaged." He gave me his card. "Your alarm scared him away, but if you're feeling nervous, you might want to stay with someone tonight."

"Thanks, I may do that."

Mrs. Bolton had stepped inside my front doorway and looked at me like a concerned grandmother. "I think you'd better come up to my place tonight and use my spare bedroom. You won't sleep a wink if you stay here."

I didn't argue. I grabbed my pajamas, toothbrush, and a comb and dutifully followed her up the outside stairs to her unit. She insisted on showing me the binoculars she had sitting by her bed. "I don't sleep well anymore so I spend a lot of time just watching the other units and the part of the sidewalk and street that I can see through the trees to the south. I was watching a bunch of kids out on the sidewalk who were out much too late, when Tommy knocked and asked to come in and use the bathroom. I wonder if it was one of those kids that tried to break in to your place."

"We may never know, but at least now I know that my security system works."

"And so does everyone else for a block in every direction."

We both laughed. "Thank you, Mrs. Bolton. You're as good as any night watchman."

"Well, I wasn't tonight. I told Tommy that he'll have to bring his own lunch from now on."

After I had bid her goodnight, brushed my teeth, and put on my pajamas, I climbed into the bed in her spare room. It was covered with a hand-pieced quilt that brought back memories of my own grandmother. I lay and wondered who was behind the attempted burglary. *Should I call Steve? He can't do anything. I'll tell him in the morning.*

I turned over, but my thoughts wouldn't be quiet. *There are plenty of suspects, and of course, it might have just been some petty thief. Whoever it was, I doubt he'll attempt it a second time.* I finally drifted off to sleep about two o'clock.

CHAPTER 17

Since I had no car on Monday morning, I called the office and left a message for Roger that I wouldn't be in until Tuesday. I added that I wanted him to call me if anything important came up, especially if he heard from Ed Gomes.

To increase my sense of safety, I jammed a straight-backed chair under the doorknobs of both the front and back doors and hooked the chain on the door, in addition to the security system. It was only symbolic but somehow made me feel a little safer. I spent several hours working on the quilt for Percy's new baby.

I finished about the time Mrs. Bolton called. "At the next meeting of the condo owners, I'm gonna push for a real night watchman. Tommy feels real bad about last night."

"Tell him not to. He tried to catch that burglar and I'm sure that man won't come back now that he knows Tommy's here and that I have the world's loudest alarm."

The next morning, while I waited for Steve to bring Uncle Bob's Pontiac from the police garage, I stood in my living room and watched the rain through the louvered interior shutters on the front window. After only a couple of weeks, the novelty of the unseasonable rain was wearing thin. The ground was saturated and the creeks and arroyos were running high, each a churning rush of water, dragging

163

debris with it in its hurry to spread out across the desert. Many roads were running like shallow creeks, awash in places with gravel and stones large enough to damage the underside of a car. Most folks, myself included, were tired of wet shoes, wet coats, wet umbrellas. Who says that deserts are always dry?

I had mixed feelings as I put Uncle Bob's gun in my purse before I left home. *Surely now I can take care of myself,* I thought, but then I remembered the moral implications Steve had urged me to think about. *Could I actually shoot someone if they threatened me?* I firmly hoped I would never need to find out.

It was nearly nine o'clock before he parked by the sidewalk that led to my front door. I hurried out and climbed into the passenger side of the big car. While he drove back to police headquarters so he could get his departmental vehicle, I used most of a box of tissues to wipe the fingerprint dust off everything he had missed.

"The CSI techs didn't find anything. We shouldn't be surprised. Anything new you need to bring me up to date on?"

As I was wiping a few last spots of dust, I responded, "I spent Saturday night and Sunday at my sister's, tending her four little girls so her husband could rush her to the hospital to have her baby. After I got home about midnight, I discovered that someone had tried to break into my condo. In addition to the report from the alarm company, Mrs. Bolton called the police."

"Why didn't you call me?" His voice was sharp.

"Steve, it was midnight and my life wasn't threatened. All the officer could do was check out my condo and take a report. What good would it have done to get you out of bed?"

"If anything like that happens again, don't hesitate to call me. I don't care if you don't think it's serious. It might have been."

"Okay, if you want me to." I was learning that when he was worried or upset, his voice took on an edge.

"Did you spend the rest of the night in your place?"

"No, I slept in Mrs. Bolton's spare bedroom."

"Good." He seemed to be relaxing a bit and his voice became apologetic. "Lexi, I wish I could offer you special around-the-clock protection, but the department doesn't have enough personnel to use like that. The police are really good at solving crime, but not very good at preventing it. I guess your common sense and me are all you've got."

"And that should be sufficient. Since the security system has been tested, I'll sleep better at night—and it'll take a few nights to get caught up on my rest after taking care of my nieces."

He laughed, sounding more like his usual self. "If the day comes when you have a family of your own, how are you going to handle several little ones—or do you plan on having a family?"

"I'll start one at a time, and work up to four or five gradually."

"So you plan on a big family?"

"Someday, but first I'll have to find the right husband."

He didn't say anything for a minute, but he grinned broadly. He had nice teeth. I liked that.

He changed the subject. "I have some new info of interest regarding Tiffany and Corstelli. Corstelli's law license was suspended several years ago for unethical behavior. Apparently, he had some really skuzzy clients and a few of them did time for drugs. Several disappeared after becoming key witnesses for the government. I can't figure out why LL would use an attorney like him."

"Maybe Tiffany chose him. I think he drew up their prenuptial agreement. LL had access to our corporate attorney, who could have referred him to someone more reputable—but frankly, I'm just speculating. Have you learned anything about Tiffany?"

"That's another matter. She showed up in state DMV records seven years ago and her social security number is of recent numeric vintage. No other records such as birth records have turned up in the Department of Vital Statistics under her maiden name or her professed birth date here in Arizona."

"Hmm. Maybe Tiffany's not her real name," I responded. There had always been something almost artificial about Tiffany in my mind.

"Possibly."

A nebulous idea tapped me on a mental shoulder. Then the

possibility of an explanation apparently hit us at the same time. He turned and looked at me as we spoke the same thought: "Maybe she's in the witness protection program."

He turned back to watch the road and rubbed his chin thoughtfully. "If we're right, that will be a brick wall. We'll get no help from the feds."

"But someone in the witness protection program wouldn't have a relative in it too like she does, would they? What about her sister?"

"Something like that could be arranged."

When he reached headquarters, he asked, "Can you get your contact at the senator's office to go back to the Pentagon for a copy of Bergman's fingerprints? I can go through regular channels, but it could take a couple of months—or more—to get anything from the military."

"I'll try."

He started to get out but paused as if another thought had occurred to him. "Can you get me a set of Roger's fingerprints?"

"He has at least one soda every day. The trash basket by his desk usually has a few cans in it."

"Good. Call me when you have one so I can run his prints."

"You suspect he may have a criminal record?" I was surprised at the thought but could understand Steve's need to be thorough.

"I'm just trying to cover all the bases." I nodded as he slid out of the car and, with a quick wave, disappeared into the building. I slid into the driver's seat and made my way through morning traffic to the office.

• • •

That afternoon, when Roger left the office a few minutes early, I put in a call to Ted Jorgenson in the other office. "Ted, do you have that audit I asked for done yet?"

"No, not yet, Lexi. I've had a couple of really sick kids at home and my wife is pregnant again, and her morning sickness is so bad that I don't dare leave her alone with the sick kids. I promise I'll get it done as soon as I can, but right now I'm headed out of the office with an armload of stuff to do at home. I hope that's okay with you."

"Sure, Ted. I hope your kids get feeling better—and your wife too. Take tomorrow off too since Thursday is Thanksgiving. There's no reason for you to come in before next Monday—and even then, only come in if everyone at your house is feeling better."

I got up from my desk and took two of the soda cans from Roger's trash basket, carefully holding them by the edges of the top and bottom. I called Steve and told him that I had the cans and that Roger was gone.

"How long will you be at the office?" he asked.

"I can stay as long as you need me to."

"Okay. I'll come out and pick up the cans ASAP. I can have the prints run by tomorrow morning."

When he got there, he carefully put the two cans into a large plastic evidence bag. "I'll let you know if his prints turn up in AFIS. When should I pick you up Thursday morning?"

"About ten would be great."

•   •   •

The next morning I called Steve from the office. "Did you check the fingerprints from the soda cans?"

"Nothing showed up in AFIS."

"I'm relieved—and glad to hear that. I like Roger. He just seems a bit immature at times—but like him or not," I sighed, "if he's made a hash of the records of Sunnyville Estates or any of the other accounts, we're going to have a very long talk."

"How's your working relationship with him going right now?"

"Everything's okay there. He's so focused on cultivating a friendship with Tiffany that he hardly pays any attention to me. He's called her from the office a couple of times since the funeral. He hasn't been able to get any information from Ed Gomes's secretary, so I gave her a call. She told me that Ed had called her a little over a week ago and said he had a "family emergency" and that we'd be hearing from him as soon as he was back in town."

"She didn't say what kind of family emergency?"

"No, and she wouldn't speculate."

"Well, good to talk to you, but we've both got work to do."

He was right, but I sure hated ending our conversation.

•   •   •

Thanksgiving morning, when I climbed into Steve's car, it felt natural to ride and chat with him. I brought the quilt for the new baby that was finally finished. I was so glad to have chosen yellow and green for the colors. No problems with gender that way.

As we reached the front door, Aunt Betty opened it and with a pleased smile, ushered us in where we faced Percy's two oldest girls who were standing in the foyer. They had obviously been waiting for our arrival so they could begin their interrogation.

"Are you Lexi's boyfriend?" Pamela made it clear that she was not going to be put off. "Well, are you?"

Her directness caught Steve off guard, and he burst out laughing. "I guess you'll need to ask Lexi that question."

I responded in self-defense, "She asked you, Steve."

He shrugged and grinned. "I think I'd like to be. Is that okay with you?" he asked Pamela.

"Yes, that's okay. I think you're handsome and," she paused mischievously, "Lexi needs a boyfriend." She giggled behind her hand and ran into the living room.

She hurried to her mother and said loud enough for everyone present and maybe even the neighbors in the houses on either side to hear. "See, I told you that he wouldn't come to Thanksgiving if he wasn't her boyfriend."

We made our way past McKenzie, who had stood unmoving during her sister's questions. She caught up with us and now seemed to think it was her turn to interrogate him. "Are you going to marry Lexi?"

There was apparently no end to his good nature. "Well, I don't know. She hasn't even kissed me yet. She might not want to marry me."

McKenzie's eyes turned their full power on me. Her little eyebrows were drawn together with seriousness. "Are you going to marry him, Lexi? You know, you should get married pretty soon. You're getting kind of old."

168

Before I could answer, Percy handed the baby to Richard and rose from the couch. She had flushed a bright pink. She hurried to Pamela and McKenzie and took their hands. As she led them to the couch and pointed for them to sit by their daddy, she admonished firmly, "Girls, we don't ask grownups questions like that. That's their business. They'll tell us what they want us to know." McKenzie pouted and Pamela grinned mischievously.

After getting over the first major hurdles of questions from my two oldest nieces, the day went well. Steve and Richard had an animated discussion of the potential of some of the NFL teams with Uncle Bob. The discussion on politics that followed lasted until the pumpkin pie was served.

After the meal, I slipped into the bathroom to touch up my lipstick and try to powder away some bruises that were showing through my makeup. Percy followed me in and closed the door. She leaned against it and asked, "Well, is he? Are you?"

I knew what she meant, but in my best Scarlett O'Hara voice, I answered, "My deah sistah, what evah do you mean?" She just glowered at me. I relented and responded, "He's a friend—a good friend. I guess he's as close to a boyfriend as I've had in a while—but it hasn't gone beyond friendship. If it does, I'll let you know. Please feel free to tell Aunt Betty since she's probably listening at the door."

Percy opened the door, and sure enough, Betty was standing about a yard from it, drying a serving bowl. I said nothing but returned to the living room, where the baby was getting fussy and Olivia was sleeping on the couch by her daddy.

Having learned all that she was likely to about my relationship with Steve, Percy said cheerfully, "Richard, we need to get these kids home so we all can have a nap. Are you ready to go?"

After they had taken their leave, Steve and I talked a while with my uncle and aunt. I was pleased and relieved to see how comfortable he was with my family members. His relaxed manner and natural humor made him pleasant company. We were both quiet on the ride back to my place. I was self-conscious because of the questions that the girls had asked that still hung in the air between us.

When Steve parked the car, I reached for the door handle. He touched my arm. "Wait, I have something to tell you." He cleared his throat. "I think children can sometimes sense things that don't register with adults. I like you—I like you a lot. That complicates our situation, because I should hand off any investigation where I find myself emotionally involved."

I started to say something but he raised his hand to stop me. "I don't think either one of us wants to bring in another investigator, so the only way around the situation that I can see is that I will try to resist the temptation to kiss you, and we will continue to consider ourselves officially just friends. Will that work for you?"

I nodded, feeling that if I told him how I was feeling, the whole matter would become even more complicated.

He crossed to the passenger side of the car to open my door. As he walked me to my front door, I waved at Mrs. Bolton. At the door, I turned to thank him for spending the day with me and my family. He leaned over and gave me a tentative and tender kiss, which I willingly reciprocated. He pulled away slowly, as if he didn't want to. "Oops, I lost my head for a minute. Let's just consider that a kiss between friends. Okay?"

I couldn't speak for a moment so I just nodded. That kiss made me feel as if 220 volts had surged through me. I finally whispered, "Okay, but I think you'd better go . . . my friend." I went inside and melted into the recliner.

I took Friday off from work, and spent a quiet weekend with my thoughts full of Steve and that kiss.

• • •

He called me on Monday morning. "Hey, let's get together for dinner tonight. It'll give us a chance to compare notes on what's going on."

"Sounds great to me." The thought passed through my mind that we were sharing regular phone conversations nearly every day, so there wouldn't be much new to talk about, but I was always glad for the opportunity to spend time with him—and he seemed to feel the same about me.

He took me to dinner at a nice little Italian place run by a husband

and wife who excelled at making marinara sauce. After we had ordered, I shared the most recent information I had. "This afternoon I had a phone call from Corstelli. He called me immediately after he talked to Tiffany. He managed to get the probate court to finalize the legal gyrations required to settle LL's estate quicker than expected. It all fell to Tiffany, of course."

"Has Tiffany said anything more to you about her plans for the company?"

We were quiet while the server put our plates and the breadsticks on the table. When she had disappeared, I answered, "Tiffany called me right after I had talked with Corstelli. She asked if I would continue running the company for the time being, with the understanding that I can quit or she can fire me at will."

"Have you made a decision?"

I spoke slowly because I was still struggling with the decision. "I think I'll take it in short leaps. I'm going to tell her that I'll try it for six months. If we both feel good about it at that time, then I'll hang on for another six. That should give me the opportunity to decide if I want to make a long-term commitment, and she can reevaluate whether or not she's happy with my leadership." I looked up at him to see if his expression confirmed my decision. It was noncommittal. "Let's face it, it's hard to see that far into the future."

While we waited for dessert, he pulled a small package out of his sport coat pocket. It was wrapped in silver foil with a red ribbon. It looked like it was from a jewelry store. As he handed it to me, it suddenly dawned on me that my life had been so full of challenges and threats that I had forgotten that tomorrow was my birthday.

He was waiting for me to open it so I took a deep breath and pulled off the ribbon.

"Oh, Steve, it's lovely." I was thrilled to find a beautiful diamond pendant. It wasn't more than a quarter of a carat, but I loved it.

"Happy birthday, Lexi."

"Thank you, my friend," I said with a slightly embarrassed smile. "It's beautiful. How did you find out about my birthday?"

"The day after Thanksgiving I called your aunt and asked. Good thing I didn't wait or I'd have missed it. I decided to ask you out a day early, so you wouldn't suspect that I knew."

That wasn't exactly rocket science, but I thought it was clever—but then, I was biased. When he took me home, as per our agreement to be "just friends" until the investigation was over, we shook hands, even though we both would have liked to set aside the agreement for at least a minute or two.

• • •

I went in to the office on Tuesday, December first, my birthday, as usual. While I was in the office alone, I received a telephone call from Comandante García. "Lexi, I have asked around and it seems that the man you asked about may be—and I stress *may be*—known here in Mexico by another name. There is an American of that description who calls himself Humberto Street and is known to have some old connections down here with the Sinaloa Drug Cartel. There is an arrest warrant and an extradition request for him working its way through official channels from my government to yours, which means that he probably has four to six weeks before anything formal like an arrest can be carried out. Extradition is a slow and cumbersome process. Does that information help?"

As he talked my heart began its descent into my shoes. I took a deep breath. "Yes, Luis, thank you so much. Let me return the favor in the future if there's anything I can do for you." I could hardly believe it. It looked like Glade Schmidt had been right after all. I was thoroughly disgusted with myself for allowing Bud to talk me into going to the warehouse.

I immediately called Steve. He said he would notify the FBI so a watch could be put on Hebestreet until the extradition papers came through. While he was talking, I was thinking about the likelihood that if Bud Hebestreet went to prison, that would end any possibility of the company getting paid for the completed warehouse project. The seriousness in his voice drew me back.

"Lexi, now that you and Tiffany have made some decisions about the future of the company, I want you to move someone else into that office with you in addition to Roger. I'll feel better if the two of you aren't there alone—especially with Roger working in the other office a part of every day. If Hebestreet calls you about any more work on the warehouse, have Roger deal with him. But don't tell him about the problems Hebestreet may shortly be having with the law, so he won't give anything away."

"Okay, I can do that. And I'll invite Ted Jorgenson, our head accountant, and Bernie Ziggler, our company attorney, to move over from the other building. It may take them a couple of days to arrange it, but there's plenty of room, and admittedly, I'd feel more comfortable." I paused as something floated into my consciousness. "There is one thing that's really bothering me."

"And that is?"

"Where's Ed Gomes? I'm beginning to think he's left the country. After all, considering the amount of money he still owes LL Construction, he'd have quite a nest egg in some small country where they don't extradite to the United States."

"It's time I filed a missing person's report on him. I'll bet I can get enough information from his secretary to get the ball rolling." The seriousness in his tone lessened. "Hey, my friend, have you got any plans for dinner tonight? You need a real birthday dinner."

"Any offer you might make would be gladly accepted."

"Then I'll pick you up at your place at six. Is that okay with you?"

"That would be more than okay. It would be great."

CHAPTER 18

When I arrived at the office on Friday morning, Roger's car was not in the parking lot. I was somewhat relieved, not sure how to act around him now that I suspected that I might have to fire him if the audit came back really bad. As I entered, I was startled to find him standing in the middle of the floor, holding a blue file folder of the type Ted Jorgenson used in the accounting office.

I tried to cover my surprise. "Hi, Roger. Where's the Corvette?" Suddenly, I realized what he had in his hands—it had to be the report of the audits I had requested Ted to do right away on the QT.

It was his eyes that made me really nervous. They were as cold as an arctic harbor. Somehow, he didn't look like the young man I had been working with for 18 months.

"Ted had one of his accountants bring this over and leave this for you yesterday after you had gone home. Ted's wife was taken to the hospital so he left work early. The note on it says, "Here's the audit you ordered. Sorry it took so long."

If that audit showed any kind of irregularities in the accounts Roger had been handling, I knew I might have a serious problem. His eyes told me that I didn't want to be around him when he was angry. This was a side of him I'd never seen before.

I walked to my desk and sat down with what I hoped appeared

to be a natural nonchalance and put my bag on my lap. I opened it, pulled out my compact, and put it on the desk as if I were planning to use it. Then I reached in and pulled out a package of gum, the kind with each rectangular piece individually wrapped in clear plastic. Holding it up, I asked innocently, "Gum?"

He gave a quick, contemptuous shake of his head and returned to looking over the information from Ted. I put my hand back into the bag, and, with the package of gum covering it, I picked up my cell and hit the speed dial button for Steve's cell phone. Then I surreptitiously dropped both into my jacket pocket. I prayed that when Steve answered, he would be able to hear me but wouldn't speak so loud as to draw Roger's attention.

I pulled out a yellow legal pad from my top right hand drawer as if there were nothing on my mind except getting to work. My heart was pounding so hard I could hear it in my ears. Swallowing the knot in my throat, I said, with what I hoped was a slightly critical tone, as if I were reacting normally, "How long have you been reading reports addressed to me? That was expressly meant to be private."

He looked up from the file folder. "Yeah, that's what the note clipped to the front of the folder said." He waved the note at me as if it were all a big joke. He smiled with a tight, mean smile. "I've been reading your correspondence and notes whenever you've been out of the office. How do you think I caught on to what LL wanted in an assistant so quickly?" He stood still with his feet planted and his eyes narrowed.

I heard the faint ring from where the cell was muffled against the scarf in my pocket, and I knew that if Steve didn't answer, his voicemail response would begin. I raised my voice to cover it. "Roger, LL and I trusted you. What was so important that you were willing to violate that trust?" I kept up the insistent questions in a forceful voice in the hope that when Steve's cell recorded my message, it would be audible despite being in my jacket pocket. "Was it Tiffany? Is she worth selling your integrity? How long have you been fluttering around her like you were at the wake, currying her favor? Even with your phone calls, do you think she would ever take you seriously?"

He stepped over to his desk and laughed as he deliberately dropped the report from Ted into his trash basket. He turned and leaned against his desk, with his arms folded across his chest. "Oh, I've been going out to Tiffany's place for a couple of months. How do you think I've been spending my evenings and weekends? She's really quite lonely and was so glad to take me under her wing. After all, I'm just a poor orphan boy with no family, just as lonely as she is." His voice was simpering and sneering at the same time. "We usually play billiards for a while, and a couple sets of tennis, and then we cool off in LL's pool and talk. She has improved my tennis and I've improved her billiards. We formed quite a fast friendship, right under LL's unobserving nose."

Everything about him—his voice, his expression, his body language—made me feel threatened. I really wanted to pull the gun out of my bag but had no justifiable reason, at least not yet. So far, we were just having a strained conversation.

Trying to sound as normal as I could, I cleared my throat. "Have you heard from Ed Gomes?"

He shook his head as if to shake off the question. "Let's talk about some important issues. I suspect that you have some questions for me." He moved around the office as if surveying his domain before he paused to lean against the file cabinets with his arms folded across his chest and a smug expression on his face. He wanted a confrontation.

Maybe he would give me enough reason to pull out the gun, so I decided to ask the big one—what I really wanted to know. "Did you kill LL? Did you kill him so you can step into his shoes by marrying Tiffany?"

"Now that's a big question." He gave me a tight-lipped smile and stepped over to where his jacket hung on a coat rack near the copy machine. He pulled a nickel-plated Colt .45 automatic from the outside pocket and pointed it at me. He motioned with the barrel and his meaning was clear.

I had waited too long. I felt sick. My hand instinctively went into my bag, but his voice grew as hard. "Put both your hands up or I'll kill you right here and now." His eyes said that he would do it, and with satisfaction.

I lifted both hands. He walked leisurely over to where I was still sitting and looked down into the bag that was on my lap. He put his hand in it and came up with the revolver and my set of car keys. He laughed and dropped them into his jacket pocket. "This isn't much of a gun. You need something more like this." His voice hardened even more and he shoved the barrel of his gun into my face, hurting my bruised cheek. I leaned back to try to put a few inches between my face and the muzzle of the weapon.

"You're going to write a suicide note and then go out and kill yourself." He gave a tragic sigh, clearly feigned.

"You can't really think that anyone will believe I killed myself."

His voice hardened. "It doesn't matter what they believe; it only matters what they can prove."

"Roger, the truth will come out." Before, I was frightened. Now, I was terrified. He seemed to be moving away from rationality.

He put his face in mine. "Truth! Where truth is concerned, there's what people want to hear, there's what people want to believe, and then there's the truth!" He stood up straight and turned to look around the room as if truth might be found hiding somewhere there. "And it's never welcome. Now pick up the pen!" Without hesitation, I did. "Write: 'To Whom It May Concern; I can't handle the pressure. I don't want to disappoint Tiffany.'" He waited for me to catch up. "'I can't do it the way LL would want.' Now sign it." I did. "Now put the purse on the floor. We're taking a ride."

I dropped my bag to the floor and stood with my hands raised to shoulder height. He kicked it under the desk and shoved me toward the door. When we got to it, he said, "Hold it." He pulled a long, black zip tie from his pocket.

"Put your hands behind your back." I did, and he stuck his gun in his belt and put the tie around my wrists. Then for amusement, he yanked my hands backward, hard, hurting my shoulder joints. "That ought to do," he said with satisfaction.

He opened the door. With the muzzle of his gun in my back,

hidden by my body, we stepped outside. He said, "Turn left." I did, and when we reached the front corner of the office, I could see a Yamaha road bike leaning against the side of the building.

"Hold it." He shoved the gun into his belt again and pulled on his driving gloves before he walked over to the bike, which he pushed toward the Pontiac. He smiled the coldest smile I've ever seen. "If you try to run, I'll shoot you without hesitation." He nodded toward the car, making it clear he wanted me to precede him. He walked me and the road bike around to the rear, where he opened the big trunk and lifted the road bike into it. For such a skinny guy, he did it with amazing ease. The handlebars were too wide for the trunk lid to close completely, so he pulled a bungee cord from his other pocket and lashed the trunk lid down. Then he pushed me around to the passenger side door. "Get in."

As I was climbing in, I looked up in time to see one of the accountants arrive at the other building and give us a wave as he got out of his car and started toward the office. I looked toward him with what I hoped was a pleading expression. As he put his hand on the doorknob, he looked back at me with a questioning glance.

"Say something, and he's dead too. Now, get in," Roger hissed.

When I had pulled my legs into the car, he pushed the lock button down and slammed the door. His smiling confidence was especially disconcerting. It made the saliva gather in the bottom of my mouth, making me swallow hard several times to control my nervous reaction. He put the car in reverse and stepped on the gas with a malicious grin. The tires whipped gravel toward the front of the office.

It was easy to see how he had gotten rid of LL's SUV. He had put the road bike in the back and after setting the vehicle on fire he'd ridden it back into town.

As he turned left onto Adobe Road, I asked quietly, "Where are we going, Roger?" My legs were quivering with nerves, and the urge to vomit rose up and shook every bone in my body. I knew I was going to die. I made a slow, conscious effort to breathe deeply to calm my stomach and clear my head. I have always told myself that I wasn't afraid of death. After all, if you live a good life trying to consistently make right choices and a minimum of bad decisions, you should feel that you could stand before the judgment bar with confidence. But I was overwhelmed with the instinct of self-preservation.

"What does it matter to you? You won't be coming back."

I felt that I needed to keep him talking. Why did I feel a need to have an extended chat with a killer in circumstances like these? Was I desperately hoping against hope that I could talk him out of killing me, or stall until Steve could respond to my phone call, or in the last desperate possibility, extend my life by a few precious moments? "Have you been planning this for a while, or are you improvising as you go?"

"I never improvise." His voice had an edge as hard as flint. "I've had this plan in the works since I heard that Tiffany wanted you to run the company while she waited for the court to complete the probate of LL's estate. She called last night to tell me about the estate settlement and about your agreement to run the company for the next six months, and if all went well, to stay on indefinitely. She thought I'd be pleased since—as she put it—'you work so well together.'"

He was becoming agitated and his face was getting red. "Don't you know how you screwed up everything? It was supposed to be Stan Bergman that took over the office. I'd been telling Tiffany for weeks what a capable guy Bergman is. He's a natural for the job, but you women . . ."—he spoke the word 'women' with an acidic contempt—"you women and your emotional baggage ruined everything, so I had to change plans." From the set of his jaw, it was evident that making him change his plans was a grave offense.

"Is Bergman in this with you?"

"Not so he would know it. He's easy to manipulate. He was sure he was going to take LL's place heading up the company."

I had so many questions. If I was going to die, I wanted answers. "Did Stan follow me home from the wake, trying to scare me?" He ignored the question. "Did you promise him a lot of money?" Still no response. "Is someone else in this with you?" Silence. "What was in the report from Ted? Did it show that you had diverted funds from the Sunnyville Estates project? Did Ed Gomes find out and confront you?"

He finally responded. "Yeah, he got mad when he found out that according to our records, he hadn't missed one payment but was really behind two installments, plus the one due last week. He was going to make a real stink about it."

"Where is Ed? Did you kill him?"

He didn't answer. He just looked at me like a cat that was about to eat the canary.

"How many other accounts have you diverted for your own use?" My arms and hands were going numb behind my back and my shoulders were hurting. I shifted and put my bent left leg on the seat between us so I could turn and see his face better.

"Just a few. Hebestreet's loft project has been very productive for me; and he can't say anything. He's caught between the cops and the cartel. Why do you think he cooperated with me and asked you to inspect the ceilings in the loft at night? Why do you think he wanted the suspended ceilings put in the lofts in the first place? So he can stash drugs that come up from Mexico. He's the north end of a major smuggling operation."

"Did you put the bomb in my car at the government center?"

He smiled and refused to answer. We turned onto Highway 101. I started to rock forward and back and side-to-side in an attempt to ease the spasms in my back.

"Sit still," he snapped.

"I can't help it. My muscles are in spasms." I lessened my rocking motions only a little. "What started this plan of yours? Why did you target LL? If Bergman stepped into LL's shoes, was he going to have some kind of an accident so you could replace him?"

We were moving with traffic toward the Cave Creek area north of the metro area, the same place LL's SUV had been found. I shivered with the realization of what he had planned.

He was quiet for several seconds before he responded. "I'm LL's son. This company is mine by right." My amazed expression must have prompted him to continue. "Yeah, she told me all about him when I was a kid." His voice had dropped to a chilling, hate-filled whisper. "She told me how he deserted her after the company began to make money. How he left us both with nothing." He spat out the words. "She had to go to work as a waitress in a greasy spoon to support us until Joe Hartzler married her and adopted me." He spoke slowly and with deliberation. "This company is *mine* by birthright, not Tiffany's." Every word was like the bite of a viper.

"Your mother was named Louise?"

"Yeah, Louise O'Mally Lattimer, until she married my stepdad."

"Your mother told you LL was your father?" I was having trouble absorbing what he was telling me. Gradually, things began to make sense. She had raised the kid on hate. I said the only thing that came to mind. "You're Joe Hartzler's son, not LL's."

As if to confirm the truth of my words, a flash of lightning tore open the sky and a roll of thunder shook the car. The rain began to pound the roof like fists.

He took his eyes off the road and looked at me with frigid rage. "Lawrence Lattimer is my father," he said, emphasizing each word.

"What did your mother look like?"

That threw him for a second. He looked at me with some confusion diluting the hate in his eyes. "She was about five foot three with red hair and green eyes. She was really pretty." His words were filled with a grim pride.

"What did Joe Hartzler look like?"

He looked at me as if he wondered where I was going with these questions. "He was about six foot two and had dark hair and brown eyes. Why?"

"Hasn't it occurred to you that if you were LL's son, you'd be short and stocky? Your mother was short, a lot shorter than LL—and you'd be red headed. You're six inches taller than LL, skinny, and dark haired. You're an entirely different body type."

He looked away from the road again, and insisted. "LL was my father. He was!" He struck the steering wheel with the heel of his hand for emphasis.

"Why is it so important to you to believe that he was your

father? Does patricide make what you've done more appealing to you? Does that make it any less unnatural?" His jaw hardened, but he said nothing, so I continued, "You once told me that you were an orphan. How did your mother die?" His jaw was tight. He wasn't going to answer. "Is Joe Hartzler dead too? Why do you call yourself Roger Hartley?"

His head swiveled as if pulled by a puppet string. He yelled at me, "Shut up! Just shut up!"

If I could get him seriously rattled, maybe he would do something stupid. Despite the fear that lay like a rock in my stomach, I badgered him. "I recognize your personality type. My college psychology professor would say you're one of those people that has lied all of your life because you're good at it. You lie for satisfaction, because you can get away with it. I'll bet you've lied even when there was nothing to gain—you just couldn't resist." I paused and took a breath. "You're a calculating, cold-blooded sociopath."

He yanked the steering wheel so hard to pull over onto the shoulder of the highway that the car behind us slid on the wet pavement and the driver gave us one long blast with his horn.

He hit the brake hard and, even before the car had quit moving, shoved the gearshift into park. Without a seatbelt, I was thrown against the dashboard. He turned on me, reaching out and grabbing my throat. My badgering was working, but not exactly the way I had hoped. I was feeling pure, mind-freezing panic. He let go of me, his hands shaking.

He regained control as swiftly as he had lost it. He whispered, "No, not now, not this way." He sat back and shifted into drive, cautiously moving back into the flow of traffic.

I was coughing, my throat hurt, and my head was pounding, but he had almost lost it. If I could get him to do something stupid, it needed to be here, while others were around, not out in the desert where no one could help me.

"You didn't answer me, Roger. Is that your real name? What happened to your parents? Were they just collateral damage?" I paused. "How did they die?" He didn't respond. "Did you kill them?"

I waited for a few more seconds before I prodded him again. "Tell me how long you've been working toward taking over the company."

He turned with narrowed eyes and gave me a look of fierce pride. "Since I was fourteen, I learned that you've got to hold on tight or the world will take everything away from you. You've got to give cold and careful attention to details while you reach for your goals. You hide your impatience from those who can't keep up. You never let their stupidity get in your way." He paused as if remembering earlier memories.

Until now, he hadn't had anyone he could tell his story to. I could almost see the synapses in his brain firing off behind his eyes. He wanted to tell someone what he had been doing for so many years. He wanted an audience to impress. He started to expound like a professor before a college class.

"We all make choices in life." That grim, smug smile was back again. "I had a math teacher in junior high when I was thirteen who promised me that he would help me land a full scholarship to a good university if I stayed in school and out of trouble." His voice began to rise. "But that jerk Hartzler wanted me to help him deliver pizzas. I have an IQ of a hundred and fifty, and he wanted me to deliver pizzas!" He spat out the words like a volcano spitting out hot magma. His hands gripped the steering wheel like vices.

Both traffic and rain were light now and I feared we would soon be out of cell range. He exited onto Cave Creek Road, still moving north, hurrying further away from the metro area. The overcast sky made the darkness stretch out in all directions, the broad fields of cultivated soil occasionally marked by the lights of a house or a cluster of homes sitting in the dark. The farther we drove, the farther I was from help . . .

CHAPTER 19

He refused to respond to my questions any longer. He had regained control. He looked straight ahead with a twisted, grim look on his face. He turned off the highway, driving east. We drove through the old, small community of Cave Creek, which was located at the base of the eroded mountains north of the metro area. It had become a status location for more recent, expensive homes. We turned on Cactus Drive, moving past scattered houses with their forty-acre lots, sporting a horse or two, set back from the road. After about ten minutes, the two lanes became a winding mountain road that eventually turned into a wide, rough gravel path that wound through the hills. Small rocks popped up by the tires rattled against the bottom of the car. No homes were visible anymore.

"You know, Roger, if you had played your hand more carefully, the police would be focused on Ed Gomes. It looks like he absconded with the millions he owed the company. They would have spent all their resources trying to prove that he hired someone to kill LL and was trying to kill me. You should have kept your head down for a while longer. If you kill me, Steve Sutherland won't quit until he gets you."

He still didn't respond. We moved along the winding road as it rose and twisted sinuously over steep, desert hills, bouncing through and over the uneven places. I allowed the motion of the car to move my body around the seat, swaying from the door toward him, and coming close to contacting the dashboard a couple of times. The movement eased the muscle cramps somewhat. We had been traveling for over an hour.

He was craning his neck, looking for a specific location. He finally found it. He turned the steering wheel so abruptly that I was thrown against the door when he turned onto a wide, rough trail probably made by four-wheeled, all-terrain vehicles. It wound steeply up the boulder-strewn mountainside.

I began to understand the kind of death he was planning for me. He was going to drive up to the top of a plateau and then send the car over the edge with me in it. Suicide? Would Steve or anyone else buy that explanation? Not likely, but like he said, it was what could be proven that was important.

"Sit still," he snarled at me.

"I can't. I have no way to steady myself without my hands." I needed to draw him out again. I wanted him distracted from his goal, at least a little, so I asked again, "Was it you who tried to kill me with the bulldozer?"

He turned and looked at me with an icy stare. "Did the cops find any of my fingerprints on it?"

"No, but you use gloves when you drive."

He snickered as if I were stupid.

Lightning ripped the dark curtain of the sky. The thunder following actually made the car vibrate. I saw a high, flat mesa silhouetted in the following flashes. The storm would soon envelop us. We might have been the only people on earth. I involuntarily shuddered.

"Steve will come after you when he finds me in the car. You can't concoct an alibi sufficient to convince him. He won't quit until he gets you."

"But like I said, it's what he can prove that's important."

The car was steadily climbing the switchbacks on the hillside. As it hit a big rut, I was thrown against the door and my jacket pocket caught on the door handle, twisting my sleeve and my hands behind me. I reached toward the pocket that held the cell phone. With two fingers that still had some feeling in them, I finally touched it.

As he drove, he was concentrating on avoiding the worst of the ruts, so I pinned the cell against the door by leaning back against it, and searched for the record button by feel. I was sure we were out of the service area, but if I could just record what was going on, if I didn't survive, there would be a record of what was happening—if the battery wasn't dead.

The car finally reached the flattened top of the mountain and he drove slowly around the plateau as near the edge as he could. The hillside there dropped off the most steeply. He parked with the front tires on the sloping edge. With just a firm nudge, if the car were in neutral, it would roll down the slope. I could see the headlights stabbing the darkness, their light indirectly illuminating a few large boulders the car would hit on the way down.

"This ought to do it," he said cheerfully as he put the car in park.

My heart was pounding so hard that I could hear it pulsing in my voice. "How are you going to explain the fact that my wrists are tied together? Not many suicide victims have their hands bound behind them."

He stared out of the windshield and moved his head from side to side in a thoughtful manner, as if trying to work out a small algebra problem. "Now that's a problem, isn't it?" He turned with a malevolent grin and struck my jaw with his fist. The blow knocked me against the passenger side door where my head ricocheted off the window. Pain reared its ugly head and my vision threatened to narrow to a long dark tunnel without a light at the end. I knew if I let go and slipped into that darkness, I was dead.

I remained motionless, slumped against the door, making him believe that the blow had accomplished what he wanted. My head was spinning and fear wrapped me like an icy blanket.

I heard him open his door and slide out. I could hear his steps on the rocky ground as he walked around to the rear of the vehicle. He unhooked the bungee cord and lifted out the dirt bike. He slammed the trunk lid and walked away from the car.

I continued to feign unconsciousness. He returned to the car and slid behind the steering wheel again.

I heard the click of a switchblade. I tried to smother the shudder that ran through me. *If he wants it to look like suicide, surely he won't stab me.* I felt him start to saw through the plastic tie on my wrists, the pressure making it cut into my flesh even more than it had.

When the tie let go, I knew it was time to act or I would be going over that drop off in a car that would be a crumpled wreck at the bottom of the steep slope.

He started the engine and I felt the slight shift of the car as he moved the gearshift from park into neutral. My arms and hands were nearly useless due to the lack of circulation, but in one desperate—or inspired—motion, I threw my body back against the passenger side door and drew up my knees. With all the force that the adrenaline of primal fear could give me, I drove my feet into his rib cage and right hip. He was caught totally off guard, and the force of the impact toppled him out of the car.

As he started to stand, I scooted across the seat after him, giving myself some leverage by putting my right arm through the steering wheel to help me. As my feet hit the ground, he stood unsteadily and put his hand into the pocket of his jacket, reaching for his gun. I figured it was now or never, so I ducked into a linebacker's stoop, and threw myself at him, hitting him in the stomach with my left shoulder. The pronounced "Ooof" he made gave me some satisfaction.

He stumbled backward about four feet, within a few inches of the edge. I lunged again, this time hitting him with my right shoulder, pushing him back again as he tried to steady his aim but the wet soil and rocks beneath his feet began to crumble. He fired a shot as his arms began to windmill, and the bullet went high, over the car. The gun flew out of his hand. He reached out and grabbed my jacket pocket. We both went over the edge, rolling in a tangle of arms and legs.

Behind us, the sodden edge of the hill under the front end of the car gave way and the big Pontiac slowly started its descent down the boulder-strewn mountainside, gaining speed as it rolled. Despite my own struggles, I heard it bounce off a large boulder. I was suddenly terrified that if I survived the fall, the car would crush me.

Providence was kind. The pocket of my jacket ripped and Roger disappeared down the mountainside with my gun in his other pocket. The car hit another good-sized boulder and began to tumble end over end. I was too busy trying to keep my hands in front of my face as I rolled and tumbled to note where Roger or the car went. I heard it ricocheting off big boulders, but I don't remember hearing it reach the bottom of the mountainside.

CHAPTER 20

The sound of distant sirens eventually drew me out of the numbed stupor I was in. I opened my eyes and saw movement and lights above me. Beams from headlights of emergency vehicles sliced the darkness and rain in erratic patterns like yellow lasers pointing off into the near black around us. Red and blue lights pulsed, adding to the feeling of unreality.

I watched groggily as several blurry forms slid, jumped, and stumbled down the slope toward the place where I was laying among the rocks and cactus. Yellow beams from flashlights preceded each one. Steve reached me first. He pulled off his jacket and put it over my soaked body. The rescuers were wet, rain water dripping steadily from their yellow waterproof coats and hat covers. Several of them gathered around as he knelt beside me.

"Lexi, are you all right?" There was panic in his voice. He pulled a handkerchief from his pocket and began to wipe my face. The handkerchief quickly turned red. My forehead or face must have been bleeding. "Are you okay?" He was almost yelling.

Even in my groggy state, his concern touched me deeply. "My hip hurts," I said through a voice that was as scratchy as my body was at that moment. He had to bend close to my mouth to hear me.

"Can you move your leg?"

I tried. "Yes, a little, maybe it's not broken."

"Where else do you hurt?" The look of concern on his face almost made up for the situation I was in.

"My right knee hurts, but I'm so cold, I can't tell if I'm hurt anywhere else." He took my right hand and began to rub it. My hands were stiff and cold and almost without feeling, but I managed to hold on to his hand—as tightly as I could. "I'm so glad you're here," I whispered.

"A rescue helicopter will be here in a few minutes. Just hang on. I won't leave you until they get you on it." He reached for my left hand I saw him pause when he noted that my little finger was pointing off at a forty-five degree angle. He laid it down carefully.

I closed my eyes for a few seconds. I think it scared him.

He gently patted my cheek. "Hey, Lexi, stay with me. Open your eyes. Don't slip away."

I struggled to open them. The pulse in my head hammered a steady beat. I was *so* tired. I just wanted to be in a warm bed where I could sleep for a year. Instead I forced myself to raise my voice and ask, "Steve, how did you find me? How did you know where we were?"

"When I tried to call you, I found a muffled voicemail. The caller ID said it came from your cell phone, so I called the office. No one answered, so I called the other office. One of the accountants said he had seen you getting into a car with Roger. I had the number on the SIM chip in your phone, so I put a trace on your cell through the phone company. You'll never know how many people I had to threaten with legal charges if they didn't get on the trace immediately. At the same time someone called 911 and reported a man attacking a woman in a red Pontiac GTO in the northbound lane on the 101. I knew it had to be you so I put in a call to the highway patrol and the county P.D. to watch for the car. A county police officer spotted it as it left the 101 at the Cave Creek exit. That was about the same time the cell carrier traced the last tower your cell was pinging off. I figured that he was taking you out to the general area where LL's burned SUV was found. I had a good idea of his intentions. I called the county police and rushed out here. We must have gotten here not long after the car went over the mountainside. The steam was still rising from the wreckage and the headlights were still on, pointing up the mountain. That helped us find you."

"I'm so glad you did. I guess God isn't ready to give up on me yet."

I began to shiver uncontrollably about the time I could hear the *whoop-whoop-whoop* of the rotor blades of a helicopter. Within a minute, the beam of a searchlight covered us like a bright blanket. A basket stretcher was lowered with an EMT riding in it. As it hit the ground, he climbed out of it, bringing his kit with him.

The downdraft and noise from the helicopter made it impossible to talk, and I was too exhausted to do anything more than whisper, so I held up my hand. The EMT dabbed at the cuts on my forehead, splinted two of my fingers and wrapped my bleeding knee.

He yelled at me, "Are you badly hurt anywhere else?" I slowly rolled my head from side to side rather than trying to yell above the noise of the helicopter. I was so cold I really couldn't tell. "We've got to get you into the basket so they can get you into the chopper. Can you stand?"

I was determined to try so I nodded.

"You want me to help you up?" Steve yelled. I nodded again. He bent over me and I put my arm around his neck so he could lift me to my feet. My sore hip and injured knee made me so unsteady that he carefully picked me up and carried me over to the basket. The EMT straddled the basket and rode up with me. The experience of riding up in the cold as the basket slowly rotated in the downdraft of the rotors pushed the pain out of my mind. I couldn't help but wonder, *Wouldn't it be strange to survive a fall down the mountain but die in the basket if it fell from the helicopter?*

Once we were inside, the helicopter rose rapidly and I was able to turn my head enough to see through the Plexiglas window in the side. The emergency vehicles were spread out beneath us, the dome lights blinking and turning like a carnival, mixing with the headlights.

191

Over the edge of the steep drop off, I could see the battered body of Uncle Bob's car, now a heap of twisted metal steaming in the wet, cold air.

My head gradually began to clear long enough for my thoughts to turn to the practical problems growing out of my situation. *What am I going to tell my insurance company? How can I explain two totaled cars? What will happen to my insurance rates?*

The most important thought then hit me. *I'm so grateful for Steve. Without his determination, who knows when—or if—they would have found me?*

At that point, I slipped into a soft darkness and woke up in the emergency room with two nurses cutting the clothing off my battered body. After being fully X-rayed, stitched and bandaged, and getting my left hand put in a cast that went nearly to my elbow, I was finally pushed to a room. The emergency room physician—the same one who had treated me after my adventure with the bulldozer—told me I had a concussion, two broken fingers, a broken wrist, a massive bruise on my right hip, and torn ligaments in my right knee.

Steve waited just outside the door of the room they put me in, looking like he wanted to talk to me. I weakly motioned him in after I was in the bed.

"You need to get your hands on Stan Bergman." I think I was mumbling. "Maybe he didn't really know what Roger was up to, but somehow he was involved too. And Roger told me that Hebestreet's part of a drug smuggling ring. Bud was paying him to keep quiet. The *Federales* are going to extradite him." I was probably babbling. It was getting hard to talk and I was too groggy to answer his questions, so I slid gratefully into that soft darkness again.

• • •

The sun was brightening the morning sky when I woke to find Steve sitting next to my bed. He was dozing, leaning forward with his head down and his elbows on his knees. The pain meds had worn off so I was hurting all over, but I had so many questions. I reached out and touched him.

His head came up and he ran his hand through his hair. He had dark circles under his eyes and his skin was gray with exhaustion. He slid his dangling tie inside his damp sport coat. He reached over and patted my uninjured hand. "Glad to see that you're finally back among the living. The nurse said that when you woke, if you were still hurting, to let her know and she'll bring you a pain pill."

"Maybe later. I want to talk right now."

He pulled a small, handheld recorder from his coat pocket. He asked, "You don't mind?"

"No, of course not. Did you find him?" I didn't need to specify who.

"Yes, he broke his neck in the fall. He'd been dead about an hour when we found his body. The death he planned for you killed him instead."

I closed my eyes and took a deep breath as I thought about that thing called karma. "So it's over. It's over." I exhaled with relief.

"It's over." He was quiet for a moment, as well. He finally added, "By the way, the searchers found your phone and your uncle's gun about a hundred feet below the lip of the plateau."

"Did the phone pick up any of our conversation? I tried to set it for record."

"It was damaged by fall and the rain, but what we could make out answered some of our questions."

"Well, I'm glad you found the gun so I won't have to explain to Uncle Bob that I lost it, on top of wrecking the car."

"I'll get it back to you from the department in a couple of days. With Roger dead, they won't need to keep it as evidence."

"Even if they did, that shouldn't present a problem now. Hopefully, I won't need to carry a gun any longer." I closed my eyes for a few seconds before returning to the subject of Roger. "He believed he was LL's son and that the company should belong to him. His mother was Louise, LL's first wife. She told him that her second husband, Joe Hartzler, had adopted him after LL had deserted them. He had been planning to take over the company one way or another for a long time."

"That explains his motive."

"He brought a road bike to use to get away after he sent me down the mountainside. Did you find it?"

"It was sitting on the top of the plateau, waiting for him."

Something new crept into my mind. "Steve, were you able to talk to Roseanna Gardner, the lady who cleans our office? I'm worried about her. The last time she came in was the Saturday before LL was killed. When I tried to call her, no one answered, and I haven't been able to call her again. Too much has been happening."

"One of the teams helping with the investigation has tried repeatedly to reach her, but they've had no luck. Neighbors told them she and her husband left on a trip the same day the media reported that LL's body had been discovered."

"It's strange that she didn't at least leave me a message. I hope nothing has happened to them." I was growing tired. "That's everything I can remember right now."

"I'm going to try to get some information on the death of his parents, now that we have their names. I'll give the Colorado Department of Vital Statistics a call. In the meantime, you get some rest. I'll come back this afternoon."

I promptly followed his advice. He was hardly out of the room before I was asleep. He returned around four to tell me that he had finally reached someone in Colorado who was willing to give him some information.

"I didn't have much luck getting information out of the folks at the Department of Vital Statistics on the phone. They wanted a formal, written request submitted, but one woman took pity on me and suggested that I contact the Colorado State Fire Marshal. He was more responsive. According to his records, a Joseph Hartzler died in a fire when Roger would have been about fifteen. Two years later, Louise Hartzler died in a similar manner. He checked the records of the investigation of both fires. He remembered the second case especially well—the one that killed Louise. He said the fire was of suspicious origin, but nothing could be proven. In both cases, there were no batteries in the smoke detectors."

I took a deep breath to get past the pain. "While he was driving me out to the plateau, he told me that he had a full math scholarship to ASU, but that Joe Hartzler demanded that he drop out of school and deliver pizzas for the pizza shop he was running. I think that was Joe's death sentence." I paused and thought for a moment. "Surely there's *some* way to prove whether or not he's really LL's son, as he insisted?"

"It may be possible. If Tiffany still has a toothbrush or a hairbrush of LL's, then maybe we can obtain his DNA for comparison."

• • •

When Steve returned to the hospital that night he brought me up to date. He told me that while I was sleeping under the influence of some pain medication, he went looking for Stan Bergman. When he and a couple of officers arrived at Bergman's home, they found him dead on the kitchen floor. The autopsy showed that he had died of a heart attack brought on by a heavy dose of cocaine he had ingested, probably unknowingly. There were no other drugs in his home or office, so Steve didn't believe that he was a user. He told me that he personally believed that Roger poisoned him.

When the Mesa P.D. searched Roger's home with Steve as part of the team, they found a shotgun, a blue sport coat with one button missing, and a stash of drugs. Evidently, he had joined Hebestreet in his drug dealing.

Steve was pleased that Tiffany had been able to find a used toothbrush of LL's so the CSI team could set to work doing a DNA comparison with Roger. When she found out that her "friend" Roger was full of ulterior motives and was guilty of murdering her husband, she became distraught. She turned to Corstelli for comfort, and her sister came to stay with her.

• • •

Percy brought me some clothes the following day, and the day after that, I was released from the hospital with a pair of rented crutches. With a cast on one hand, I found the crutches unwieldy, so I resorted to using only the right one. On the way home, Steve shared two pieces of information of special interest. "The DNA results are in. Roger was not LL's son."

"Somehow, that's a comfort. What's the second item?"

"The county police think they've found Ed Gomes's body. Early this morning out north of Cave Creek, not far from where we found you, some hikers came across his remains. It'll take a DNA or dental match to get a positive ID."

"And all this time I've been accusing him of absconding with the money he owed the company. I feel bad for thinking all those unkind things about him. Do you think Roger killed him?"

"He had two slugs in him. The lab did a comparison to Roger's gun—which, by the way, we found on the mountainside, not far from where we found you. The slugs matched, so yes, it looks like Roger killed him. I called Ed's secretary as soon as I heard about the body. She said that when Ed called and told her he had that family emergency that was taking him out of town she thought he sounded really stressed or nervous. Roger was probably holding a gun on him at the time."

CHAPTER 21

It was after one when we reached my place. "Do you feel well enough to go out to lunch? Either that, or you'll have to let me fix you some frozen waffles and scrambled eggs again." He grinned as he made the offer.

I knew I was a pretty pathetic sight, so I wasn't ready to face the world, and I was hungry. "If you're willing to do the cooking, I'd love some waffles and eggs."

I teetered on my crutches to the front door of my place, and I waved at Mrs. Bolton as best I could. Once inside, I turned off the alarm. He pointed to the couch and ordered, "Stay there until I can get it ready. Then I'll help you up."

When she called, as I knew she would, he handed me the phone. "I'm all right, Mrs. Bolton. I was just in a little accident." She immediately sounded very upset. "Yes, yes, another one, but it looks worse than it is. I'm sure I'll be good as new in a couple of days." She offered to come down and take care of me for the next few days. "My friend Steve is fixing me lunch right now, and after he leaves, if I need help, I promise I'll call you."

When he was finished with the eggs, he put two waffles on my plate and helped me over to sit on one of the stools.

As I poured blackberry syrup over my waffles, I asked, "Has any of the money that Roger embezzled from the Sunnyville Estates project or from Hebestreet been located? Has there been time to get into his bank account?"

He shook his head. "Not yet. We're sure the FBI is working on that and will get there first, probably tomorrow. The Bureau asserted its authority in the case, because you were kidnapped."

"That will complicate things, won't it?"

"Probably."

"Are there any theories floating around as to what he most likely did with it? It looks like he got away with at least four million from the Sunnyville project, and I can only wonder how much he took under the table from Hebestreet. Do you suppose that he squirreled it away in some offshore bank?"

He put down his napkin. "Personally, I think so, but even the FBI and the IRS will have a tough time tracing the funds. The bank has got to be identified as well as the account number." He finished his waffle and wiped his hands on his napkin. "If the Bureau is making any progress, they aren't sharing it with us. Admittedly, they haven't had much time as yet."

I'd been thinking while he talked. "Steve, last March, about the time we thought Ed Gomes had missed the first payment, Roger took a two-week vacation. He came back very sunburned, which for him was not unusual, so I didn't pay any attention to the fact, but now that I think of it, the time frame coincided with a trip Tiffany took to Bermuda." I looked him right in the eye. "There are probably several offshore banks in the Caribbean."

"Do you have Tiffany's number in your cell?" I nodded. "Will you call her and tell her that we need to come out for a visit right away? You might get a better response from her than I would."

When she answered my call and I explained our intentions, she responded, "Well, my sister and I are flying out to San Juan tonight, so you'll need to come out right away. What's this all about?"

"Just some little details about the investigation." I was deliberately evasive as I suspected that she didn't want to talk about Roger and would put us off if she had any idea what we wanted to talk about. "We'll be right out."

When I ended the call, Steve looked at me with concern. "Look, Lexi, I don't mean to drag you back out if you're hurting or too tired. I can interview her alone."

"No, I'm slow on these crutches, but I don't want to miss anything. Please let me go with you. Just give me a couple of minutes to check my email. I haven't been home for a while and I had some inquiries in the works."

Steve had followed me into the room and stood behind me. I found a response from Diana waiting for me. It was dated three days earlier.

Dear Lexi,

Sorry to be so slow in responding. I've attached what I've found so far regarding that inquiry you made about a former student, Roger Hartley. The first is a page from the yearbook the year he was a freshman. Additionally, I've asked around and learned that at the end of his freshman year, there was an incident that was reported in the newspaper, involving him and another student. They were renting an old house off campus that caught fire. He and the other young man were sometimes called the Hart twins because their last names were so similar and they were both attending on math scholarships. I took the time to locate the articles at the university library—hence the delay in answering your email. I remember hearing something about the boy who survived being a 'trust fund' baby without family. He was taken to the hospital and his burns treated, but the next day, after he had identified his friend, he had a total emotional collapse and remained in the local hospital psych ward for a week, sedated and without visitors. After he checked out of the hospital, he left the campus and didn't reenroll the following fall semester. All of this information is in the public domain, so I haven't violated any confidentiality laws.

Hope this is of use.

Your friend,

Diana

I printed out the attachments. The attachment was a copy of a page of pictures of freshmen from a yearbook that included young men and women with last names beginning with H. I studied the photos closely. There were humorous captions under each one such as "Born to make a million" or "Destined to be a general" or some such comment. There were two pictures that shared the same caption, labeled "The Mathematical Hart Twins." The name under one was Donald Hartzler and the other was labeled Roger Hartley. Donald Hartzler had a prominent cowlick in the front hairline of his dark brown hair and very familiar eyes. I didn't recognize the photo of the young man listed as Roger Hartley. I handed the page to Steve.

The next attachment was a copy of a newspaper article. The headline read "Fiery Death of ASU Student." As I read, part of it leaped out at me. *The body of the young man was burned beyond recognition, but was identified as Donald Hartzler by his roommate, Roger Hartley, from a ring and watch the victim had been wearing. Mr. Hartley was also injured in the fire, suffering first and second degree burns on his face, hands, and arms. The cause of the fire is still unknown but is being investigated.*

I handed the article to Steve while I checked my other emails. Dr. Landgrave at Stafford University had responded to my query. My hand shook a little as I hit the print button to retrieve the attachments with it. The copies of pages of three sequential yearbooks printed out; sophomore, junior, and senior classes where the students with last names beginning with H were pictured.

He had simply written, "This is all I can send you without violating the university rules of confidentiality. Hope it helps."

It did. There was no Donald Hartzler on those three pages but there was a Roger Hartley who had a familiar and very prominent cowlick in his front hairline. Under the picture was written, "Born to succeed, graduated *summa cum laude.*"

I put the pictures side by side and studied them. I sat speechless for nearly a minute before I could whisper, "Well, I think we've got our answer. Donald Hartzler, the son of LL's first wife, made the switch to being Roger Hartley through arson and murder." I put my head in my hands. "I wish we had seen this information three or four days ago, before Roger gave me that ride out beyond Cave Creek. I almost died because we didn't know this sooner."

Steve put his hand on my shoulder while he took another couple of minutes to read the newspaper articles and the information from Landgrave. He laid the pages on my desk, and said simply, "But you didn't." I stood and he pulled me to him for a careful and tender embrace. When he released me, he said quietly, "It looks like we have our answers. Now let's go out to visit Tiffany and see if we can locate the money."

After we climbed into his car, he reached over and opened the glove compartment. He pulled out Uncle Bob's gun and handed it to me.

I opened my bag and regretfully dropped it in. Roger was dead and gone, and for that matter, so was Stan. But that loaded gun made it clear that Steve wasn't sure we knew the entire story.

We got to Tiffany's within twenty minutes with the use of the lights and siren. Steve was really charged up about the possibility of our uncovering a lead that might take us to the money.

When the housekeeper opened the door, we could see several suitcases sitting in the foyer. It looked as if they were going to be gone a while. Emma led us to the white, sunken living room and pointed to the couches. Steve was too agitated to sit so he stood while we waited for Tiffany.

My appearance startled her. "Lexi, you look awful. Did Roger do that to you?"

I nodded. "I'll heal. It looks worse than it is."

"You poor dear. I'm so sorry you're injured." From her voice, I wouldn't have guessed it. She turned toward Steve. "What's so important that you've rushed out to see me?" Her perfect eyebrows were arched. "I thought the investigation had been completed."

"We needed to ask you about a trip you took to the Caribbean last March. Lexi mentioned that Roger took his vacation about the same time you took a trip to Bermuda, and we were wondering if he might have accompanied you or might have met you there."

Tiffany looked genuinely perplexed. She shook her head. "No, I've traveled with girlfriends or my sister on some of those trips," her voice began to show irritation, "but never with Roger or any other man." She looked at me with narrowed eyes, as if I had been going around slandering her reputation.

Steve cleared his throat. "Let me explain the situation, Mrs. Lattimer. We're trying to locate the money Roger embezzled from the company. Apparently, he got away with at least four million from the Sunnyville project alone, and probably substantially more from other projects, but we're sure it's not in any US bank. An amount like that, even if divided among several banks, would draw the attention of the IRS. So it has occurred to us that perhaps he took that vacation trip somewhere where he could arrange to put the funds in an offshore bank. The Caribbean seemed to be a likely spot."

He had managed to smooth her ruffled feathers. She said simply, "Oh, I see." She looked off into the distance, perhaps seeing those sun-drenched islands in her mind. "There are several prominent banks there that come to mind, such as the Bank of Aruba, the Mercantile Bank of the Caribbean, and the National Bank of Bermuda. There must be others, but I can't think of any at the moment." She paused and added, "I do remember Roger asking me if I had ever hired a private jet that could make it to the Caribbean from here. I laughed and told him to look in the Yellow Pages. I didn't think he was serious." Her brow wrinkled just the slightest bit. "Even if you knew the bank someone used, I've heard that they use numbered accounts, so if Roger put the money there, how would anyone find it?"

Steve looked like he had just come face to face with a harsh reality. "You're right. Even if we knew where he put it, we may still not be able to get at it." He stood and offered his hand. "Thank you for your time. I hope you have a good trip."

"With my sister along, I'm sure I will. She needs to get away as much as I do."

We were led to the door and when it closed behind us, Steve said, "I was hoping for some easy answer, but it looks like there aren't any."

I suppose this is probably what most investigative work is like—rush here and there in the hope of gaining new information but coming away with crumbs. We climbed into the car and he pointed it down the long driveway.

"Steve, if I had a numbered account in an offshore bank, I'd be sure to keep the account number somewhere safe but where I could get to it in a hurry, if I needed to. I'd make sure it wouldn't likely be found by anyone else."

He didn't respond for a minute, but then glanced over at me and grinned, "Are you too tired to take a look at Roger's place?"

"No. I'd love to see it. Do you think we might find the account number there?"

"Yesterday afternoon, I was part of a team from the Mesa P.D. that went through it, and the Bureau will have gone through it by now, so to be realistic, we aren't likely to locate anything, but who knows? Anyway, why don't we take a look?"

CHAPTER 22

It was about two thirty when we parked in front of a two-story Spanish hacienda that was painted a pale cream color. Steve helped me climb the stairs to the front porch that was almost hidden by Spanish arches supported on graceful columns that extended across the entire lower floor. Each window was protected by decorative wrought-iron grating. I assumed that Roger had a small apartment in the building as several of the large, older homes in the neighborhood had several mailboxes on their porches.

Steve explained, "When I tried to locate Roger at the address he had given me in that first interview, and I couldn't find him, the tenant living at that address told me that he had bought this big house across the street some time ago and had steadily renovated it. His neighbor said that several people had come looking for him at the old address, and packages were occasionally delivered there. When that happened, the neighbor just sent the delivery men or visitors across the street."

"So when he wasn't with Tiffany, he was probably working on this. Frankly, I'm impressed."

I could see a computer-printed, eight-by-eleven sheet of paper taped to the front door that read, "Restricted. No trespassing." He dropped to his knees and pulled out a leather pouch of locksmith tools. He talked as he worked. "Both the Mesa P.D. and the Bureau had to enter without a key, but this isn't a difficult lock."

When we walked in, I was startled by the size of the room. Roger had taken out the walls between what probably had been the master bedroom and the living and dining rooms, making the entire first floor, with the exception of the kitchen, a display of exquisite furniture. Pillars had replaced the support walls. Everything was remarkable in its uniqueness. The walnut plantation shutters inside the windows were the only modern touch to the room. Steve tipped them open and I could see dust motes dancing in the streams of afternoon sunlight.

A dark gold and blue Oriental carpet of superb quality covered the floor. As Steve moved around, I ran my eyes over the room. "Wow," was all I could say.

I had learned a fair amount about antiques from my mother and Aunt Betty as I grew up—whether or not I wanted to. They were both antique hobbyists and had dragged Percy and me around to antique shops every Saturday—or so it seemed. Our coffee table in the living room was always covered with magazines about antiques.

I immediately recognized a Victorian campaign loveseat with its swept-out sides. A Hepplewhite table sat in what had been the master bedroom, and a Tudor Regency table with Sheraton dining room chairs sat in the dining area. On the opposite wall, there was a Victorian double-end, show-frame sofa. A full set of Spode china was displayed in a breakfront.

"Wow," I said again.

Steve nodded at me and used his public library voice, "Remember that the place has been searched before, so we need to look in places that were missed, if there are any. We know we're looking for an account number. They didn't."

I had the feeling that we were trespassing somehow. While he carefully pulled out drawers and turned them over to check the bottom of each one, I slowly explored the rest of the house with the help of my crutches. A Newport grandfather clock stood on the landing of the stairs. I hobbled up the stairs to an upstairs bedroom, where there was a fourteenth-century Tudor chest with Saint George and the Dragon carved on the front. It sat at the foot of a nineteenth century four-poster bed. Also in that room was a chiffonier that I though might be a Riesener. The house was filled with rare, remarkable pieces.

I limped back down to the main room where, with Steve's help, I carefully pulled the backing off several fine paintings but found nothing. We systematically made our way around the house, trying not to damage anything. "Wherever it is, it would be somewhere easy to access," Steve mused as he examined the interior of a cabinet.

I was bending over a refractory table when the thought struck me. I stood up abruptly. "Steve, how stupid can we be? We're looking at the money. It's right here."

He pulled his head out of the lower portion of the cabinet and asked, "Come again? What do you mean?"

"This house is filled with rare antiques. That's where he put the money—at least a big piece of it. I'll bet these items collectively are worth a fortune."

I turned and looked at the bookcase. "Take a look at the books. I'm almost positive they'll all prove to be first editions." I read some of the titles aloud. "*A Passage to India* by E.M. Forster; *Journal of a Voyage to New South Wales* by John White; Dante's *Divine Comedy*; Poe's *Tamerlane*. These titles are too eclectic to reflect his reading tastes. He's obviously collected them for their value. He must have been intending to sell them soon, or they would have been put in a temperature- and humidity-controlled environment. If kept here for any length of time, they'll deteriorate."

I looked around again. "The value of the furniture, art, and books might rise to the level of—oh, I don't know—maybe as much as a half a million dollars, but I doubt that these things represent all of the money. Surely, he would want cash that was easily accessible."

Steve stood up and brushed off his knees. "If the furniture and books are worth so much, why is there a bunch of worthless stuff on the built-in shelves on that wall near the kitchen door? Do you suppose that he has a sentimental side and those are childhood treasures?"

I turned and from where I stood I could see four children's blocks on the top shelf: an uppercase *M* and a *B*, a lowercase *o* and an uppercase *C* facing the viewer. Next to the blocks was a low, inexpensive ceramic dish holding (I counted) nine marbles. Next was a cluster of five nesting dolls probably from Eastern Europe of the kind that you can buy in any tourist market. A vacant space left me wondering if something had been removed. Next was a cluster of four dice. A single, inexpensive bud vase stood on the next shelf with three artificial roses in it. The last item was a large, low bowl with four, shiny red Christmas ornaments in it.

"Could it be a code?" I wondered aloud.

Steve's face lit up as he caught my drift. I picked up my bag, which I had set by the door, and pulled out my cell phone. With one click, I had a picture of the odd arrangement. "Take out your pen and notebook and let's see if we can make this into an account number. Let's suppose that the blocks stand for the Mercantile Bank of the Caribbean that Tiffany mentioned, and the first number is nine, the second five, and—I hope something isn't missing. Let's say the vacant space represents a zero." Steve was writing as I talked.

I walked over to the dice and picked up each one, noting that each one was a deuce. "The spots total eight, but perhaps four twos are part of the number. On the next shelf we have one vase with three flowers in it. Could be a three, or a one and a three, or a thirteen. The last number could be a four. That gives us several potential sequences."

Steve looked up and smiled broadly. "We don't have to figure this out ourselves. Let's take that picture and our notes to the FBI office and talk to Castello, the agent handling this case. He can point us to someone who can tell us which sequence is most likely an account number for an offshore bank. They should know things like that."

We locked up the place and headed downtown. He handed me his cell phone. "Bring up the directory. There's a number in it for the local FBI office. Call and ask for Castello. Tell him we need to talk to someone who has some expertise in offshore accounts."

Special Agent Mel Castello transferred me to an agent by the name of Smithfield who invited us to discuss the matter in his office at four fifteen. It was three forty five at the time. When we arrived, we parked in the lot behind the square block of a federal building with the façade of identical square, inset windows. Cement-filled posts along the sidewalk in front were meant to keep vehicles away from the entrance.

Knowing that there was a security check inside, I put the gun Steve had loaned me into the glove box. He was forced to leave his weapon when we identified ourselves for the security guards. "You can pick it up on the way out, Detective," one of them said as he pointed toward the elevators. "You want the fifth floor."

We rode up in the elevator, passing two floors of social security offices and two other floors of unlabeled federal offices. The remaining two floors were given over to the FBI, ATF, ICE, and several other agencies designated by abbreviated alphabet labels.

The receptionist in the FBI lobby smiled in a businesslike manner and responded when we identified ourselves. "You're expected. I'll tell Special Agents Castello and Smithfield you're here."

We waited there until a tall man with dark hair entered and extended his hand. "Hello, I'm Special Agent Castello. I understand you may have some information on matters related to the Benson kidnapping and the Lattimer murder and embezzlement case." He pointed us to the chairs in front of his desk. We sat.

I vaguely remembered him. It seemed to me that he had come to the hospital while I was still groggy from pain medication after falling down the mountainside, and had asked a few questions I could no longer remember. Evidently, he obtained all the information he needed from Steve's reports, since I had had no more interaction with him.

Steve introduced himself and added, "And this is Lexi Benson, the kidnap victim that brought the Bureau into the case."

He stepped over and shook my hand. "Glad to see you're doing so well, Ms. Benson. A lot of kidnap victims don't fare as well as you." As I stood there on my crutches in my bruised and battered condition, I wondered what he meant. Then it dawned on me—he meant that I was alive.

He turned to look at Steve. "I've got the file on the case on my desk. Please follow me and we'll talk in my office."

Castello held the doors for me as we moved down a hall to his office. It was almost spartan, though it did have carpeting in an olive green. One wall was nearly covered by tan, government-issue file cabinets. He pointed toward two chairs arranged in front of the desk. "Special Agent Smithfield will be joining us in a minute or two."

We didn't say anything more until Smithfield entered the room. He went through the usual greetings and handshakes before he pulled up another chair and sat next to me.

Castello looked from one of us to the other. "Now you've got our attention."

Steve looked at me. "Lexi, I think these men are going to want to see the picture on your phone."

I pulled it from my bag, pressed the buttons to show the picture I had taken in Roger's home, and handed it to Castello.

"We think that the display of items on these shelves may be a code for a numbered offshore account," I explained.

Castello's eyebrows pulled together in puzzlement before he handed the phone to Smithfield. As Smithfield studied the picture, Steve pulled out his notebook. "We went through the suspect's home after your agents finished their search, looking for a clue as to where he might have put the money he embezzled. Lexi suggested that the items on the shelves might be a clue to an account number. In order they are—" He proceeded to list each item.

When he got to the four dice all turned to two dots, Smithfield stopped him and asked, "Miss Benson, what gave you the idea that these things could be some kind of a code for an account?"

"The apartment was full of valuable antiques and first editions, but these two shelves are just kitsch—junk. We thought for a moment that perhaps our suspect had a sentimental side and they held some childhood memories, but we gave up that idea fast." I looked at Steve and then back at the two men. "We both suspect that he set the fires that killed his parents, as well as a former roommate, so he's not the sentimental kind."

The two agents looked at each other. "Is there evidence of that?" Castello asked.

Steve shook his head. "It's all pretty circumstantial." He nodded toward me to prompt me to continue.

"The four blocks at the beginning of the top shelf made me think that they might stand for the Mercantile Bank of the Caribbean. If that's so, then each item or cluster of items could suggest a number in the account. If this is the case, the dice could represent four twos or an eight. The bud vase and three artificial roses could possibly represent a one and a three or maybe thirteen. Do you see what I mean?"

While I had been talking, Smithfield had been writing the numbers on a yellow legal pad, arranging them in alternative ways. He looked up. "What else was on the second shelf?"

I responded, "A shallow bowl with four Christmas ornaments in it."

"You're sure they were Christmas ornaments?"

"Yes."

I watched him make a capital C and a four. Then he held it at arm's length and showed it to Castello. He nodded with satisfaction.

Smithfield stood and asked, "Do you have any other photos like that on your phone?" I shook my head.

He stood and shook our hands. Castello followed his example. We were being dismissed. "I need to have a copy of the photo. I'll have one of our tech people take the phone and get a copy. We'll get it back to you in a few minutes. Can you wait?"

"Sure." I looked at Steve.

He smiled and said, "No problem."

We returned to the waiting area, and in about twenty minutes, a woman wearing a white lab coat entered. Approaching me, she asked, "Miss Benson?" I nodded. "Here's your phone. Special Agent

Smithfield asked me to thank you for coming in." With that she was gone.

I started to put the telephone back into my bag, but Steve put out his hand. He pressed a couple of buttons and then began to laugh before he handed it back to me. As we rode down in the elevator, he said, "They made sure to delete the picture."

"Why would they do that?"

"Apparently, they don't want us to share it with anyone else. They'll be going through that house again before an hour has passed."

CHAPTER 23

Against Aunt Betty's wishes, I returned to work on Friday. My bruises were still evident but I was getting better with the crutch. The first thing I did when I got to the office was locate an empty box in one of the closets. I put everything from my desk in it and managed to push it over to LL's desk with the crutch. There, I sat down in his chair, leaned the crutch against the desk, and put my purse on the floor by my feet.

I decided to keep LL's awards on his desk to remind me that I needed to take the place of a good man who left very big shoes to fill. I was looking forward to having Ted Jorgenson and the company lawyer, Morton Zigler, joining me on Monday.

I was expecting a telephone call from Steve. He had suggested that we get together for lunch. I began collecting all the paper clips that had accumulated in the middle drawer of LL's desk and putting them into a clip holder when I heard a knock on the front office door.

I called out, "Come in!" Not many people ever knocked. I called out louder, "It's open. Come in."

The door opened and all I saw was a huge floral arrangement and two legs. A deliveryman was literally hidden behind it. In the parking area I could see a brown delivery truck with *Flowers Abloom* printed on the side. Below that in smaller print, it read *Free Delivery*. I started to laugh, thinking that Steve had really gone overboard.

"Who sent me flowers?" I stood. He leaned against the office door, closing it behind him.

"Put it on the table over there," I said as I pointed to one of the large tables where we read blueprints. "Do you have a card or something to tell me who sent them?" I still hadn't seen his face.

An arm appeared from behind the arrangement and he handed me one of those tiny envelopes used by florists. I opened it as he carried the flowers to the table.

I read two words, "From Roger." Anxiety suddenly became a cold, heavy mass in my chest. I looked up as he sat the floral arrangement on the table, straightened up, and turned to face me. He wore a brown jacket with the emblem of a wireless floral service on it, but I immediately recognized the head of straw-colored hair. It was Chuck.

A malicious smile distorted his face. At that moment, his expression had all the charm of an awakened cobra. "I see *you're* using LL's desk now, sitting all alone in the office like a queen." His eyes glistened as hard as polished stones.

His behavior had awakened a primal fear, the same fear roused by Roger five days before, and I felt as if I had suddenly fallen into a cold, fast-flowing stream. I tried to steady my voice. "Hello, Chuck. . . . What brings you here?"

He laughed. The sound could have frozen prey in its tracks— and I knew I was that prey. Trying to use some bravado to hide my nervousness, I asked somewhat curtly, "Why are you delivering flowers? With Bergman gone, is the Phoenix office so chaotic that you've gotten another job?" I looked at my watch as if checking the time.

As if to answer my wish, the phone began to ring, but with narrowed eyes, he ordered, "Don't answer it. You don't have an appointment this morning." The phone continued to ring. "Did you forget that Roger had a key to the office? He gave me a copy weeks ago. I've been coming and checking your schedule. I've been watching to see if you were sharing the office with anyone." He added in a whisper filled with pure hate, "But the queen likes her space and her privacy." The phone finally quit.

I felt like a moth in a jar, batting its wings against the glass, my thoughts unable to offer a way to escape. *How stupid could I have been? Why didn't I think to change the lock? We all thought our problems were over once Roger was dead.*

Ice crystals began to form up and down my spine. I was suddenly so angry with myself and frightened of him that I felt dizzy. I vaguely remembered seeing a floral delivery truck pass my car on Adobe Road that morning. I had wondered what would bring a delivery truck for a floral shop way out here, so far east of the metro area.

I raised my voice and demanded, "Why are you here, Chuck?" When he didn't respond, I filled the silence with more questions. "Have you been part of this conspiracy with Roger all along?" He continued to stand there, arms folded across his chest, silently enjoying my quiet panic. "Was it you who tried to kill me with the bulldozer? Was it you who followed me home after the wake?" The expression on his face was one of malicious pride. "Was it Bergman who tried to blow up my car," his eyes looked disappointed, as if I had suddenly robbed him of well-deserved praise, "or was it you?"

An expression of grim satisfaction told me it was him. "Everybody except Roger always treated me like a dumb farm boy from Minnesota—simple, hardworking Chuck; harmless, not quite bright Chuck." His voice went hard. "Well, I'm not simple or harmless, and Roger was smart enough to realize that."

"But what was in it for you? Was it money? Are you looking to move up to running the Phoenix office? Were you in it together—killing LL, I mean?"

He finally spoke. "Roger offered me money—a lot of it. And with LL gone, we knew it wouldn't be hard to get rid of Bergman. Roger and I were a team, a good one—until you killed him."

I was immediately defensive. "I didn't kill him. He tried to kill me and died in the attempt."

"What does it matter? It's still your fault." He stuck his face in mine and whispered. "Yes, I drove the bulldozer. It was me that followed you home from the wake. And I put the explosives in your car—not Bergman. I've been handling explosives for years, taking out tree stumps on my father's farm. Roger asked me to handle the situation there at the warehouse as well because I know every square inch of that building."

In my purse, my cell phone began to ring. Instinctively, I reached for it.

"Don't touch it," he yelled, but I had the clasp of the bag in my hand. I had never wanted anything as badly as I wanted the gun that was in it. I popped the bag open and was bringing the gun up to point at him when he lunged. He grabbed the gun with both hands and literally pulled me up from the chair as he tried to yank it out of my hand. His hands were wrapped like a vice around my hand and the cylinder of the revolver so it wouldn't fire.

I hit him on the side of his head with the cast on my left hand, crushing his ear against his skull. It seemed to stun him so I hit him again. He staggered backward, the gun flying from away from both of us and sliding across the floor.

He rushed at me again in a full-blown rage, lunging and striking me on the chin with his full strength. I fell hard against the desk, feeling it bruise the flesh across my back. I tumbled to the floor with the room spinning.

The force of my fall moved the heavy desk at least six inches and knocked over LL's three awards and the trophy. I struggled to my knees. I felt an urgent need to get up off the floor for fear that he might charge at me and start to kick me like an angry child in a temper tantrum.

As I struggled to pull myself up by leaning against the desk, he pulled a small automatic from the pocket of his uniform jacket. "Stay where you are."

I was full of adrenaline. I reached behind myself to locate something on the desk to use to defend myself. My fingers wrapped around one of the awards. I threw it with all the strength I had, and for once, my seventh grade softball team would have been proud of me. It hit him full on the sternum. He staggered back against one of the file cabinets. His gun went off, but the bullet passed over my head and through the wall.

As he tried to regain his balance, he aimed the gun at me, so I grabbed another award and threw it. As it hit his shoulder, the gun went off again and I heard another bullet zing past my ear. A window behind me shattered.

I made an inarticulate sound that I hoped was a scream, trying to draw someone's attention in the other office. I grabbed the third award and threw it, and with the help of Providence, it hit him in the forehead. He stumbled back into the file cabinet and went down to his knees and then to his face in slow motion.

I rushed at him and knelt on his back with one knee, while I pulled the gun from his hand. "Stop it, Chuck. I've got the gun. Just give it up. Don't make me shoot you." I was talking a hundred miles an hour.

In the hope of getting help, I pointed the gun toward the window and squeezed the trigger twice. He rolled over as I squeezed the trigger the third time, toppling me onto the floor. He grabbed my hand with the gun in it and held it against the floor like a vice. His other hand went around my throat.

He hissed through clenched teeth, "Let go of the gun or I'll snap your neck." Someone pounded on the door. It was locked for some reason I couldn't fathom. Then in a flash, I realized that Chuck, as the innocuous deliveryman, had managed to turn the deadbolt when he had closed the door, hidden behind all those flowers.

I began to make chuffing sounds like a dog in a choke collar as he increased the pressure on my throat. He put his face in mine, the malevolent grin back on his face. I could hear a humming in my ears and the room was beginning to fade to black. I hit him in the head again with the cast on my left hand. He straightened his elbows, pulling away from my reach. That eased his grip on my throat and I pulled my right wrist loose but the gun slipped out of my grip.

I grabbed a breath and tried to scratch at his eyes but only took in a handful of air. He was leaning away from me. His arms must have been three inches longer than mine. I heard someone throw himself against the door.

With all the strength in my adrenaline-filled body, I twisted at the waist enough to pull up my knees, almost against my chest. My right knee and bruised hip screamed with pain as I shot out my feet as hard as I could and hit him in the gut. He grunted, and the momentum of my kick pushed me away from him.

I rolled onto my hands and feet and tried to scramble toward the gun on the floor, but from where he was lying, he reached out and grabbed my right foot. I kicked at his face with the other foot. I caught him in the jaw.

I was pulling air frantically into my lungs as I struggled to stand. I grabbed the desk and twisted so I could stomp on the hand around my other ankle.

That forced him to release his grip, allowing me to pull away and turn on him, but he reached out and picked up his gun. I leaped on him with both elbows pointed like spears, pushing him flat against the floor. The impact made my elbows hurt like I had run into a brick wall but his hand was still holding the gun. I bent and locked my teeth onto his right wrist.

He yelled in indignant rage and rose to all fours, throwing me off onto my back. He brought his fist down on my head. Flashes of light filled the sudden darkness that engulfed me, but even in my stunned condition, I could hear the sound of breaking glass.

"I'll kill you if you try to come in," I heard him yell.

When the room stopped moving, I tried to focus my eyes. I saw Chuck pointing his gun at the heads of three of the accountants, including Ted Jorgenson, who had broken the window above the blueprint tables. They paused in response to his threat.

Ted pleaded with him, "The police are on their way. If you take off right now, you can get away. Look, you can take my truck. You'll be halfway to Mexico before they get on your trail." Ted threw his keys at him. "It's the black Dodge Ram."

"You think I'm scared of the police?" He was still yelling.

They were distracting him, allowing me to inch away from him. I looked around for my gun. I was within six feet of it so I scooted on my backside until I reached it. As I grabbed it from under the desk, I could hear sirens in the distance.

Chuck rose to his feet and, still holding his gun, bent to pick up the keys Ted had thrown at him. As he stood, I pointed my gun at him and yelled, "Put up your hands or I'll shoot you." My hands were shaking from fear and exhaustion.

He stared at me and the gun I was holding as if he didn't believe me. He raised his gun so I fired. The bullet hit him in the left upper arm. He looked surprised but it was evident that he wasn't feeling a thing.

I had been so sure I would hit him in the chest, but I had missed. It hadn't even entered my head that he wouldn't go down if I shot him. I wasn't mentally prepared to squeeze that trigger a second time, a nearly fatal mindset.

"Put the gun down, Lexi. I'm a much better shot than you." He didn't believe that I would shoot him again, even though I still had the gun pointed at him. "Get up. We're going on a little ride and you're my ticket out of here." As he waved his gun at me, I squeezed the trigger again. It hit him high in the left shoulder. The impact made him take a small step backward.

His jaw tightened. "If I shoot, I won't miss." He spoke each word separately to convey his seriousness. "Now put it down and get up."

I put it down, looking at it as if it had betrayed me. I struggled to stand on my injured knee and raised both hands. He took three steps over to me, put the gun to my head and wrapped his left arm tightly around my throat. I grabbed his arm with my right hand to try to ease the pressure. Dragging me along, he backed toward the office door while he faced the accountants watching through the broken window. The sirens were getting louder, but he showed no sign of hearing them.

I was so close to him that I could smell his body scent. It was strong with the sharp smell of sweat. Rage was pouring from his skin.

I was soaked to the skin with the perspiration of fear. With the gun against my temple, I didn't hesitate to cooperate. As he backed toward the door, I offered no resistance. When he reached it, he pivoted, pulling me around so I was facing it. "Open it," he hissed into my ear.

My right hand was slick with sweat, but somehow I managed to turn the deadbolt and the doorknob. My heart was beating against my ribs like the frantic wings of a dying bird.

As he pushed me through the doorway, I could see red and blue dome lights blinking in the distance accompanied by the wail of several police cars that were rushing along Adobe Road toward us. He paused to look around for only a fraction of a second. Suddenly, I was sprawled across the ground in front of the building.

When I looked over my shoulder, I could see that Steve had jumped on Chuck's back when we came through the door. As they struggled over the gun, they went down in a heap in the gravel of the parking lot.

I labored to my feet and watched in horror for a fraction of a second. I hobbled close enough to grab Chuck around the neck as he rolled on top of Steve. With his neck in the crook of my right arm, I pulled with all my strength. I wasn't strong enough to be a real threat to him, but at least I could be a distraction. He hardly seemed to notice, so I hit him on top of the head with my splintering cast. That left him stunned just enough that Steve was able to throw him off and onto the ground, the gun dropping from his grip.

As police cars braked in the gravel and slid to a halt, the officers dropped out of the vehicles behind their open car doors with guns drawn. Turning my head, I noted at least a half dozen guns pointing at us with more to come as other police cars arrived.

Someone with a bullhorn ordered, "Hands up. Put down your weapons." I put my hands in the air. Steve stood and identified himself, displaying his badge. "This man's under arrest," he yelled.

Chuck paid no attention to the police. Instead, he reached for the gun on the ground and, grabbing it, stood unsteadily. He lunged at me, screaming, "You ruined everything! Everything!"

I tried to back away from him, but my knee buckled and he pulled the trigger as I fell on my back. Several of the police officers fired, and Chuck seemed to melt there in the dusty gravel parking lot, folding into a lump of what had once been a man.

When Steve reached me, I could see blood running down his face. He wiped the drops from his chin with the back of his hand, leaving a bloody smear. "How bad are you hurt?"

"I'm okay. Are *you* all right?"

He looked at the blood on his hand. "I don't think it's serious." He put out his hand to help me up.

"Thank you for saving my life," I whispered.

He pulled me to him and whispered, "It's over now. It's finally over." I clung to him.

By this time the police were swarming the place. The ranking officer approached Steve. "Detective Sutherland, there's an ambulance on the way." He called out, "Johnson, Beyers, escort Detective Sutherland and the lady into the office. Find them a place to sit until the ambulance gets here. Maybe we can get some questions answered."

Steve helped me limp toward the office. "How did you know he was here?" I asked.

"Your sister Percy called me. She was almost frantic by the time the dispatcher figured out who she wanted to talk to. She was talking so fast I could hardly tell what she was saying, but when I got her to slow down so I could understand, she insisted that she had some kind of premonition telling her that you were in trouble. She said that she ignored a similar premonition a few days ago, and as a result, you nearly died on that mountain. She demanded that I do something. To pacify her I told her I'd call you right away." About the time we found a place to sit in the office, the ambulance arrived.

Steve told the EMT that he wasn't hurt badly enough to go to the hospital. "That guy on the ground needs you more than I do."

The second ambulance attendant had just checked Chuck's body. He responded, "He doesn't need anyone."

The officer in charge ordered, "You *will* go to the hospital. That's department policy." He looked at me. "You go too. You're covered with blood and the way you're limping, you need to see a doctor as well." It was then I realized that I had a lot of Chuck's blood on the back of my shirt.

After we had climbed into the back of the ambulance, Steve's bleeding head was examined. My cast was in bad condition and my hand hurt—a lot.

Steve continued his explanation. "When you didn't answer the office number, I tried your cell. When you didn't answer it, I called the other office. While I was talking to one of the architects, he told me they heard what sounded like gunshots, and that a florist's van had been in the parking lot much too long for a delivery. Ted and a couple of accountants went to investigate."

"God bless them. They distracted him long enough for you and the cavalry to ride to my rescue." I was caught off guard by the tears that nearly overflowed. I forced them back.

He gave me a tender smile as the attendant taped a gauze pad over the cut on his forehead. "When I realized that you were in danger again, I decided then and there that if we both came through it, I was . . ." His voice was suddenly too tight to continue.

When we were pushed into the emergency room in wheelchairs, I was pleased to see the same doctor who had treated me after my adventure at the Sunnyville golf course and on the mountain. He knew my name. It was almost like he had become my own personal physician.

As I was pushed into a cubicle in the emergency room, he shook his head. "Well, Miss Benson, it looks like that cast I put on your hand will have to be replaced. What have you been doing with it, using it as a pile driver?"

"You might say that."

The X-ray showed that I had broken another bone in my wrist while hitting Chuck, but I considered it a small price to pay to be alive.

I could hear someone questioning Steve in the next cubicle. The voice sounded like the officer who had ordered us to the hospital. The interview ended with him stating firmly, "Come into headquarters and complete your report as soon as the doctor says you can."

"I'll be in tomorrow. Can someone give me a lift back out to the site so I can get my car?"

"You left your keys in it so I had an officer drive it over here for you. It's in the parking lot." He was evidently through with Steve. He spoke through the curtain separating the cubicles. "Doc, when can I talk with Miss Benson?"

I responded. "The doctor is just replacing my cast. You can come in right now if you want to."

While my cast was replaced, I answered his questions. He admonished me in the same way he had Steve. "Come in for a more formal statement tomorrow when you feel up to it."

When we were both released, I waited in a wheelchair while Steve brought the car around to the emergency entrance and picked me up. We were both pleased to see that my crutch had been put in the back seat. When we reached my place, I insisted that he come in so he could sit down and relax. I was so grateful that we were both alive, and I wanted to just sit and enjoy that feeling, but after a frantic telephone call from Percy, we were quickly overwhelmed by her and Aunt Betty, who had both been waiting for a report on what had brought on Percy's fearful intuition. Within two minutes, Mrs. Bolton had joined us. I decided to just relax and enjoy the attention.

CHAPTER 24

I've thought a lot about Roger and Chuck and how their disregard for any kind of moral code destroyed or injured so many people. I'll never understand their choices, but at least some questions have been answered. Some have not. The county M.E. did a postmortem on both of them, and both showed meth and cocaine in their systems when they died. That was why Chuck hadn't been stopped by Uncle Bob's .22 revolver.

"I would never have been able to subdue him if you hadn't put a couple of bullets in him. He was like a raging bull when we fought," Steve explained.

"My aim should have been better. I never dreamed that two bullets would hardly slow him down."

"We should see that you get some target practice in the future." He was smiling when he said it, but he meant it.

"Okay, but I fervently hope I never need to shoot anyone . . . ever again."

Roseanna Gardner and her husband returned home a week after Roger's death made the news. She called one of the detectives who had interviewed her neighbors and explained that on the Saturday morning before the contract signing at the office, she had pulled LL aside and told him about the white powder she found while cleaning the restroom. She suspected it was cocaine, something that had taken the life of her son a couple of years earlier. LL knew that only the three of us used that restroom, so he was sure that he needed to talk to Roger about it. That was probably what had gotten LL killed sooner than Roger had originally intended. Fearing that LL had said something that would motivate Roger to go after her, she and her husband had fled.

Bergman was the author of the note that was pushed under the office door. His handwriting matched. He may have been trying to frighten me into stepping aside so he could fill LL's shoes.

Steve believes that Chuck probably planned to take Bergman's position at the helm of the Phoenix office, at least in his own mind. In all likelihood, Roger planned to take LL's place running the company with me out of the way and would have continued to court Tiffany in the hope of actually owning the company. If that had come about, Tiffany would have probably died young. But let's face it; we may never know all the answers.

As part of the investigation, Steve confiscated the mail that came to the office in Roger's name. The statements from the trust department of the National Bank showed regular deposits to the checking account of Roger Hartley in the amount of five thousand dollars a month from the trust account of Mr. Jasper and Mrs. Wilma Hartley, deceased. Those monthly payments must have been the motive for the death of the real Roger Hartley in his freshman year of college. He would have still been alive if he'd shared a room with any other guy.

We soon determined that there was a relationship between Tiffany and Corstelli—or at least, one developed quickly. They slipped off quietly three months later to be married in Bermuda.

• • •

The company is doing well and I think I can take at least an itty-bitty part of the credit. I regularly use the expertise of the local project managers, which makes all the difference. Like LL, I know that I don't know it all.

One of my first big decisions once we had fully measured the financial damage done by Roger was to follow Bergman's advice. We bought Sunnyville Estates from the bank at auction.

The extradition order for Hebestreet came through within two weeks once Steve talked to the FBI and they put their efforts into the situation. The bank foreclosed on the warehouse lofts, and with Tiffany's blessing, my second major decision was to have LL Construction buy that project at auction as well.

I offered Bergman's job to Rocky Steelman from the Tucson/ Casa Grande office. He's proving to be a good choice.

Steve and I laughed heartily when we saw the story in the paper about how the FBI had located the funds embezzled from LL Construction in a bank in the Caribbean. Our theory about the account number must have paid off—though the Bureau never admitted it.

I've requested that our corporate lawyer file the paperwork to claim both the embezzled funds and the property in Roger's house, and the house itself. It may be tedious, but I expect that we'll eventually get back a large portion of the money that was stolen.

I'm glad to report that the insurance company came through with a check for my Sebring, and for Christmas, I bought myself another car, a candy apple red Buick Lacrosse, the same color as Uncle Bob's Pontiac. The bad news is that I've got to make payments on it for another two years since the check didn't cover the entire cost, and my auto insurance rates have nearly doubled. No big surprise there. I'm lucky my agent was able to talk the company out of dropping me.

The brightest thing in my life is how I'm feeling about Steve. He has proven that he is solid, caring, sometimes funny, and often earnest—and he wants a big family. We laugh at the same things. Our faith is important to both of us, and I found his love of the Lord refreshing, considering how many men in his line of work are cynical and embittered. I've never experienced such a gentle tenderness in a man. Considering his occupation, I never cease to be amazed—and touched.

We both love music, including the heavy stuff like Beethoven, Liszt, Rachmaninoff, Tchaikovsky, and the other great composers—

and we both like the Beatles. When I finally convinced him to sit down at the piano and play for me, he didn't so much play the notes as he caressed them, calling up melodies and embroidering them, embellishing them, until the composer's themes were adorned and enriched. I love the emotions that pour from the keys under his fingers.

The episodes with Roger and Chuck taught both of us that we had begun to care for each other in a very real emotional way. With the case solved, we're free to admit that we're so much more than just "friends."

• • •

The rain finally stopped and Christmas Eve was mild. The desert seemed to glow in a burst of color that precedes the sinking of the sun. The sky was silver gray, layered with pink and lavender clouds that darkened to magenta. A hot gold light radiated above the ball of fire that had just been hidden by the horizon. I hated to leave the sight to go into the little restaurant, but we were both hungry.

When we reached the dessert of cherry pie à la mode, he pulled out a small, black velvet box from the pocket of his sport coat. The pie was immediately forgotten.

As he opened it, he looked into my eyes and said quietly. "We've been though a lot in the last couple of months, and I know there are those who would say we haven't had time to get to know each other very well, but I hope you know me well enough that you can tell me if you would be willing to spend your life—and beyond—with me."

I looked directly into his eyes and answered in as much seriousness as I could muster, considering the rate my heart was beating; "I could handle being crippled and blind, being stricken with shingles and pneumonia, and living in an open boat without warm clothing or food with a storm coming on—as long as I was with you." I didn't even look at the ring. I was trapped in those remarkable eyes.

He started to chuckle and the chuckle turned into a full-bodied laugh that drew the attention of the other diners. He laughed so hard for a minute that he had to wipe his eyes with his napkin.

After regaining his composure, he leaned over and kissed my

forehead. He smiled into my eyes. "I think I can offer you more than that."

"But you wouldn't have to."

As he slipped the simple solitaire on my finger, he leaned in and gave me an extended, gentle kiss. The other diners applauded.

Few men have ever appealed to me, not so much because I'm picky, though I am, but because I'm protective of myself. That means I disqualify most men before they show an interest. I couldn't pinpoint what allowed a man to occasionally get through my defenses. But Steve had penetrated those defenses. Maybe that can happen when a good man saves your life.

It goes without saying that Percy and Aunt Betty are nearly as thrilled about my engagement as I am. They are so glad to see their sister and niece looking seriously at marriage to a man they both approve of.

Hoping to find an occupation that will be more conducive to family life, Steve has spent some time looking into several different lines of work, and a few days ago, he received an offer to head the security at the local division of a major aircraft manufacturer.

When he told me, I insisted, "I'm willing to make you the center of my life no matter what job you have. Don't change just because you want to please me."

"But I want a job with time for home and family."

What more could I ask?

EPILOGUE

Occasionally, when I'm sitting quietly enveloped in my thoughts, a shadow falls across my happiness. I've continued to dwell too much on the death of LL—and of my parents.

But last night LL came to me in a dream. The contents of the dream were confused. The landscape was almost familiar, but not quite. Events around me didn't make sense but he was there, alive and whole, and completely like himself. Somehow, I knew he had come to say good-bye. I'd never taken the opportunity to tell him how much he had meant to me. I had always thought there would be time for me to share my feelings with him. It hadn't been a lifetime of friendship—just three years of working for and with him—but his influence on me was profound.

In that dream, I clung to him, and for a brief moment, he turned into my father. I coaxed him to stay, but he wanted me to let him go. He didn't say anything, but I knew. He didn't chide me for trying to keep him there, but I could sense that he wanted to move on. In the end, I set him free with gratitude and affection. He smiled and waved before he disappeared.

When I woke, I was weeping for him, for my parents, and for everyone I'd ever had to let go of.

After a few minutes, I got out of bed and went to my front door.

I threw it open. The sun was rising above the jagged peaks of the Superstition Mountains and tinting the underside of the streams of clouds in the eastern sky. Violet, deep rose, and pink ran together on a background of azure like watercolors on a canvas. The smell of the desert air was sweet and brisk, and seemed almost radiant as if permeated with suspended gold dust.

For a few moments I watched the birds frolic from branch to branch in the orange trees, as they chatted with each other in satisfaction at the change in the weather. A mockingbird was singing his entire repertoire in a tribute to life.

To the south, beyond a swath of blue sky, cumulous clouds were piled like a bubble bath. The air was washed clean. I was ready to give freedom to all those who had gone on ahead. Their mortal lives were written but mine had much yet to compose.

I would never want to go through something like I'd been through with Roger—or Chuck—again, but I'm deeply grateful for the insight I gained into myself and, more especially, for the man I'm going to marry in September. Without Roger, who knows . . .

DISCUSSION QUESTIONS

1 Do we let the death of someone we love paralyze us or do we direct our steps through the grief and embrace the resulting altered life?

2 Do we accept positions that may intimidate or do we refuse them or flee, hoping to eventually become better prepared or more confident?

3 When we feel threatened, do we withdraw or hide, or hold on for the better good?

4 When faced with challenging problems, do we actively seek solutions or expect someone else to do it for us?

5 When we make a choice or a decision, are we prepared to deal with the attached consequences, or do we believe sometimes we can be free of those consequences "because no one will find out"?

6 How does the disregard of the moral laws of God on the part of one person threaten or injure others?

ABOUT THE AUTHOR

Born in Ogden, Utah, **Jean Holbrook Mathews** attended Weber State, where she met and married John Phillip Mathews. His job took them to St. Louis, Missouri, where they raised their family. There she completed her education, receiving her BS in education and English from University of Missouri–St. Louis. After teaching briefly, she was elected to the Missouri House of Representatives, where she served for ten years. During that time, she received her MPA from the University of Missouri–Columbia. Upon leaving the legislature, she was appointed by Governor John Ashcroft to serve as the public member of the state medical licensing board, where she became the only non-physician ever elected as president of the board. She taught state government and public administration at UMSL as an adjunct professor. She and her husband served a humanitarian mission in the Philippines for the LDS Church and they have traveled extensively in Europe. After her husband took early retirement, they moved back to Utah for several years, where she took up writing. More recently, they have relocated to their present home in Mesa, Arizona. She has authored seven novels.